SYNCHRO
BOY

SHANNON MCFERRAN

SYNCHRO BOY

ARSENAL PULP PRESS
VANCOUVER

SYNCHRO BOY

ARSENAL PULP PRESS
Suite 202 – 211 East Georgia St.
Vancouver, BC V6A 1Z6
Canada
arsenalpulp.com

The publisher gratefully acknowledges the support of the Canada Council for the Arts and the British Columbia Arts Council for its publishing program, and the Government of Canada, and the Government of British Columbia (through the Book Publishing Tax Credit Program), for its publishing activities.

Arsenal Pulp Press acknowledges the xʷməθkʷəy̓əm (Musqueam), Sḵwx̱wú7mesh (Squamish), and səlilwətaʔɬ (Tsleil-Waututh) Nations, speakers of Hul'q'umi'num'/Halq'eméylem/ hən̓q̓əmin̓əm̓ and custodians of the traditional, ancestral, and unceded territories where our office is located. We pay respect to their histories, traditions, and continuous living cultures and commit to accountability, respectful relations, and friendship.

This is a work of fiction. Any resemblance of characters to persons either living or deceased is purely coincidental.

Cover photo: istockphoto.com
Cover and text design by Oliver McPartlin
Edited by Shirarose Wilensky
Proofread by Alison Strobel
Printed and bound in Canada
Library and Archives Canada Cataloguing in Publication:

McFerran, Shannon, 1973–, author
 Synchro boy / Shannon McFerran.
Issued in print and electronic formats.
ISBN 978-1-55152-744-4 (softcover).—ISBN 978-1-55152-745-1 (HTML)

 I. Title.

PS8625.F47S96 2018   jC813'.6   C2018-901868-2

C2018-901869-0

To Tim and Sandy

ONE

Today I catch the eye of the synchro girl with dark hair and good dimples, just before I dive off the starting block. It's the last race of the meet—if I swim my triple-A time now, I've got a shot at the national team.

That is, if Geoff doesn't kill me first.

The girl with the good dimples smiles at me. I smile back. I've been watching the synchro girls for ages, so it's fun that they're all lined up along the wall of the dive tank now, watching me. When I watch *them*, they don't even notice me looking. Well, if they do, they don't show it—and I get it. They're performers. I danced for seven years, so I remember what it was like to be behind the fourth wall.

But they're the dancers now. I'm just a fish. I crouch on the starting block, ready to propel myself into the water.

I wonder if she thinks I belong here. Because some days, I don't even feel like I fit in with the guys on the Rosa Waves team. I don't think like them, or joke like them—and I may be great at long course, when we swim fifty-metre laps, but I don't look the part. I'm the only guy on the blocks with long, lean limbs, the only one with slender shoulders. I don't have a swimmer's hunch. I spent too many years in front of a mirror with my shoulders back, working my core, before I found my way to the pool.

Yeah, I'm the pretty one. That's probably what all the synchro girls are thinking.

Swimmers, take your marks. I look down at my reflection, staring back at me from the pool's still, flat surface. Behind me, my best friend, Riley, waits his turn for the freestyle relay.

Then Andy, then Geoff.

The horn sounds.

I push off and dive as far as I can, holding my head down.

When I surface and breathe to my right, the swimmer in the lane beside me is already ahead by a stroke. He's a big guy, shoulders twice my size. It's okay. I just pull harder. When I breathe left, I glimpse the pace clock.

When I breathe right, Giant Shoulders is still in front by a head. I tell myself I just have to be fast enough for the qualifying time.

Left breath after the turn. The pace clock says thirty-one seconds. Too slow. Pull harder. Kick harder.

Last breath on the right side.

I pull with everything I've got, forcing myself to keep my head down, no more breaths, no more drag. I'm going to make it to nine strokes this time.

Eight more strokes. Seven, six, five, four.

Pull harder.

Three more strokes, then I slap my hand on the deck. Riley dives over my head. Do I have my time? The pace clock says fifty-seven seconds by the time I look up. If the timer has the same time as the pace clock, I made it—but it's too close to know for sure.

I get out, and the timers in my lane are both standing up. The guy's helping the lady dry spilled coffee off of her clipboard, her clothes.

The other two lanes are well behind us now, and the stands are scream-ing—you gotta love that about a qualifier at your home pool. It feels like all of Victoria's crammed into the stands.

Riley gets out, and I raise my hand for a high-five.

"We could have had first." He shakes his head.

"We might still!"

"You at least get your time?"

I go to look over the timer's shoulder, but the box on the sheet where my time should be written down is empty.

"Hey, sorry ... What happened to my split time?"

"It was an accident," she says. "Someone knocked my elbow and—"

The official walks over to us. "Get off the deck! You know you're not supposed to talk to the timers."

"I know, but ..."

I go to the back of the deck and watch Andy get out, and Geoff jump in. I know exactly what happened.

See, Coach Cragg put me first in the medley so my time could qualify—but that meant there would be no anchor—instead, the pressure's on Geoff to bring up the rear, so he was shooting daggers at me when I got up on the starting block.

Let's just say that, uh ... Geoff takes his racing very seriously. Not that I don't—the national team trials is my program goal, signed by me *and* my mom at the Sports Institute at the start of every school year. I just don't feel like it's worth getting mad at your teammates, you know? But Geoff's been pissed at me ever since I got faster last year.

He bumped the timer's elbow. At just the right moment.

Geoff's giving it everything he's got, trying to make up for lost time. But it's clear. He's not going to make it. Giant Shoulders' team comes in first. Geoff gets out and rips his goggles off. He looks amused.

"So, Princess, you get your time?"

Princess. That's it. "You bumped the timer, you jerk!" I lunge for him, and Geoff jumps back, but he slips, his feet coming out from under him, his head hitting the tile.

I wasn't going to hit him. I swear I just wanted to scare him. But now some officials are coming over here, and Geoff's holding his head as everyone clears tables and chairs off the deck. The meet's over.

"What the—?" Geoff sputters. "Oh my God."

"I'm so sorry, man. So sorry." I try to catch his eye, but Geoff just keeps his head down. When he opens his mouth, there's blood.

"Oh, Geoff—I think you're bleeding."

"'Cause you made me bite my fucking tongue, you asshole!" Geoff kicks my shin.

"Ow!"

I look up at Coach Cragg, who's telling the others to back off. Great. Then he helps Geoff stand up and sits him on a deck chair. Coach checks his eyes and holds up fingers to see if Geoff's concussed. When he decides he's okay, he turns to me, and stares. Everyone on the team is quiet. I hear the screams of the kids in the wave pool and the thwanging of diving boards. I feel stapled to the ground under his glare.

"That's it, Bart."

"I'm sorry, Coach. I didn't mean to hurt him. But he sabotaged my *time*—"

"I don't care." Coach shakes his head. "You don't breathe when I tell you to breathe, you don't focus, you stare off at the bloody synchro team when I'm trying to get your attention, and now you're playing around like you're in god-damn Aquatots or something. How old are you?"

"Sixteen, sir."

"You're not acting like it."

I stare at the tiles by my feet. I can't look at anyone. Certainly not over at the pool, where the girl with the good dimples could be looking at me and thinking I'm a wound-up jerk. Not at Riley, my oldest friend, the one who got me here, into the racing pool. My eyes drift up to the empty spot on the plaque where my name's supposed to go at the end of this season. As long as this shit with Geoff doesn't screw it up.

"Go get changed, Lively. You're done for today."

"You want me to leave?"

"Yeah, get out of here. Get yourself together. Come back next week."

"*What?* You're suspending me?"

"Yes. And when you come back, I want you here every day, doing your best. No picking fights. You hear me?"

"This is unbelievable! What about Geoff? Did you see what *he* did? I don't have my time because of him."

"I don't care. I can't be concerned about your time if you're going to attack your teammates." Cragg shakes his head. "You're up for national competition for God's sake."

Fine. This is bullshit, but I know better than to push it with Cragg. When I do, it just gets back to my dad, which leads to him calling me from the oil patch for the express purpose of making me feel like crap. Then Mom gets on the phone and yells at him. They might as well still be married.

I take off to the warm pool to do a few laps to get the stress out of my system. Then Geoff stops on his way to the locker room.

"Geoff, look, I'm sorry about your head. I really am."

"You wanted me to hit the deck."

"I did not!"

I keep my eyes on the synchro girls swimming laps of egg beater kick across the dive tank.

"You know, you're such a fucking ballerina, you should just go join them."

"Who?"

"The goddamned water ballet, Bart. Isn't that what you want?"

"No! Geez."

"Oh, come on. You've been staring at them every chance you get."

"Well? So what?"

"So ... it's Try It day. You should go."

The sandwich board's at the edge of the dive tank like it is every Sunday in September: *Synchro Swimming—Try It! Free session, Sunday, 11 a.m.* And for the first time, I'm not in a practice with the Rosa Waves.

But this is a trap. Geoff just wants to get more fuel for teasing me.

On the edge of the dive tank, Chelsea Gates, Synchro Star and Queen of the Sports Institute, is doing that weird thing synchro swimmers do with their arms to run through a routine—they call it land drilling. When she stops I try to catch her eye, but she's not looking at me. Maybe *won't* look at me. That's nothing new—Chelsea's always looked past me to the real athletes. The buff guys. We've been going to school together since grade six, and I know she'd never look at a slim and bendy fish like me.

"It's okay, Princess. If you're too scared to go over there and join them, I understand. Those girls *are* pretty scary. Especially that one." Geoff nods at Chelsea, who slips into the water with her teammates.

"Don't call me Princess."

Geoff just grins. "Look at you. You *are* scared—but, of what? The girls? Or doing what you want?"

His question guts me. So Geoff thinks I'm some chickenshit? That's it. I am so sick of him, and Coach, and all the macho guys on the Rosa Waves giving me a hard time—and for what?

"I do what I like."

"Yeah?"

"Yeah. Watch me."

Before I can fully appreciate what I'm doing, I start crossing the ten tiles between our pool and the dive tank. Halfway there, I think, *Crap. What am I doing?*

Geoff calls at my back, "Enjoy your holiday, Princess."

I flip him the bird over my shoulder.

TWO

I walk over to the podium and sound system where the synchro coach usually stands. The girls in the water look up at me. On deck, Chelsea stops talking, and just stares. Then the girl with the good dimples turns around to see who Chelsea's looking at—I smile and give her a little wave.

Then I turn back to look at Geoff, but he's already walking off the deck. Instead, I'm looking straight at Coach. He just shakes his head.

The girls break their stare when a short, fit woman with her hair up in a messy ponytail comes up to me.

I hold out my hand.

"Hi, I'm Bart."

"Hi, Bart. I'm Su-Yun. What can I do for you?" she asks me as we shake. I'm surprised her voice sounds so familiar. But of course I've heard her shouting over the noisy pool at the girls so many times.

"Um ..." I motion toward the sandwich board. "I'm here to try synchro?"

She looks behind me, then meets my eyes. "You swim with Dennis Cragg's team, right? Does he know you're doing this?"

"Uh, he didn't ... until now."

"Oooh. He won't like this."

"I know."

Su-Yun smiles slightly. "So you're here to try synchro in protest?" She chuckles. "I like this. Protest synchronized swimming ... Okay, Bart. The girls call me Sunny. I'm the head coach."

"Thanks for having me."

Sunny calls the girls over and makes introductions. A couple of them say a shy hi or hello. The girl with the good dimples is Erika. Sunny introduces the tall Black girl from my school as Julia, and she smiles warmly. Casey, Kyoka, and Huiyan, who all go to a different school, don't say anything. Huiyan whispers to Kyoka.

Chelsea raises one eyebrow. "Bart Lively?" she asks, like she can't believe it's me.

"Yeah, hi."

She goes to say something else, but Sunny cuts her off.

"Okay!" Sunny shouts. "Warm-up time."

I hop in, and just about sigh at the warmth compared to our lane pool. It's got to be thirty degrees Celsius in here.

Sunny gets us to do a lap of egg beater.

"Bart, line up behind the girls and see if you can match their speed. Twenty-five metres."

I start off swimming egg beater as upright as possible, arms furiously pulling me ahead in time with Chelsea, who's in front of me. I don't want to be left behind ... But seriously, these girls are fast. I can't keep up! It's a killer! It's almost funny how this tires my legs out.

After that, Sunny says, "Okay, we're going to do sculling and figures, then we'll try some lifts, for fun. Bart, have you done much sculling?"

"Sure, hands only, right?"

"You got it. We'll do forward, backward, and support scull today—support scull keeps you vertical in the water."

"And what are figures?"

"Those are the movements between the different positions in synchro."

"Yeah, and most of them have you upside down with your legs out of the water," Chelsea says, shaking her head. "Bart, what makes you think you can do this? What are you even trying to do?"

"I'm just ... trying synchro."

"Oh yeah, 'cause guys don't have enough of their own shit to do, they have to come take over our sport too?"

I hold my hands up. "Whoa. I'm not taking over anything."

"Chelsea." Sunny shoots her a look. "Come on." Then she says, "Bart, go grab two water jugs."

I swim to the side, and Erika follows.

"I can show you where we keep them." She pulls herself out of the pool and onto the deck effortlessly. Erika's not like the girls in my swim club—all big shoulders and biceps. Her physique's more balanced—like a dancer's. I follow her into a little room off the pool deck, and she grabs two big, empty, collapsible water jugs out of a big bin and passes them to me.

"I guess you've seen us use these?"

"Yeah, for balance or something?"

"They help keep you floating so you can focus on the figures." She smiles again, and I notice her deep brown eyes and amazing dimples. But even more, I notice she has an energy around her, like she's wired and ready for something. Not like the way the lane swimming girls drag themselves around at practice. She's lit up.

Erika waits for me to open the door back to the pool deck, but I take a sec to peek out the window first.

"Is something the matter?"

"Uh, no. It's okay." I lean on the door, and it opens a crack.

"Are you nervous?"

"Perceptive." I smile at her.

Erika raises her eyebrows.

I sigh, and open the door all the way. I hold one of the giant bottles up on my shoulder as we head back to the pool. Erika bonks me from behind.

"What? You're afraid one of your teammates are going to see and make fun of you?"

"No. They know I'm here."

"You know, everyone thinks this sport is only about looking pretty, but just wait until you sprint free for a hundred metres and then do an under."

"What's an under?"

"A length of the tank—twenty-five metres without a breath."

"Oh, yeah—I saw you doing that."

"It's not easy. And get ready for some bruises."

"What?"

Erika comes up so she's standing toe to toe with me. "We swim really close to each other. It's pretty much a contact sport."

"Oh."

The first figure they show me is sailboat—knee bent, making a little triangle above the water.

Then they get me to swim the ballet leg—one leg on the surface, and the other straight up.

"Not bad! You've got a lot of core strength already," Sunny says.

When we finish practising some basic figures, the girls demo their team routine. I dunk my head to watch them under water, and I can hear the music as clear as if it were playing in air.

The power in their legs puts the girls on my racing team to shame—some of the guys too. And they have such powerful cores, they can lift each other out of the water, propel *themselves* out of the water, upside down. Watching the work on the surface is one thing. But watching what they do under water ... I don't even know how to describe it. It's like I'm watching goddesses.

"Okay, your turn, Bart. Let's get you and Chelsea and Erika and ... Julia? No ... Kyoka." The shortest girl turns her head toward Sunny, her eyes wide. She shakes her head, just a little. "Yes, Kyoka. You four. Let's see you put something together. Bart, you'll need one of these." Sunny passes me a nose clip.

"And, girls, nothing hard! Basics. One lift. You all lift Kyoka." She smiles mischievously. "Bart, you saw how the girls positioned themselves into the stack lift before? I'd like to see you try the base. Erika and Chelsea, you be the pushers. Kyoka's feet will be on your shoulders, Bart."

Kyoka looks away, into the stands, where the synchro moms sit watching, clutching paper coffee cups. She looks at them like a puppy that's been told to sit and stay.

When I get up on the bulkhead, the movable wall that spans the width of the pool, I look back over at the racing lanes. Everyone's gone home. No one's here now to care that I'm doing this. I feel so free for a moment that it's like I'm a little kid playing at the pool. I somersault into the water, just for the fun of it.

"You're not bad, you know," Erika says. "You haven't done this before?"

"No. But I danced for eight years."

"No way!"

"Come on," Chelsea orders us to get out of the pool. She picks a song on her phone and sets it to repeat. "Get back up here, Bart. We're supposed to dive in together."

Erika gives me a look like I should just ignore Chelsea. "So when did you start swimming?" she asks.

"I was about twelve when I joined the Rosa Waves."

"Do you miss dance?"

I pretend I don't hear her question as I climb the ladder. Chelsea starts moving us into position on the bulkhead, two in back, two crouched in front, ready to dive. She runs through the drill, telling us what to do on which count.

We dive on eight.

Once I'm under water, I position my shoulders under Kyoka's feet. I hear metal-on-metal tapping—Sunny keeping count for us with a little wrench against the ladder. I feel the girls below me grab my feet. On four, they egg beater up. As powerfully as I can, I stand up from the squat, pushing Kyoka out of the water. From underneath, it doesn't look like much. But it must have been something, because Kyoka shoots back into the water in a stream of bubbles. We surface, and she's squealing and waving her hands.

"That wasn't just a lift. Bart!"

"What?"

"I *somersaulted!* Bart, I was *totally in the air. Do it again!*"

Chelsea scoffs, "Kyoka, come on."

"You did a somersault?" I grin at Kyoka. "That is so awesome!"

Chelsea nudges my side. "Try me. I'm heavier. And see if you can get me out of the water on your own. No stack."

I draw a deep breath and sink down beneath the surface. Chelsea's calves are solid muscle in my hands. I launch her and surface, and the first thing I see is Sunny, staring at us from the deck.

"Wow. You are hired!" she jokes.

"For all our lifts! Yes!" Kyoka shouts. I'm the big brother now, suddenly popular at the lake because all the little sisters just found out he can toss them so high they fly over the water and land with a splash. Chelsea tries not to look impressed. "Okay, fine. But can you do *this?*" She gets out of the pool and steps into a front split, flat on the deck. She's getting cheeky.

"Right or left?" I ask, all bored.

Behind me, Erika laughs. "Left, then side!"

I hoist myself out of the pool and step into a left front split, and stick my tongue out at Chelsea. Then I shift into side splits and lift my arms into the air, facing Erika. She splashes water up at me.

"Where did you come from?" Sunny asks.

"Just the swim club."

"No way. Those aren't swim club moves!"

Then Erika outs me as a dancer. Sunny asks me to show them a pirouette, so I do.

"No, I mean under water. And upside down."

It takes me a sec to figure out what she's got in mind, but then I get it. I corkscrew down, spinning ... I swim down deep, where the volume of water presses against my ears. A feeling runs through my body to my pointed toes, as my arms gather water, like I'm hugging the deep. I remember messing around like this in some hotel pool on a road trip. Mom sitting on her deck chair, reading a book.

"You've just done a vertical spin, Bart," Sunny says when I surface. Wow—another figure! Without even having to be taught the moves.

I immerse myself again, and there's no sound now but the hum of the filter. I like this. It's not like the racing pool, where I could spend a whole practice on just a couple of strokes.

The girls' legs float above me like strands of seaweed, with sun streaming down in between. I swim up to the surface and burst out as high as I can, legs beating fast until I push out, almost to my waist, and take a full breath.

Erika looks at me like she feels what I'm feeling. She smiles.

I smile back.

"Okay, we're done! Good work today." Sunny claps. The lifeguards start rolling lane dividers across the dive tank.

"Hey, Sunny," Casey says. "Now that Elizabeth's moved away, we've got a spot for Bart! He could join the team, right?"

"Don't you think he should learn some more figures first? One step at a time, Casey." Sunny laughs, but then her smile falls away as she looks past me. "Uh-oh."

I turn around and see two of the moms who sat in the stands making their way across the deck. I recognize Chelsea's mom—she's always here. And judging from the look on Kyoka's face, the other must be her mom.

"What are you doing?" Kyoka's mom comes right up and asks me. "Are you making fun of the girls? There are no boys allowed in this club."

My heart sinks.

Sunny sighs behind me. "We have no rule against boys joining. He's not making fun, Mrs Shiozaki. He came for the Try It session."

"She's right," I say. "Your daughter's super talented, and—"

"And what, now you're going to join synchro?" Chelsea's mom interrupts. "These sessions are to get new girls interested in joining. They're not for racers to come over here and waste the girls' time, *and* their coach's time." She darts a look at Sunny. Then she shoots her fire gaze back at me. "You may not realize this, but these girls are elite athletes."

"I know," I say. I shake my head and walk away to get my bag. But Chelsea's mom follows me.

"This isn't a boys' sport!" she snaps at my back.

I turn back to face her. "Why not?"

"You can't compete against girls. That's entirely unfair. The girls work hard to get the strength to do what they do. We can't have boys coming in and making it look like it takes nothing."

"Nothing? No way! I just busted my a—"

Erika grabs my arm and pulls me away before I can say anything else. But I hear Sunny tell Amanda Gates that the girls are more flexible, and more buoyant. "Bart wouldn't have an advantage," she says.

"*I* think you were great," Erika says, half laughing at Amanda Gates. "Don't listen to her. You should come back."

"I don't think so."

"What, didn't you have fun? 'Cause it looked like you were having a pretty damn good time."

I sigh. "I did have fun. Thank you."

"So that's it?" Erika sighs. "But you're so flexible, and you're *that* good at the dance stuff, but ... you're a *long course swimmer*? I don't get it."

I shrug. "I like the water."

She smiles. "So do I."

"I gotta go." I shoulder my bag, and head. But walking down the deck to the locker room, I sense her eyes on my back. I get the feeling she isn't going to let this go.

I change, and when I get upstairs, I stop to look at the dive tank through the window. Now I know—I can swim like those synchro girls. I can dance under water.

I'm also the best long course swimmer on the Rosa Waves. I've been swimming with them for five seasons. There are always ups and downs. And maybe it's down now, but it'll go up again—I *know* that. The racing pool is where I need to be.

But this down feels a little different. This time—my buddy Riley aside—I can't stand the Rosa Waves. I can't stand the racing pool.

God, that's scary.

A guy runs and spins off the dive platform, his perfect figure defying gravity for a moment. I'd be lying to myself if I said I wouldn't rather be in that pool—swimming synchro, or maybe diving, gracefully plunging into deep water. If only I could get the guts to go up that ten-metre tower. But ... there's nobody in the *world* who could get me up there. Damn, I can't even go high enough to go down the waterslide.

And like hell I'm going to join an all-girls synchro club.

THREE

On Monday, I stay at school, taking the rare chance to do homework on a weeknight. When I get home, Mom's not back from the law office where she's an assistant, so I don't bother starting dinner. I eat two sandwiches. Then I make a protein shake, and then I have a bunch of crackers. I want cheese, but I'm too exhausted to get it out of the fridge and slice it. Instead, I use the crackers to scoop peanut butter out of the jar.

"Bart, use a knife," Mom says, coming into the kitchen, still wearing her shoes, keys in hand.

"Sorry. You just get home? Did you eat?"

"Yeah, no worries. We ordered in. But Bart?"

"Mmm-hmm?" I mumble.

"Coach Cragg called me."

"Um." I chew my mouthful of peanut-butter-cracker and swallow. "To tell you how great I'm doing?"

"No, to tell me you got suspended! A week off's a pretty big deal right now. You want to tell me what happened? Cragg said you pushed a guy."

I can't take the way she's looking at me right now. "It's just stupid stuff."

"It isn't just stupid. Bart, this isn't like you. Trying to start a fight?"

"I wasn't trying to start *a fight*, Mom. I just got fed up. It's just—it's nothing."

"It can't be nothing. What started it?" She crosses her arms. The clock on the kitchen wall ticks too loudly, waiting for me to tell her everything.

"It's *nothing*."

I can't sell her on it, though. She just looks at me like she knows exactly what's going on at the pool, but she doesn't say anything. She just waits until I break her gaze, and then she sighs. She takes the box of crackers from me and fishes a couple out, then passes me the box. "Here. Clean up, okay?"

"I will."

The blender's dirty. The peanut butter jar is open, the lid and an open bag of bread on the other counter.

"Don't forget."

I kiss her cheek, and she heads upstairs.

So I start cleaning up my mess. While I'm putting stuff away, I keep thinking about what it felt like to swim with the synchro club. Not just what it was like to swim so differently. What it was like to hang out with the girls—Erika, in particular. And by the time everything's put away and I've wiped the counters, I'm hardly thinking about Geoff or the suspension.

I look up the Rosa Pacific Synchro Club website. Like Sunny said, there's nothing saying boys can't join—it just says the club is open to "athletes of all abilities"—but it's all photos of girls against a purple-and-pink background.

I check out the photos of the team that will go to the national competitions and recognize Chelsea, Erika, Julia, and Kyoka. It's a small club. Looks like they've only got recreational classes for younger swimmers, and the national stream team this year. That's it.

I search around for guys' synchro, or mixed synchro, but I can't find anything for my age group. So I search for men's recreational clubs.

Nope.

There aren't any in my city. Or ... my country.

Well. So much for that.

●●●

On the third day of my suspension, I'm already restless as hell. Riley and I pack up our stuff after our last block, biology, on the second floor of Rosa Pacific Secondary School.

"It's Wednesday, and I haven't spotted Erika yet," I complain. "You sure she goes here?"

"Yeah, she just started in the Sports Institute this year. I think she's in my speech arts class."

"I can't believe you still take that."

"I can't believe you *don't*. Dude, it's the easiest English credit in grade eleven."

"Well, unlike you, I don't actually mind reading books."

Riley whacks me one.

Rosa Pacific Secondary School, home of the Sports Institute, or SI, has about 800 kids—so I've got a small chance of running into someone I don't have classes with. But that doesn't stop me from keeping an eye out for Erika, 'cause I've been thinking about her all week.

Riley and I are in compressed classes the Sports Institute offers so we can spend the better part of our days training. It's only one thirty, and we're free for an hour before we have to be on deck.

Geoff and Andy come down the stairs behind us and start goofing around. They get up on the railing and pose like they're a couple of synchro swimmers waiting for their music to start. Then Geoff leaps off to the stairs below, but he fumbles and bumps into our bio teacher.

"Watch it, Mr Chan."

The guys crack up and motor down the stairs, heads down.

"Losers," Riley says. "But, dude ... I gotta ask you. Do you want to be a synchro swimmer now? Wait, no. If you do, I don't want to hear about it."

"Why?"

"'Cause." Riley laughs. "Synchro's gay. We could see you from up top, you know."

The café at the pool has floor-to-ceiling glass, looking down on the pool below. My teammates were all headed there after the meet. Of course they watched.

"So Geoff starts going off about how he's going to bring you a tutu tomorrow and make you wear it. So I told him to shut up, because you're in hot pursuit."

"I'm in *hot pursuit?*"

"Yeah, of a synchro girl."

"Well, I'm not."

"C'mon, dude."

"You didn't have to tell—" I don't bother finishing my sentence. "Never mind."

I hurry down the stairs and push the door open. Outside, I breathe in the fresh September air, getting the smell of musty building and pine cleanser out of my nose.

Riley laughs as he follows me out into the parking lot. "Hey, where's the fire?"

We get into his car.

"I'm ... just done. Like, this bullshit's non-stop."

"Sorry, man. I just meant *synchro's* gay. I didn't mean *you're* gay. Unless ... like, did I just touch on something there?"

I whip my head around. "No. Are you saying ...? No. No, you did not." I shake my head.

"Okay, then." Riley gives a weak smile.

"*Okay,* then." I look straight ahead. Riley starts the car, and we head out into traffic. We drive in silence for a while. Instead of taking the Pat Bay Highway, Riley drives the long route through the Mount Douglas Parkway, cutting through the forest, and then up through neighbourhoods with views of the ocean and Mount Baker, before heading down toward the pool.

"Is this because of health class in grade seven?" I ask. "'Cause I thought we put that to rest."

"No ..." Riley says, but then he can't think of anything else to say. "Okay, maybe."

"Shit. This all over again?"

In middle school, when we had the class that was supposed to introduce sexual identity—I made the huge mistake of asking if it was normal to think about people of the same sex *and* people of the opposite sex *that way.*

"Sure," the teacher said. "It would be totally natural—and you wouldn't be alone."

"Oh, I didn't *say* I was attracted to anyone," I backpedalled. "I was just ... talking in general."

But it was too late—as far as everyone was concerned, I was queer.

Riley pulls up to the pool and cheers when he gets his favourite parking spot near the back door. I unbuckle and start to get out, but Riley doesn't open his door.

"Hey, I didn't mean to ..." he starts.

"Yeah, no worries."

"Look, if you ever want to talk about anything, I just ... You know ... I'm not going to ..." Riley sighs. "It's okay. You can talk."

"Okay."

He's still not opening the door.

"Riley, I got nothing to say."

He sighs again, and opens his door. The interior bell *ding ding dings* until he remembers to unbuckle his seat belt and get out.

FOUR

I can't tell my mom I tried synchro. She'd probably wonder why I don't just go back to dance. Why don't I just go back to the studio, if I miss it so much?

It goes back to the first week of middle school, when our homeroom teacher asked us all to write down our favourite video game, the name of our best friend, and our favourite sport.

My middle school had team sports, but I didn't join any of them. I didn't play video games, and I had a hard time picking a best friend out of the group of girls I hung out with all the time. Guys from my elementary school got me, for the most part, even though we weren't friends. I was the super flexible, skinny boy who didn't move like they did—but they were cool with me. Guys from the other feeder schools weren't. All they saw was a boy who didn't look Boy. Didn't speak Boy.

Our teacher put each kid's answers on a poster with their photo—then hung them up around the room. Riley's best friend dropped him by October, and there he was, stuck with the reminder all year.

And me? I was the kid stupid enough to put ballet as my favourite sport. It took all of one day before a kid wrote *fag* on my poster, and the teacher had to take it down. She said she was going to print a new photo, but the gap on the wall stayed. We got busy with other projects. And then, after a while, nobody noticed the crap on the walls anymore.

The teasing got worse through the fall. When Chelsea Gates saw me at the Christmas dance, she asked if I was going to show them the sugar plum fairy, and all her friends laughed. After I danced my solo for the school talent show, Geoff and Andy followed me all the next day. I'd be leaving a class they weren't even in, and they'd be waiting so they could follow and call after me, "Fag, fairy, faggot, fag boy ..." At the end of the day, I thought I'd lost them. I packed up my bag as fast as possible, but when I got to the stairs to leave, there they were.

"Where's your tutu?" Geoff asked.

I ignored him and started walking across the front yard of the school.

Somebody called Geoff back, and I took the chance to run.

"Yeah, you better run. We're coming!" Andy yelled.

So when I got out of their sight, I picked up the pace and headed down a footpath in the opposite direction of my townhouse. I walked home a different way, up the extra blocks and back along an alley, in case Geoff and Andy were waiting.

The gate to our townhouse complex clanged shut behind me. Mom wasn't home from work yet. I ran upstairs to my room.

I started with the competition ribbons, hanging on hooks mounted by my desk. Blues, reds—into the garbage. Mom came home when I was taking the framed certificates for my Royal Academy exam levels off the wall. I stacked them up and took them to her room. I don't know what she saw first—them or my red eyes.

"Bart? What are you doing?"

"I can't—" My voice broke. "I can't have these in my room."

"What happened?" Mom took the stack of frames from me. She looked through them, laying each one out on the bed.

I shook my head. I didn't want to talk about it anymore.

"You know, you can't let a bunch of kids who don't know any better make you ashamed ..."

"They're not just a bunch of kids! They were following me. They were going to take me down."

"Who? Those same two? Because, Bart, I can go down there ..."

"No! Please don't."

Mom held my gaze for a breath.

"Please?" It's not like I was some complete social outcast. It's not like they would have just found something else to harass me about if I wasn't a dancer. It was *dance*. Ballet was in the way of a normal life.

I sat down beside her on my bed. Mom pulled me into a hug and rocked me a little. She kissed my head, then whispered into my curls. "Okay, hon. I won't go."

I sniffed hard and sat up. "I'm not going to my recital."

She looked sadder than me. "Oh, Bart. Are you sure?"

I sat up taller. "I'm not going to any more dance classes, either."

Mom picked up a frame from the stack and ran her sleeve over the top, wiping the dust away.

"Are you sure this is something you're done with?"

I nodded.

"Well." She forced a smile. "Look at you, growing up. Moving on."

I watched her put the stack away in a drawer in her closet. It hurt, watching her put my certificates away. We'd been in it together, all these years, just the two of us.

"You know, you used to dance whenever we put music on. Whenever you even heard music. Even in—"

"I know. Even in department stores."

Mom knew I needed to dance. So she signed me up for ballet. Up to that point, all I wanted was what she wanted. And all she wanted was for me to do what I loved.

As a last-ditch effort, she made me watch that ballet movie *Billy Elliot* with her. But the movie didn't change my mind—I just felt sorry for Billy's friend, left behind in that homophobic town when Billy moved away to train.

And when I came home from school the next day, Mom had put a framed photo of me at a recital, mid-leap across the stage, on my dresser. There I was, skinny arms outstretched—one pointing ahead of me, one behind.

She left a note tucked into the gold frame: *Never forget what you are capable of.*

• • •

At eleven, Riley was scrawny and geeky like me, and he never gave me a hard time for not acting Boy—so at least there was one kid. We started hanging out at lunch, and playing basketball, even though we both kind of hated ball sports. It was just something to do together. He invited me over to his house, and when I saw the five pairs of goggles on his dresser, I asked, "What the heck?"

Then he explained swim club to me. "It's hard. You practise a ton. But there aren't any balls flying at you—no contact. Most of those guys who are always picking on you used to give me a hard time. But since I've been swimming? They just leave me alone."

I came home and begged Mom to sign me up for swim club. Riley was waiting in the hall. I just wanted her to say yes quickly so we could go to the skate park like we planned that day—'cause, you know, falling off a skateboard would get me more cred than doing a pirouette.

"Bart, this is a lot of money, more than dance."

"Yeah, but ... it's a big sport. It's a big deal. Riley says guys in this club end up going all across the country to swim."

Mom sighed, and picked up her pen. "You're sure this is what you want?"

"One guy on the team even went to the Olympics, Mom! From this club!"

And even better? When Dad found out, he was overjoyed. Not only was I doing just what he did in high school, but his old swimming buddy Cragg would be my coach. Then in grade nine, I signed up for the Sports Institute with Riley. We get extra coaching, and our training counts for credits toward graduation.

Dad was so happy he told Mom he'd pay for all of it—coaching, the program, travel, the works.

So I got what I wanted. The teasing ebbed, and swimming filled the empty space that dancing left when I quit. Sure, stroke correction was a shadow of the work required of ballet positions, of body alignment. Getting up on the blocks at a meet was so many shades lighter than the thrill of getting up on a stage. But it was demanding, and I constantly set myself new goals for better times. And I kept meeting them. And when Dad would come visit from Alberta, we'd have something to talk about. So I had that, and I had Riley—and finally, the respect of other kids. And that was all I needed.

But now—it's not enough.

FIVE

When we get to the aquatic centre, we go in the back door and stop at the railing before Riley heads downstairs to the pool deck and I head upstairs to the gym.

Riley nods down to the deck. "Oh, look—" Riley elbows me. "Chelsea's checking us out." He puffs up his chest.

"Yeah, Chelsea's not looking at me." I want to say, *She's not looking at you, either, Riley,* but I let him have his fantasy. Riley and I, well—we may be Sports Institute fish, but we're no catch. And both of us know Chelsea's standards.

Erika stuffs her dark hair into her purple cap and dives into the deep end. The coach starts some music and the girls in the water lift their legs straight up out of the pool, toes pointing to the blue sky on the other side of the glass ceiling. Even their hips are out of the water.

"Whoa," says Riley. "How do they do that?"

"I don't know. But isn't it awesome?"

"They're freaks of nature."

In the dive tank, the girls do a lift—the smallest one flies off the shoulders of another girl. I can't help but stare.

"Look at *that*," Riley says, checking out a girl on the deck practising a headstand on a board with hand grips.

"Yeah, that's awesome."

"*She's* awesome. I wonder if she'd be into some Riley."

"Oh, come on."

"*What?* Maybe I'll ask her out. You never know until you ask."

"You just go ask her? You just say, 'Hey, you into this?'" I point down at my body.

"You got the product, you might as well do the market research."

I shake my head.

Erika warms up with some fast laps. I lose sight of her after she tumble turns, but then she pops up again on this end and I realize she swam entirely under water—the full twenty-five metres.

"Did you see that?" I ask.

"What?"

"She didn't even take a breath. A whole lap."

"Holy shit," he says. Then Riley smiles at me. "You're falling in love."

"No, no. I just ... I keep noticing her."

Back in middle school, after the Health Class Incident, Riley said, "You know, if you like girls, you can just like girls." And that's true for me—I like girls. And Erika? Yeah, I like her. She's pretty cute.

"Okay, here's what we should do."

Riley raises a brow.

"We should ask synchro girls out to the SI barbeque."

"Yeah. Sure." Riley nods. But he looks scared, now that I've challenged all his talk. "It's at Chelsea's house this year, you know."

"I know. Look, don't you think it's a good idea? We've never actually gone out with a girl."

"Well, if you count the grade seven dance ..."

"I don't count that."

Riley nods.

"Especially the part where I asked Chelsea to dance."

Riley aims his finger like a gun at me. "And got shot down. I still can't believe you got up the guts to do that."

"I just wanted to show her I was a good dancer."

"Riiiight. Well, you got to dance with Anika."

"Yeah, but we didn't ... I mean, I never even kissed her."

"Yeah, okay."

"And you didn't even kiss Zara."

"Dude, she was way tall. I couldn't reach."

I laughed, remembering them dancing together. I think Riley came up to just below her chest.

"Let's do it, Riley." I slap my palms down on the railing. "We'll just ask a couple of synchro girls. We'll go to the barbecue with them, and then ... who knows?"

Riley gives me a funny look.

"Okay, I know. Not what you'd expect from me." I laugh. "So? Doesn't mean you're not into it, right?"

"Yeah." He laughs. "Sure, I'm into it. Sure ... who knows? Maybe they'll even say yes."

"So, we got a deal?"

Riley pauses before answering, like he's trying to process the role reversal. He studies my face, wondering if I'm serious about this.

"Okay, deal. And if you back out?" Riley raises his chin a little. "You have to see *90210 Shark Attack* with me."

"Aw, no way, man." Riley and I both have a monster flick obsession— but he has no taste, so I've resigned myself to some really awful flicks to appease him. "I have to draw a line somewhere. Besides, you said I didn't have to after I watched *Cute Little Buggers* with you."

"That one wasn't that bad."

"Seriously? Possessed bunny rabbits?"

"Come on, Bart! We've seen every other monster flick from 2014."

I shake my head. "Fine. But you have to get vanilla. No disgusting German cherry delight crap." Cake is Riley's other obsession, so we usually pair the two if it's his choice. Sometimes we get the bakery to write *Happy Birthday, Riley* on it, even if it's not his birthday. If it's my choice, we get ice cream.

"No Black Forest?"

"Yeah, none of that garbage."

Riley slaps my back. "'Kay, gotta head. See you after."

I stay at the railing a while, watching the synchro. Erika's body slips through the water without making a ripple, and she surfaces in the centre of the tank. The coach starts some music with keyboard and guitar. After a few bars, I recognize it—a wistful song about a river, a singer wishing she could skate away.

She spins in a circle under water, her leg held above the surface like a dancer's graceful arm. A twist and a spin, and then she's describing shapes like she's skating on ice. I never thought a *leg* could communicate anything. But I've got to admit—her body's expressing the emotion in the song so perfectly that I can feel all of that sadness and longing deep down.

• • •

When Riley drops me off at home, Mom stops me from heading up the stairs.

"I just went to the gym. I gotta take a shower."

"Why didn't you shower there?"

I sigh and drop my hand from the bannister.

"No, it's okay. You don't have to explain. Just give me two minutes first?"

We go sit at our fifties dinette set, the kitchen lit just by the range hood. I turn the salt shaker around and around, until Mom puts her hand on mine to stop me.

"You got suspended, so I thought maybe you were ... Well, I thought maybe you were thinking of quitting."

"No, I'm not."

"I just don't want you to think you have to keep doing something that makes you miserable."

I shrug.

"Okay, then. If this is what you want, there's no sense in half-assing it. You know there's scholarship money on the line, right?" Mom gets up and starts drying dishes from the rack and putting them away in the cupboard. "I suggest you get your head back in the game next week and focus."

I mumble, "I will."

"Look, have you told your dad about your suspension?"

"I haven't talked to him."

"He'll be—"

"Pissed. I know."

She stops and looks at me.

"Well, are you going to call him?"

"Cragg'll have beat me to it. He called you, right? He'll have already talked to Dad."

"Well, you better not mess around when you get back to practice next week. If you're sticking with this, then stick with it, okay?"

I don't say anything. Best to just keep quiet, and then maybe I'll get to go upstairs.

"And *you* should talk to your dad. He's funding your ride. You need to tell him yourself."

"Fine. I'll call him and tell him I was fighting. He'll understand, right?" Ugh, that's so bitchy I want to take it back.

Mom puts down the dish towel. "Bart."

"I know." I start spinning the salt shaker again. "It's not why he left you."

Mom says Dad didn't get into fights until after he left her. For a while, he'd show up on our doorstep after too many beers, sporting a gash in his forehead, a black eye ... Mom would give him a spare room to sleep in and send him on his way in the morning. I was like two, three ... I don't remember any of it. But it makes me mad that he'd take advantage of her like that when he was "down on his luck," as he says.

You make your own luck—I know that.

Before Dad went to work in the oil patch, he was out of work for a while. Mom used to say she didn't know how anyone could be an electrician and be out of work, the trades were in such huge demand. But I think it was just Dad's lack of self-control. At some point, he got it together and moved to Fort McMurray. Now he's a maintenance tech at a substation, and he makes decent money. Comes to see me twice a year.

"Bart, he's going to be here in about a week. Will you make sure you talk to him before he comes?"

"Yeah, all right."

Mom softens. "Look, I know it gets monotonous when you're working toward a long-term goal. But listen, everything worth doing is hard sometimes. Right? You remember what your teachers tell you? About how much this dedication and this perseverance is training you for all kinds of stuff in the rest of your life, and—"

"And *for* the rest of my life. I know, I know."

Mom sighs. "Okay. Hey—how about we go for brunch on Sunday? You and me?"

"Um ... I think I might be at the pool."

Mom frowns. "I thought you aren't back at practice until Monday?"

"I'm not. I'm just going to have my own workout ..."

"All right. I know when I'm being blown off."

"No, Mom. I'm not—"

"It's okay." She smiles. "Another time."

"Can I *please* go have a shower now?" I get up and she puts her arms around me and gives me a hug.

"Yes, smelly boy." She pushes me away jokingly. "Go."

SIX

On Monday, I call Dad and get his voice mail—so I just leave a message asking him to call me back. Then I hit the pool for my first practice after my suspension. I grab a flutter board and get in, ready to warm up my whip kick. I can't help but think that egg beater in the dive tank would get my legs in better shape, though.

Riley and I hang on to the wall, waiting our turn. He squints in a beam of sun coming in from the skylight.

"Bart, you've got a halo."

"I'm just glowing."

"Yeah, I'll bet. You've charmed those synchro chicks. Did you ask Erika out yesterday?"

I shake my head.

"She turn you down?"

"I didn't ask her."

Riley frowns. "Oh."

"You ask anyone yet?"

"I'm gonna."

"Who? I met them all, you know. They're all pretty cool. Well, except maybe Chelsea."

Riley smiles. "You'll see. It'll be a surprise."

"No way. Not Chelsea."

"Nah. Gotta walk before you can run, man."

A guy on the top platform of the dive tower has abs so cut I can count the six-pack from here. His shoulders are so much wider than his hips he's like some inverted triangle cartoon of a guy. Below, on the five-metre platform, a taller, leaner guy with dark brown hair steps up to the edge, shaking out his legs and slapping them with a chamois. I look down to where they're going to dive, into the deeper blue water, next to the synchro practice. The synchro girls get to look up and watch the divers from below, watch those perfectly cut bodies fly and spin and land.

"Check it." Riley nods to the bulkhead, where Chelsea's posing, her graceful arm uplifted, frozen until her music starts. With a flutter of her hands, she breaks the pose and dives in on the downbeat, cutting the water without a splash.

"How do they do that?" he asks.

"It's practice. Hours in. Like what we do, but then they've got that to show for it." A performance. Something beautiful. "You know there are guys doing it too now? Their coach came and told me before practice today."

"Sure. But, like, what about the crotch lift?"

"What?"

"That thing they do, where they lift one girl out of the water by her crotch? The girl on the bottom's upside down, and her foot's right there in ..."

"Yeah ... She's called the base."

"Who?"

"The swimmer on the bottom."

"Okay. But have you seen it? She pushes this other girl out of the water by the crotch ... with her foot. Dude. A foot on her crotch."

"I get it, Riley."

"Okay. So what happens when they have to lift a *guy*? Do they have to shove their feet in *his* crotch?"

"Riley."

"I'm just sayin'."

"Shut up, Riley."

I watch Kyoka get propelled out of the water.

"See, Bart? How would a girl do that to a guy?"

"She wouldn't—I mean, if he was bigger than the girl. It's always the smallest bod in the pod that gets lifted. It's just physics ... nothing to do with being a guy."

He doesn't get it. I shut my eyes and let myself sink under for a second. Two. Three. Ten. Twenty. How long could I hold my breath in a routine?

A hand taps me on the head. I pop up and see Erika kneeling on the tiles. She's not wearing her cap now, just a grey cotton T-shirt over her suit. It's getting wet where the suit touches.

"You done already?" I pull my goggles up onto my forehead and rest on the edge.

Riley pushes off for his lap, grinning at me.

"Just a break. What are you doing?" Crouched down, covered in a T-shirt, Erika looks smaller. Like her majesty is muted. She's less athletic goddess, more regular girl.

"Um, swim practice?"

"You should be in our pool."

"Well, that was just a trial session."

"I don't care, mister." Her brown eyes are amused, and angry. "Mister ... What's your last name?"

"Lively."

"You sure are!"

"Watch it, Erika. I've been hearing that joke for, like, sixteen years. What's yours?"

"Tenaka."

I like the way it sounds. "Okay, Miss Tenaka. But I have a lot to catch up on here. I've missed a whole week."

"Yeah, I noticed you were gone."

Huh. She noticed.

"But seriously, Mr Lively? You need to be practising with us. You're wasting your talent over here."

I laugh and splash water up at her. "I'll have you know I'm going to trials for the senior national team this year. I just got my times."

"The national team? So what then, you're headed to the Olympics?"

"Not ruling it out."

"Okay, Bart Lively. But I think synchro would be good for you. You'd get strength, conditioning, endurance—all the stuff you get from lane swimming but different challenges."

I know. I was more worn out after the Try It session than I am after most Rosa Waves practices.

Erika continues. "*And* there's an artistic element that you're missing out on over here."

"Oh, yeah." I look down into the water, to the touchable bottom of the lane pool.

"I nailed it, right? That's what you want."

I shrug.

"You know we have national teams in synchro too? I'm going to trials for the junior national squad," she says, all false modesty. "You know, so I can swim for Canada one day."

"Oh. Congratulations."

"Well, I'm not there yet. But I'll get there. Sunny says you're a total natural, and I don't know how to tell you this, but that's super rare."

"For her to compliment someone?"

"No, for someone to be a natural at my sport! For real, most people can't do what you could do their first try. Sunny said you have a lot of potential for the mixed event. And even if you didn't want to compete, you could still enjoy all the routines, and music, and you know, the *show*."

Geoff swims to the end of the lane where we're talking, and instead of just passing me, he stops, like he's waiting for me to go.

"Well, I don't need *show*," I say.

Erika looks confused.

"I don't mean ... I just mean ... I like watching you guys. You're great."

"So why were you a dancer, Bart?"

Geoff pipes up. "Because Bart's a fag."

Erika gives him a look to shut him up, and I kick him under the water.

"I want to swim a mixed duet routine," Erika says. "It's a new event this year—a duet with a guy and a girl."

"Well, if you need a *guy* you don't want *Bart*," Geoff says.

I push his head under water. He comes up and wags his eyebrows at Erika.

"Oh. You want to swim synchro?" she asks sarcastically.

"Yeah, no." Geoff laughs. "I'll leave that to the ladies," he says, and splashes up a bunch of water as he swims off.

"Boy, he's a treat," says Erika.

"Yeah. You said it."

She rocks forward.

"Okay. So why *were* you a dancer?"

"I dunno." I bob under, then back up, blinking the water out of my eyes. "My mother signed me up?"

"I call bullshit."

I slip my goggles back on and look down the lane.

"Okay. I get it," she says, standing up. "I know the decision can't be easy for you. But you should know that we want you to join."

"Who wants me?"

"Well, me and Sunny, and some of the other girls."

"Chelsea doesn't. Not her mom."

"Ignore them." Erika stands up. Burgundy letters on her grey cotton T-shirt spell out *Breath is for the weak*. Ha. You bet. You'd think she was my soulmate.

"How much time would it take?"

"Maybe three times a week?"

Three times a week? I'm already practising five days a week with the Rosa Waves. Even if I practised with her on my off days, I'd still have to double up on one day. And then I'd die.

Coach walks down the deck, having caught me hanging around talking. Erika takes the hint and leaves, and Cragg shouts, "Lively! Four freestyle, four whip kick no arms, four fly. Now!"

Erika mouths *Think about it,* then walks back to the locker room.

Then I start in on my laps. Back and forth. Back and forth. Trying to come up with a plan.

SEVEN

After practice, I stop Coach Cragg as he's wheeling the whiteboard back into the supply room.

I exhale and look up at the empty stands, then back to Coach. "Hey, I was wondering if I could ask you something."

"If it's how to kick your feet higher out of the water, I can't help you."

I chuckle, like he's made a joke, not a jab. "For real, though, I have a proposal."

"A proposal? Where's my ring?"

Oh God, I want to whack him. When I rehearsed everything I was going to say, I didn't factor in the jokes.

"I'm interested in reducing the hours I spend swimming with the Rosa Waves so I can do a cross-training activity."

"Cross-training? What, you want more time in the gym?"

"Not ... exactly."

Then Cragg shakes head. I see the gears moving as he figures it out on his own. "No. I saw where you went last week."

"Yeah. It was cool. And I thought maybe I could spend some of my pool hours training with the synchro club. It's really tough, and I think it could totally complement my development here ... Maybe the hybrid training is just what I need to really, you know, launch myself to another level."

Coach Cragg looks like he's trying to understand what I've just said, like I've started speaking another language. My heart's thumping hard. I'm more than a little afraid.

"In a girls' synchro club?"

"It's not—there's nothing that says guys can't swim with their club. And, well ... if I could get out of practice early on Thursday maybe, then Sundays ..."

"You want to skip out on practice for water ballet?"

"It's not ... water ballet."

"No. My answer's no."

"Come on, Coach. I'm doing really well. I won't fall behind, I promise."

Cragg looks away, and then steps right up close to me. Pointing a finger at my chest, he growls, "You have no idea. You're so privileged you haven't a clue what I've put into your training, or what your parents have."

I cringe. I know he's put a ton into me. It's not like I'm not thankful. And beneath whatever insensitivity Coach Cragg sports, I know he cares about me.

"Have you even asked your dad about this?"

"I'm going to."

Cragg stands there, waiting me out. I hate that. I'm standing here, trying not to fill his silence with a bunch of meaningless words, but it's hard. The silence is too uncomfortable.

"Swimming's important, Coach, but this feels important for me to try out too. Sunny really thinks I have a lot of promise."

"Oh, you're a natural, are you?"

The way *he* says it I know it's not a compliment.

"I just don't want to have to choose between—"

Cragg shakes his head. "Choose? Is this really a big decision for you? You can't split your focus. God, Bart. You know what this sport is offering you. And if you want it, you have to give it *everything*. You know that. You've got a job to do here."

I know. I know the job is to win, and the job is to get my name on that plaque on the wall with the record times in our club from every year, going back to the early nineties.

"So what are you going to do?" Coach asks.

I hear the blood rushing past my ears, my quick pulse. I know what he expects me to say. And it's not just him—I would have to ask Dad eventually. And if Coach won't say yes, there's no way Dad will.

"Well?"

"My job."

"Good." My heart sinks into my feet. Coach keeps talking, but I can barely process what he's saying. "Oh. I forgot to tell you since you were away last week, but there's a school meet here on Wednesday, so our pool time's bumped later. We start at seven."

I groan.

"I know you guys hate late practices, but come on—you just had a week off. Suck it up!"

I drag myself over to the hot tub, and this guy I've watched from the dive club—my height, good shoulders, cut abs—slides in too. I close my eyes and lean my head back on the tile, let the heat from the water and his stare unfreeze me.

Okay, I don't really know if he's staring. But when I open my eyes, he's looking at me.

"Hey," he says. "You're the synchro boy, right?"

"Uh, no. I mean, yeah, I *tried* some synchro, but I'm not a 'synchro boy.'"

Dive Boy leans back and holds his hands palms up. "I just asked a question."

Sure, but he's probably thinking *water fairy*.

"It's a high-performance sport," I tell him. "Just like diving."

"Sure." He grins. "You liked it?"

"It felt right. It just felt like something my body knew how to do. Not that it's easy, though, you know? It was super hard."

Dive Boy leans his head back and relaxes into the jets. "I can see the appeal."

I close my eyes and try to relax too. When I open my eyes, Dive Boy isn't looking at me.

But I look at him.

His shoulders, so smooth and cut and perfect, make me feel like touching them. And I guess most people would think, *Oh, that's it. Bart's gotta be gay. He wants to touch that boy's shoulders.* But that's just ... simplifying it.

I'm just admiring his body. Letting myself think about what it would be like to be that perfectly formed.

Or ... to touch someone that perfectly formed.

Yeah—even if the hot tub isn't raising my blood pressure, my cheeks are burning. It's time I got out.

• • •

I go to the team locker room, and Geoff and Andy walk up and strike a pose, their arms in the air, like they're at the start of a synchro routine.

"Oh, fuck off."

They can barely contain themselves. I look at Riley, but he's keeping out of it. Some of the other guys are just smiling to themselves. Yeah, it's totally hilarious. Then Andy starts singing, "La la la la la ..." and they spin around. Geoff puts his hand over his mouth and says, in an announcer voice, "It's the Rosa Pacific water ballet ... now with more homo!"

"It's seriously demanding, okay? It's harder than what we do. You guys don't even know. They're really strong."

"Oh, so something for you to look up to?" Andy asks. "It's good to have goals. Maybe you can get as strong as the other girls one day, Bart."

My heart starts pounding. This isn't good. It's like the ground I gained the other day when I made them shut up has been ripped out from under me. I grab my shampoo and go to the showers, and there's Dive Boy.

"Hey."

"Hey." I pick a shower head two over from him and turn on the tap. I shut my eyes and tip my head back, soaking my curls. Geoff and the other guys will be coming in here any minute, and suddenly, I just want to be out of here as fast as I can. I soap down and reach for the shampoo bottle, but it slips out of my hand. I bend down to pick it up just as Geoff and Andy walk in. Too late.

"Oh no! Bart's dropped the soap! Andy, it's your turn."

"I'm not going near that fag," Andy says, laughing.

"Shut the hell up!" I lunge for Andy, but he backs away. Then they both stand in the entryway to the showers, daring me to walk around them.

"You're just an attention whore, aren't you?" Geoff asks, coming in closer. "You just like it when you're acting like a girl and everyone's watching you, don't you?"

"No!"

Dive Boy shuts off his shower. He looks at me like he's keeping tabs on the situation, and I don't want him to come to my rescue. I don't want to be a princess in a fucking tower.

"Maybe they're watching me because I'm getting better times than you. So why don't you just leave me alone."

"We'll leave you alone when you stop acting like a girl, Bart. Stop trying to make our swim club gay."

"I'm not the one who's standing around in his Speedo, paying too much attention to other guys in the shower. Leave me alone, Geoff."

Dive Boy laughs and takes his towel off the hook. I so wish he wasn't here to see this. I don't know what he thinks. But I find myself wondering if Dive Boy thinks I'm gay, or if he thinks I'm *not* gay now. Or if he thinks I'm just a jerk, crowing about my times.

Geoff and Andy wait for Dive Boy to leave, then they lay into me again.

"Oh, sorry, Bart. We didn't mean to interrupt your date."

"Fuck you."

"Uh, no thanks," Geoff says, and finally, they go turn on their showers and leave me alone.

I grab my towel and quickly go change. And I can't help but notice that Riley's only now going to take his shower. Well. I'm definitely not waiting down here in the locker room. So I head upstairs and grab a bench.

"It blows," Riley says, coming up the stairs. "Putting up with those idiots." He looks away, like he can't meet my eyes. "It sucked last week when you weren't at practice."

"Yeah. I don't know why they're getting worse all of a sudden. For a while there, we never really had to deal with this bullshit, right?"

Riley nods. After I joined swimming, we became Bullet and Bigfish. Just a couple of water rats. Nobody really gave us a hard time, not even when we started waxing our legs. Now? It's like middle school all over again.

Riley keeps leaning back on the railing and bouncing forward. All kinds of energy, even after a three-hour practice.

"Just don't get suspended again. Don't make me deal with these assholes myself, okay?"

"What do you mean? What happened?"

"Just the usual."

The usual, but I guess I wasn't there to be the one to take it. "They give you a hard time?"

Riley shrugs. And there's my answer. Even if I wanted to ditch the Rosa Waves—even if it were possible—I can't leave my bud behind to deal with this crap.

"Hey. I'm not going anywhere now. We'll do something about it."

"What, like go crying to Coach about the big bad bullies?"

"Well ... I don't know. Don't you think we should try to talk to Cragg?"

"Just forget it," he says, pushing himself off the railing one more time, before heading up the stairs. He stops halfway up. "We still going for Mickey Dee's?"

"Yeah."

"Good. Fucking starving."

• • •

After dinner, I'm just stressed—and mad. The assholes have got under my skin. But worse, I couldn't get Riley to talk. No, he just hinted at stuff happening, letting me imagine the worst—stuff that Riley makes *me* responsible for, the way he says, "Don't leave me alone with them again."

Fuck.

In my bedroom, I throw my bag on the desk and click on the fairy lights that frame the window. Then I turn on my little Bluetooth speaker and start a playlist of my current favourite pop songs.

It's a guilty pleasure. Just like the poster of dancer Sergei Polunin above my night table, the one I take down before anyone comes over.

I kick my rug under my bed, pull off my shirt, and spin out some fast pump turns, leap and kick as much as the space between my bed and my desk will allow, which isn't much.

I'm bulletproof, nothing to lose ...

Sometimes this is enough—enough to burn off stress, to shake it off like a dog who's scrapped with another dog.

"Bart?" Mom knocks and opens my door. "It's a little loud."

"Sorry."

"Have you called your dad yet?"

Ugh. So much for stress-busting. I turn off the playlist.

"He wasn't home."

"Well ... try again, okay?" Mom pushes my door open wider and comes in. "He'll be here this weekend. I don't want him not finding out until he gets here—"

"Yeah, okay. I will."

She drops a fresh set of sheets on my bed and looks at the row of swimming medals that hangs on the wall above. She picks up my pillow and slowly starts taking the case off.

"Mom, leave it. I can do that."

"Okay. You have any homework?"

"Yes." I look at the clock—it's nine already. I just feel like going to bed.

"All right, then. I guess I can't make any more excuses to be here."

"You don't have to make excuses, Mom."

"Well, you don't want me to stay here and watch you do your homework, do you?"

I laugh. "No. Okay, get lost."

Dad's an hour ahead, so I hope it's not too late to call—but, like my homework, I just want it over.

I get his voice mail again.

"Hey, it's Bart. Your son. Just leaving a message." I hang up and think: *Idiot. Of course you're his son.*

I switch over to Messages, but then I stop myself. I can't tell him by text or I'll look like I copped out.

I'll just have to wait.

EIGHT

After school, I watch Erika, Julia, and Chelsea walk to Chelsea's little Nissan in the parking lot, and I just about laugh watching Erika and those tall girls try to pile in there. It's like a clown car.

I unlock my bike and am just about to get on. But wait. They're going to the pool, of course. The dive tank's not taken up for the meet.

They're practising.

The Rosa Waves *aren't*.

But—it's my night to make dinner. Since we have a short practice on Wednesdays, I cook when I come home. But today I told Mom I'd come home and make supper for her before I go to the pool, since we're bumped later.

I take my phone out and text her.

> Hey mom so so so sorry got a chance to do some stuff at the pool. Make u an aMAZing dinner this weekend k?

Stuff? Okay, but you owe me dinner AND a gelato.

> It's a date

I hop on my bike, and turn in the direction of the pool.

• • •

Half an hour later, I'm in the dive tank with Erika, treading water while she explains duet competitions.

"So every pair has to swim a technical routine, then a free routine.

55

The technical's where both swimmers have to swim all these required elements in a certain order at the same time, facing the same way. You can do a highlight—like a lift or a throw—but other than that, it's gotta be the same."

"Okay. And the free?"

"In the free routine, you can do anything you want.

"And that's the same for girl–girl and mixed duets?"

"Yeah, with mixed, though ... the free is even more cool. 'Cause there's more opportunity to interact, and it's not just matching each other all the time. It's less like a chorus line. It's like ... Well, it's like a real dance."

"Like pas de deux?"

"Yeah, but not like the prissy *Nutcracker* ballet crap."

"Hey!"

"No offence ... I just mean that it's more like modern dance. Contemporary music, more expressive."

"I love contemporary."

Erika smiles at me. Those dimples pop in, and I can't help but think about how pretty she is.

"Cool. Okay, so do you remember back layout position from before?"

"Yeah, sure." I float out on my back, toes pointed, sculling at my side.

Erika coaches me through a figure that I learned last time.

"You need to keep the toe of your bent leg in contact with the inside of your extended leg, 'kay?"

"Okay. Try again?"

She patiently adds steps to the figure until I can do the whole thing. I've lifted my legs together while my back is arched—hard, so hard ... I've got a strong core, but it's still not easy. A twirl, a twist, and then descend. I come up and take a giant breath.

"Your breath control's seriously good. I don't know guys who can hold it for that long."

I raise a brow. "Thank you?"

"But you can't gasp when you come up."

"Oh."

Erika builds a short, easy sequence of three figures strung together. We swim them side by side, and Sunny comes over and counts for us. When I come up, she holds up her iPad. "I just shot video. Do you want to see?"

I groan, watching how I come in late on a count. Watching my legs be less than straight on a vertical.

Erika frowns. "You don't even know, do you? The fact you can even do half this stuff already? God, Bart. It takes weeks and weeks for a synchro newb to get to where you are."

"Yeah?"

She looks at me like, *Yeah, duh.*

Sunny nods too, her eyebrows raised.

"But ... It looks so bad compared to what it feels like."

"What does it feel like?"

"Well ... kind of electric, to be honest."

"Hey, it's like that when you start swimming something new. But don't feel bad. You keep practising and it comes together, and then ... Well, if you think *that* felt electric ..."

I raise an eyebrow. "Are you flirting with me?" If Sunny leaves us alone for a bit, I could ask her out. Now would be a good time. But Sunny's sticking close by.

Erika just smacks my arm and gets out of the water. "I'm going to get us some music."

It's a pop song. Lots of synth.

"Listen to the words!" Erika says, then she starts singing along. "'Is this my life? Am I breathing under water?' Isn't it perfect? I've always wanted to do a routine to this one."

The beat is fast, way faster than I thought you could ever swim to. But she slows the counts down, and for the next thirty minutes, Sunny and Erika direct me and correct me through a series of movements that have

Erika and me interacting. At the end, after the other girls have packed up and gone home, we can do about twenty seconds of the routine without stopping. That doesn't sound like much, and I sure am sloppy—but there's something totally delicious about doing the movements together.

I put my hand behind Erika's head like we're preparing to kiss. I lift her out of the water by her waist. Our legs interlock at one point. The water's warm. The contact is ... completely seductive. I'd probably get turned on if I wasn't so thoroughly wrung out from the hard work. And if I wasn't so nervous, under Sunny's watch ... And if we weren't whacking each other under water so much.

I get out and sit on the side.

"Bart, your control will come. You are really good at keeping up with Erika's pace."

"His swimming speed's awesome." Erika turns to me. "What do the racers call you?"

"Oh ... Bullet?"

"See? Bullet. Can you imagine what we'd look like if we practised enough?"

Sunny sees me lie back on the tile.

"Bart. You look exhausted."

"Yeah, I should head." I sit up and look at the clock. It's ten after seven, and the Rosa guys have started warm-up already. "Whoa, when did that happen?"

Erika leans over and whispers in my ear. "You love it. Time flies when you're having fun, right? I told you."

I push her away, but I'm smiling.

"Hey, Bart." Sunny squats down to talk to me. "You did so well tonight, and you really are so good at this. If you come back, you and Erika could swim a duet for the club—we might even send it to competition, if there's an opportunity. What do you say?"

"Yeah, I'd love to, but ..."

Erika looks at me, then at Sunny.

"It's a big commitment, but I think it's worth it, Bart. I can tell you right now, you have what it takes for competition in this sport. I'm serious."

Even if there wasn't a university scholarship waiting for me ... even if I felt really *done* with racing ... I couldn't. Not with Dad funding my Sports Institute program. Not with Dad and Coach Cragg so sure of my future success. What would I be leaving behind? Too much. And I can just imagine what Riley would say if I left the Rosa Waves.

"I can't. I'm sorry."

Erika looks down into the water, then up at Sunny.

"He's on an Olympic path, with racing."

"Ah." Sunny stops smiling. "Too bad."

"Too bad?" I laugh.

"Yes. I'd love to see what you're capable of."

"Well, thanks for that, Sunny. And thanks for tonight." I look at Erika. "It *was* fun."

She holds her hand up in a little wave. And that's it—I can't ask her now. Not with her looking so sad. I grab my bag and head back to the other side of the pool.

After practice with the Rosa Waves, I scarf down the protein bar at the bottom of my bag as I search iTunes for the song Erika's picked for the routine she wants to do. Then I add it to my library and put it on repeat all the way home.

NINE

This past week I've tried to focus—to just forget about the synchro stuff, and keep working on my times. At school, I'm trying to get ahead of the work, since it already feels kind of overwhelming this year. Grade eleven's starting with a bang. Five essays, all due before the end of September!

"That'll teach you to take four humanities blocks in one semester." Riley laughs. "I'm surprised they even let you do that."

We're sitting on the front steps of Rosa Pacific Secondary, and he's checking out every girl who walks past us down the stairs on the way to the parking lot.

"Ugh. I know. I'm so stupid."

"Yeah, speaking of that, have you asked her yet?"

I shake my head.

"You know, you keep going over to the dive tank to talk to her. I thought you'd have asked her by now. What are you even doing over there? Coach was pissed when you were late to practice."

"Don't remind me."

"Well? I just don't know what's going on. You've been weird lately. Ever since you got suspended. It's like you're not really here."

"It's nothing."

Riley waits. Just like Coach likes to wait for you to talk. To fill in the space. I wonder if he learned the trick from him.

"So your dad's coming this weekend, eh?"

"Yeah."

Riley waits some more. When I don't say anything, he just stands up and walks down the steps.

"Okay, then. See you at the pool."

"Wait—can I drop my bike at home and get a ride with you?"

Riley throws his hands up. "Okay, whatever."

"Hey, sorry. I'm just tired, man."

"Sure."

• • •

After practice, I get changed slowly, and walk up the stairs. I feel drained. Like I'm coming down with something. At the top, my phone buzzes.

> Hey Bart, it's Erika. I need u to look at this

I click the attached link, and there's a stream of stuff ... a hashtag on Twitter: #MixedDuetOlympics. And a bunch of images tagged with the hashtag. Facebook posts. Instagram.

I sit down on one of the benches in the hall and start looking through the links. The Twitter hashtag starts with the US synchronized swimming champion Bill May's tech duet partner Christina Jones asking people to support the event for the next Olympics by posting their favourite photo of a mixed duet. So I scroll through, and it's photos of synchro with guys. Lots of pics of Bill, but not just Bill. Lots of other guys. French guy, Russian guy, Spanish guy. Canadian guy. Wait. I back up ... the Spanish guy's not huge. He's built like me.

I flip over to YouTube and watch their duet from the world trophy last year, where they were the only competitors. It's good ... I like the way they move on deck, and in the water.

I go back and see more tagged pictures: the Japanese pair, the Turkish pair. The Czechs.

There's an article too. No—there's more than one. People writing about how guys are ready now. They're gunning to include the mixed event in the Olympics in four years.

The hall's busy. The polo team arrives for practice. The water aerobics class leaves, and parents rush their kids to and from swim lessons.

My phone buzzes in my hand again.

U there? Did u check that out?

Yeah. Hey, how'd u get my number?

Casey got it from Riley.

What?

Riley asked her out. He didn't tell u?

No. When?

idk. Last weekend?

She said yes?

Ya! :-D Tell Riley he's lucky. Casey's great.

I will. Fucker! he said nothing

Anyway, u could win a medal and really show that bag of dicks u swim with.

lol. Tempting.

I'm serious. Bean him between the eyes w gold. That'll shut him up.

Gold?

Worlds. Then Olympics. It could happen.

G getting brained w gold medal does appeal--but i'm not a violent person ;-P

fine

How many guys u think are training in canada?

none in our age group.

no juniors?

girls had to fight over the 1 guy who was ready 4 senior world champs :-D

this year?

Zero Bart. Nobody. Do it with me.

I spin around on the bench to face the pool through the window. The polo guys are getting in now. Helmets on. A respectable water sport, but I hate the constant sound of the whistle. And, you know, it involves balls being flung at your head.

Synchro has *such* a reputation. The first time I stand on the bulkhead ready to start a routine, everyone will say, "Look, Bart's gay! He's never had a girlfriend. Now this." They'll figure they know everything about me. "Well, he's gay, isn't he? He's joined a girl's sport, so that's it. Bart's gay. Now we know everything about him."

But here's the thing: they can't know if I'm gay. 'Cause *I* don't even know.

I hate this. I mean, if I wanted to do synchro, why couldn't I just do it and not have people say anything? I should be able to. Maybe in some other universe I could. But not this one. Not here at this pool. If I were to leave the Rosa Waves and go join synchro, I bet the shit I've gotten the last couple of weeks would look like nothing compared to what I'd face then.

And then there's Coach. At every step, Coach Cragg's picked out my strengths, and given them back to me. He tells me what I'm good at and helps me focus. He's pushed me harder than I've ever been pushed, harder than my mom would ever have pushed me—and I am grateful for that, really. Even if I get pissed at him, and what he lets go under the radar here, I can't walk away from his coaching. That would feel like rejecting everything he's given me, the *path* that he's given me.

And Dad would probably kill me. Or never speak to me again. Would he even help pay for my university tuition if I don't get a swimming scholarship? 'Cause I'm pretty damn sure they don't give guys scholarships for synchronized swimming.

I stare into the deep end, at the tiles breaking and rippling as waves run along the surface. I think of all the reasons why I can't swim a mixed duet. They start with getting asked if I'm queer; they continue with getting booed off a bulkhead before my performance and assaulted in the showers. And they end with getting close to Erika only to find out that, actually, I'm *not* attracted to her that way. And then what?

sorry. I just can't.

Riley comes up the stairs. "Who ya texting?"

"Uh, Erika, actually."

"Oh, I know what you're up to." Riley drops his bag and does some kind of manoeuvre that might be a sixties dance move and shakes his hips a little. He starts singing—"Erika ... nobody does it like Erika ... Let's do the swim ..." He grabs his nose and mimes a cannonball, then laughs.

"Look, Riley. I'm not trying to ..."

"Get in her pants? I know. Because she's not wearing any. She's wearing a swimsuit."

I sigh.

"Can I go home now?"

"Oh, you wanna ride?"

"You think I'm hanging around here to look at your pretty face?"

Riley shoves me. I shove him back. So at least it feels a little back to normal.

"I can't give you a ride to the SI party, though, 'kay? I'm gonna go get tortured with those big acupuncture needles."

"Your shoulder still bugging you?"

"Yeah. Physio said I shouldn't drive the same day."

"Cool. But I'll still see you at the party?"

"Yeah, I'll be there."

With Casey. But he's not saying it. What's he waiting for?

In the car on the way home, my phone buzzes again.

U can! Don't be scared. Pls? I've got u

I'm not *scared*. Am I?

• • •

After I've eaten, I go up to my room and watch Bill May's last performance with his duet partner Christina Jones on YouTube, the first time men competed in the synchro world championships. Bill's in a bright coral Speedo. His deck work starts off with him running in and pulling off three back hand-springs. Then he dives through a little square Christina makes with her arm and leg—straight into the pool.

Then I check out the Italian pair, and a few others from that competition in Russia last year. I look for more ... I lose an hour, easy, just bringing up video after video of guys in different competitions, but I keep coming back to Bill. There's something so compelling about watching him swim.

I'm so absorbed I don't hear my door open until it hits that spot where the hinge creaks. I shut my laptop, but that just looks suspicious.

"Mom ... knocking?"

"Sorry." She puts the basket of laundry down on my bed and nods at my computer. "But are you watching something you shouldn't?"

"*No*, Mom."

"Well, what didn't you want me to see?"

"Nothing."

"I don't know, Bart. You won't tell me what's going on at the pool, and you can't do brunch, even though you don't have practice. It feels like there's a lot you're keeping from me. Are you seeing ... ah ... someone? Is that what this is about? Because you don't have to sneak around, if that's it—"

I shut my eyes for a moment. Mom's always so careful not to talk like she has any expectations that I'd be dating *girls*. She's always choosing her pronouns so freaking carefully. I open my eyes and look right at her.

"I'm not seeing *anyone*, Mom. And this is what I was watching."

I open the laptop and hit the space bar, and Bill May is swimming on my screen.

"So you were watching synchro?"

My cheeks go hot. "Yeah."

"Show me."

She sits down on my bed. I open my laptop and play her Bill's free routine with Kristina Lum-Underwood from worlds in the summer, and then his USA gold-winning tech duet with Christina Jones.

"That move's called the cyclone."

"You're interested in this?"

"This girl from the synchro club says they do these mixed duets for their competitions now. It's a brand-new event, with guys. I was just checking it out."

"A girl? What girl?"

"Just a girl."

Mom stands up. "Okay. Make sure you bring the basket down after you put your laundry away."

"I will."

After Mom's gone, I watch Bill swim a duet with Anna Kozlova to "The Phantom of the Opera." The song's cornball musical crap, but Bill and his partner make it so much better with how they swim it. They swim another duet to that old song "Anything You Can Do." Bill's hamming it up, and I've never seen so much—well—*acting* in swimming. It's funny. And the words: *Anything you can do I can do better* ... that's gotta be a jab at everyone telling him guys can't swim in a girls' sport.

Bill's ripped. His body's like a swimmer angel and a dancer angel melded into one human form. I've never seen anyone so strong, and so in control of every movement of his own body—and in *water,* even. God, he's strong. He can lift himself up out of the water on a vertical, so toes first, all the way up to his *chest.* Just a total athletic feat. I can barely imagine what it takes to swim like that.

But I can totally see myself trying. I can see myself right there. They're making it okay, Bill and these other guys—it's like they're living a different *kind* of maleness. Something I don't see in the racing pool. Something that's not *allowed* in the racing pool. And you know what? They look beautiful doing it. And people love them! Look at them cheering and clapping like mad, waving flags.

They're making it *okay.*

I get up from the computer and walk over to the mirror. I stretch my arms up over my body like May did when he walked up to the bulkhead, so flexible his shoulders dislocated.

You know, every time I move, eight years of dance gives me away. It tattles on me. But in this sport? It just looks right. I fan my fingers out and point to the ceiling. Then I float my arms down and hold them in second position. I pirouette, spinning two complete rotations before meeting my eyes in the mirror.

TEN

The next morning, I wake up thinking about Erika. I put the folded laundry away, and on top of my dresser, I see the old recital picture in the gold frame. Mom must have put it there after I went to sleep last night. But where did she even find it? I thought I'd boxed it up ages ago with a bunch of crap from when I was a kid.

The note tucked into the frame's faded, but I can still read it. *Never forget what you are capable of.*

For a minute, I feel like the pressure lifts. All the limits. And that feeling? It's too damned good to ignore.

● ● ●

When I get to the pool Thursday night, I figure I'll tell Cragg I'm leaving the Rosa Waves at the end of practice. But once I'm downstairs, I change my mind. I can't—I don't want to spend one more practice in the racing pool.

I change fast, so I can head out to the deck to talk to Cragg before any of the other guys are there.

"Look at the keener," Riley teases. "Making up for lost time?"

"Uh, yeah. Kinda."

I duck out the door. I haven't told Riley yet. I don't even know how to tell him.

I catch Coach Cragg writing down our warm-up.

"What's up, Lively?"

"Coach, I know you're not going to like this."

"What?"

"I've decided to leave the Rosa Waves. I'm joining synchro."

"You're doing this?"

I let him steam for a minute. Wait me out. Wait for me to keep speaking. When I don't, he shakes his head.

"You know what? Getting a kid to your level? That takes commitment. I was committed to you."

Was. Past tense. Something about that makes it official, makes it real. This is really happening. I just think about that note in the frame, and take a deep breath.

"Yeah, I know."

Cragg looks shocked.

"So you're just going to walk away from this?" Cragg shakes his head. "God, Bart. You can't just mess around. You can't leave to go play water fairy and then come back here, you know."

"I know."

"I mean it. You won't be able to swim for me again. What are you going to tell your dad?"

"I don't know. I'll ... just tell him."

"I'd like to see how that goes."

It's not like leaving dance, when I was just aching to get out of what was making me uncomfortable. No. This feels numbing. This is a shock.

Riley and the guys come out on deck and start walking over here. I don't want to stick around. I've done it—I've ripped off that Band-Aid, but I still don't know what to say to Riley.

I turn away, but Cragg stops me. His voice sounds thick now, like he's going to cry. "You walk away from this, you know what you're giving up?"

I look at the plaque, the spot where my name would go up later this year, if only I stayed.

"Yeah, I know." Then I give Coach a small smile.

He shakes his head. "You think the guys here were giving you a hard time, you just wait until those girls get ahold of you."

• • •

I hold back tears as I slip into the hot tub, just wanting the comfort of hot water swirling around me. I'll just soak for a bit, then leave before the Rosa Waves are done. I'll tell Riley later.

I just quit racing.

It doesn't even feel *real*.

How do I just let go of the plan for my life?

I stay in the hot tub for far too long. The dive practice breaks, and that beautiful boy with the warm eyes gets in with a couple of his teammates. He jokes and talks easily with them—like he's completely taken up with what's going on with them. But I must be wearing my shock on my face, because every now and then, he looks right at me. And his eyes seem to ask, *Are you okay?*

I give him a sad smile that says, *No*. But *yes*.

Yes. I'm going to swim with Erika.

A voice inside me is saying *This is okay. You are worth this. You deserve to find out what it's like to be back on the stage, in your own skin.*

I'm going to do this duet, and we'll get good enough for junior worlds first. Then Erika and I will get good enough for the Olympics. I can feel it. And Sunny said I was a natural. So we'll work hard for four years, and we'll be there when they debut the mixed duet at the next Olympics. We'll be there for Canada. It's going to happen! It *has* to happen.

I'll get so good that feeling that I had when I swam the duet will be visible to anyone—under water or on the surface. And the world will see that it's ridiculous to keep someone out of a sport just because of their gender. We're going to show the world what it's missing.

But also, *no*. I'm nowhere near okay. Because now I have to explain to everyone why I'm doing this—to Riley, to everyone at the Sports Institute at school. To Mom and Dad. And what am I going to say? I've given up a sure thing for this duet, this thing that I just have a *feeling* about?

It's going to look like I've lost my mind. But it feels like I might have found my heart.

So *yes,* and *no.*

It's too complex. And Dive Boy can't possibly understand everything I'm saying if I'm not going to use any words, can he? But I'll take his look as comfort anyway.

Then I close my eyes and imagine kissing him. When he gets out of the tub, I watch the water drip off his legs. My eyes travel up to his ass, just before I squeeze my lids shut.

Fuck.

• • •

Before I get home, there's a text from Riley.

> how come u ditched?

> kinda gotta explain in person

> talk tomorrow?

Three dots appear. Riley's typing something, but he never finishes.

ELEVEN

I looked for Riley the next day. He wasn't in bio—typical for first block on a Friday. It wasn't until Socials that I remembered the big needles. He was either at physio or recovering—I never got a chance to talk to him.

The Rosa Waves don't practice on Fridays. So when I show up on the pool deck after school, Erika looks confused.

There's only water polo in the racing pool.

But I'm on deck. In my swimsuit.

"Hey, you. What are you doing here?"

I just smile.

Erika gets a glint in her eye. "Wait ... no. For real?

"I'm in. Totally in. I told Coach Cragg last night."

Erika puts a hand over her mouth "Oh my God. You did it. You quit the Rosa Waves!" She grabs my wrist and pulls me in for a hug. She yells over to the others, "Bart's in!"

Julia comes over and gives me and Erika a high-five. "Yay, we've got a *guy!*" she shouts.

"First and only junior duet pair competing in the mixed duet. Yeeeah!" Erika says. "Let's celebrate! Hey, do you want to go to Chelsea's barbecue tonight?"

"Yeah, that's the big SI welcome back. You bet! Come with me?"

"Oh, yeah, I'll be there. Julia and I are going ... We're going to get ready at her house after practice. We'll see you there."

Okay. So, not exactly a date.

Sunny comes over to us with a grin on her face.

"This is exciting."

She gives me registration papers and a welcome package, and then talks to me and Erika about practice times, and our first meet—a training meet, where we'll perform a portion of our routine to get judge feedback.

"Okay, now get in the pool! We've got work to do."

I can't help but notice the mothers in the bleachers, looking on with grim expressions.

Just ignore them, I tell myself. *You're exactly where you need to be.* Then I hop in next to Erika.

We start with the sequence we worked on last Wednesday, then add on a bit more.

When Sunny calls for break time, I look into the bleachers, and the mothers are staying put. Good. I get out of the pool and down half a litre of water. Then I grab my phone and hold it out to Chelsea.

"Hey, can you do me a favour ... Take a picture of me and Erika when we come up on the boost when we run through it again?"

"You want a souvenir?" Chelsea asks.

"More of a first-day record." I smile at Erika. "It's our first official duet practice."

"You can't be serious. That's what you guys have been doing?" Chelsea looks at Erika with a big WTF written on her face.

"Of course he's serious," says Erika. "Bart's a natural. I mean, look at his flat splits! Look at his walk-on, for crying out loud."

"Yeah, he even walks on good," Jules says.

"I thought you were just messing around," Chelsea says. "Doing this for, I don't know, for fun or something. What makes you think you can do this?" Chelsea stares me down. "Seriously, what if I said I'm joining competitive swimming now?"

"I don't know—what are your times like?" I try not to smile.

Chelsea narrows her eyes at Erika. "He is *not* seriously going to swim a duet with you."

"We *told* you. He is."

"How?" Chelsea looks back at me, from one eye to the other, scrutinizing. Then back to Erika. "How did you convince Bullet to do this?"

"I didn't do anything," she says.

"The hell you didn't."

Whoa. What's going on? Erika stares Chelsea down until she sighs and holds her hand out for my phone. "Okay, fine. Do you want it landscape or portrait?"

"Uh ..."

Erika rolls her eyes. "Just whatever looks better, Chels."

"Well if you want to have it emphasize the height on your boost, you should go with portrait. But if you want me to zoom in more, then ..."

"Portrait! God. Get in the pool, Bart."

"Yes, ma'am." I get in, and Erika and I go beneath the surface, get into the body boost set-up, our knees bent, like we've been practising. We count silently to ourselves, and on five, we kick out a powerful egg beater.

"Can I see?" I swim over and Chelsea crouches down to show me the screen. In the photo, Erika and I are out of the water almost to our waists, arms up, smiling. "Awesome!"

Chelsea looks at the screen and frowns. "You're not vertical. You're winging off to the side."

Erika says, "Let me see." Chelsea shows her, and she scoffs, "Hardly. You seriously couldn't tell unless you got out a measuring stick."

"Do you want me to?" Chelsea asks.

I get out of the pool, dry off my hands, and look over Erika's shoulder. Something about seeing Erika beside me in the photo sparks a mental image of myself with a medal and a girlfriend. The two of us, together, winning. No more Princess, no more teasing from the Rosa Waves, or from Coach. I'll speak Boy, I'll look Boy. And better still? I'll do it while I'm fucking *synchronized swimming*. Ha! That'll show the stupid gender police and their stupid rules.

"That's okay, Chelsea. This is good." I take the phone back, and flip over to Twitter. I post the picture and tag it: #MixedDuetOlympics #newbie #heyyouneverknow.

"C'mon, guys!" Sunny claps. "One more run-through so I can video you and then you guys can go to your party."

After we do the routine again, I take Sunny's tablet from Erika, laughing 'cause she's trying to hold it away from me, but my reach is way longer.

"Don't worry! I'm not deleting anything." I scroll back, replay one part.

"Okay, see where we do this facing back? I think it would be sexier if we did the front version of the figure. Then like, come up facing each other. Then ... Okay, I don't know how to do this in the water, but ..." I get out on deck to demonstrate. "We'd come up *en couronne*, then I'd inside spin and you'd outside spin, like ..." I hold up my arms, rounded above my head, and turn. "It looks more dramatic, right?"

"Okay, Bart, slow down. I'm not a ballerina," Erika says. "*En cour ...* what?"

I slow the movement down, and show her fifth position. We get in the water and run through that sequence with the new choreography—and with some adjustments, it works.

"That's awesome! Thank you," Erika says, watching the new version on the tablet. Julia swims up and gets Erika to play it for her, and I lean back and watch, feeling ... well, proud.

Erika and I run through the duet once more, while the others watch. And this time, I feel how we're more in sync. It's like we're really dancing in the deep. We swim through to the end of what we have so far, multiplying each other's energy. And it's ... a total high.

We emerge and blink hard. I look at Jules. She shouts a drawn-out yeeeeah! And then Kyoka high-fives us.

I'm half-excited, but also half wondering what bugged Chelsea so much about me swimming the duet.

TWELVE

Chelsea's house in Cordova Bay is all cedar and glass and corrugated metal, a custom design built down a steep hill so all you see from the driveway is the top, top level. This whole neighbourhood's on a slope, with views of the ocean and the Olympic Mountains.

"Wow."

"No kidding, eh?" Julia says.

Some lacrosse boys come out the front door as we walk up the steps. They're headed down the street with their backpacks and a few of the girls from the soccer program.

"They're leaving kind of early, aren't they?" Erika asks.

"Oh, they'll be back."

She looks at me quizzically.

"They're hitting the trail at the end of Chelsea's street for the side party."

"There's a side party?"

"For the lacrosse boys, yeah. Swimmers don't really party with the lacrosse guys."

"It's just weird," Julia says. "You SI guys got all these cliques. I mean, man, this is *high school*. You think you would all just grow up sometime."

"Oh, so you don't have cliques in the regular stream?"

"Not like this. It's like you don't even talk to sports that aren't yours."

I shrug. I guess she's right about some of us. But as for me, it's not because I'm a snob about my sport.

"Like, do you even hang out with non-swimmers?" Julia asks.

"I don't think swimming's better than anything else. It's just that Riley and I stick together." Speaking of Riley, I gotta find him. If another Rosa Wave swimmer found out and told him I quit first? Ugh, I'm going to feel so bad.

"Seriously, like ... I hope for their sake those guys don't have a game tomorrow," Erika says. "Don't they have games on Saturdays?"

"Well, all they have to do is chase a ball around with a net on a stick. I could probably do that hungover," Julia says.

We laugh.

The sign on the door says, *Come in—we are on the patio downstairs,* but there are already a ton of people on this level too.

"Do I, uh ... take my shoes off?" I ask.

"Ha! No," Erika says. "Chelsea's mother once told me not to or the oils from my feet would stain her carpet."

"Well, you *are* dirtier than dirt," Julia jokes.

"Hey!"

I follow them down the wide staircase to the deck, where Chelsea's handing out sparkling lemonade in fancy glasses. She passes one to a soccer player in grade eleven and gives him a look at the same time—one that says, *Hey, you're not bad.*

She turns and passes me a glass. No look for me.

"Cheers! Here's to the season," she says. We all clink glasses—except Chelsea misses Erika's ... I think on purpose.

I go and sit on one side of Julia, and Erika sits on the other. "So what's ... Chelsea's deal with you guys? Is she friends with any of you?" I ask.

Erika snort-laughs. "Yeah, no. She's not friends with any of us. She was friends with Elizabeth, but she moved in the summer."

"Was she ever friends with you, though? I thought she's been swimming with you guys forever."

"Chelsea and I started synchro the same year, when we were nine. By the time we were eleven, we were in the national stream—and swimming up an age group with permission. They said we were very 'promising.'"

"You *are* promising," Julia says.

Erika fidgets with the zipper on her hoodie. "We swam a duet every year until this one."

"So why not this year?"

Erika and Julia exchange a look.

"What? You're not telling me something."

"Nothing. It's nothing, Bart. Chelsea and I ... We swim well together, but I was done. They were just hoping I'd change my mind."

"You were done. How come?"

Erika sighs. "I dunno. How well do you know Chels?"

"I don't, really. I mean, she's in the program with me, but we don't have a lot of classes together or anything."

"We never hung out outside of synchro. There was one time Chelsea's mother dropped her off at my house for a 'playdate' before we were headed off to an event, and the whole thing was a disaster. We tried to play, but Chelsea was too worked up. We just ended up watching videos of routines and land drilling. Chelsea's idea. It was so boring. I think we were both relieved when it was time to hit the road and go to the meet."

I could picture that. The two of them, eleven years old, vibrating on a different frequency—Chelsea higher, tighter, faster; Erika lower, calmer.

"That's funny. But you spend, like, all your waking hours at the pool together. You must know a lot about each other."

"Yup, this year—" Erika stops when Chelsea passes too close. We're all silent until she passes by again.

"This year's our eighth year swimming together. But it's so weird. I've been swimming with her for *eight years,* and we've travelled together for so many comps, and we know so much about each other, right? But then there will be these major things about her that nobody knows—that she doesn't tell me. Or anyone."

"Yeah," Julia says. "Like, Chelsea never even told us when she had a boyfriend. I only found out because she tweeted a picture of them together."

"What? Chelsea's on Twitter?"

"Yeah, she mostly uses it to complain broadly."

I laugh.

"Yeah, so the boyfriend ..." Erika says. "Maybe you know him, 'cause he's from your program too. A standard-issue good-looking guy."

"Chelsea's dated a lot of guys from school."

"This one wore a lot of collared shirts."

I thought about it for a minute, then remembered a couple of weeks when she went out with Dan. Not a swimmer, but a cricket player. We all wondered what the heck a cricket player was doing in the SI, but I think the girls thought of him as a catch. And Chelsea caught him, at least for a while.

"So we slept in the same hotel room for qualifiers last year. She never said a word about Dan. She came to warm-up all distracted, and she'd been crying. I tried to ask about it, but nothing. It's like she doesn't trust any of us with her stuff, you know?"

"Well, do you tell her stuff?"

"Yeah," Erika smiles. "All the time."

Julia shakes her head. "Yeah, but you tell everybody everything."

"Why not? My life's no big secret."

"Okay. So you and Chels are ... frenemies?"

"No. That makes it sound like we really *care*. We're more like ..." Erika drifts off, thinking. "We're intimate acquaintances."

"Wow. That's deep," Jules says.

I get it, now. "So that's why Chelsea and her mom don't want me swimming with the club. She's mad at me for swimming the duet with you."

"Well, if she is, she can go ahead and be mad. I wouldn't have been Chelsea's partner this year anyway. You know why? Because anyone who partners with Chelsea also partners up with Chelsea's mother. She'll be so far into your business you can't move. Like, do you see my mother coming to the pool and interfering? No. I'm sorry, but I couldn't take another year of Amanda Gates."

"Oh, red alert," Jules says. "Chels at ten o'clock. Okay, so how much are you guys training for your duet?"

"Sunny said I'll have to do an extra ten hours a week on figures. But we'll work on our routine about six hours a week, I think?" I look at Erika.

Chelsea drops down beside us.

"More like eight," Erika says.

"That's a ton! Do you guys get time for any cross-training?"

"Well, there's stretching and land drills," says Julia.

"I run," says Chelsea. "Just twenty klicks a week."

Erika scoffs, "Yeah, *just.*"

"You *have* to run. It's the only thing that really builds up lung capacity," Chels says.

I can hear Riley's voice in my head. *Nice pair of lungs on her.* I just about tell him to shut up out loud. I guess I'm too used to him being around. Where is he, anyway?

Erika says, "I hate running. I just like to dance."

"Oh, yeah? What studio?"

Erika laughs. "Uh ... my bedroom? I mean, I dance to my own music. At home. Like, in my pyjamas."

Chelsea shakes her head. "'Cause you're a loser. Oh, excuse me. Rowers." She gets up to greet some tall, broad-shouldered guys stepping out onto the patio.

"Man, that seemed ... unnecessarily harsh." I give Erika a sympathetic look, but she just waves it off.

"Just ignore her," says Julia. "We all do."

Wow. Chelsea must be really mad that Erika's not swimming with her this year. Which says a lot about what she thinks of me.

"For real, though, I just practise extra," Erika says. "And Julia runs, probably more than Chelsea." Julia waves Erika off.

"When do you even fit that in?"

Erika blushes. It's cute.

"I think I've got permanent prune hands."

Julia nods. "Perma-prunes. That's us."

"There is nothing prunish about either of you." Oh God. Now I'm blushing. They smile, and kind of freeze, until they break the awkward silence laughing at me. Great.

Erika leans in. "Okay, I'll tell you a secret. I go to the pool at four."

"In the morning?"

"The coaches don't get on deck until five, even for the earliest practices."

"How? The pool isn't even open!"

"The custodian lets me in. He's my uncle, so I've kinda got an in."

Julia catches my eye and leans over like *she's* going to let me in on a secret now. "She's insane."

"No, I'm not. I'm just ..." Erika looks at me, and furrows her brow. "I've got the national squad trials this year. And I'm really sure about this mixed duet." She blushes again.

"So am I."

"So you guys are gonna be number one junior mixed duet in the country?" Jules asks.

"Or the only one, yeah."

It's dark now. Someone lights torches around the patio, and Chelsea cranks up the music. Soon, people start dancing. The girls and I get up. I scan the crowd for Riley and see Geoff and Andy on the far side, hopping up and down to the beat along with everyone else. Golfers, rowers, soccer players. Swimmers, divers, water polo kids. And even the lacrosse boys, back from the bush with red-rimmed eyes.

This is nice—it's reassuring, everyone still around me, the whole tribe of us sporty kids kicking off another year of training.

A familiar head comes bouncing above the crowd toward us, and when Riley and Casey meet up with us, I'm grinning with my arm around Erika. The girls are dancing with me. Casey's holding hands with Riley. I think it's perfect timing. Because I'm still here, right? I'm not going anywhere. I'm still on the deck at the pool, and I'm still here with the SI crew—even better, we're here with the girls now. Just like we planned. Kind of.

"Hey!" Riley shouts.

"Hey, man. I've been looking for you. I have something to tell you."

"He's one of us now!" Jules blurts out.

"What, Bart's a girl?"

"No, you goof." Erika shakes her head. "He's a synchro swimmer!" she shouts, going up on tiptoes, then throwing an arm around my shoulders. "He *left* your club for *mine*." Then she kisses her fingers and slaps her own butt. "So there!"

I crack up.

Julia leans over and takes the glass of lemonade from Erika. "You have to excuse her. She gets a little out of hand when she's had too much sugar."

We're all laughing. But Riley? Uh, not so much.

"What's up?" I ask.

Casey takes a step aside, like she senses the tension.

"For real?" Riley asks. "Is that true?"

"Yeah, it became official yesterday."

"Like, along with racing?"

"No, man." A couple of other Rosa Waves behind Riley are listening in now. And Dive Boy, who says something to Julia and stands watching us too. The song switches to one less jumpy, more classic rock. It's irritating.

"I'm not going to race anymore," I shout over the music. "I'm done. Erika and I are going to swim a duet." We fill him in on the details about the competition, the training.

Some Rosa Waves racing girls behind Riley whisper-yell into each other's ears. Dive Boy pats me on the back and says, "That's great!"

But Riley's shaking his head. "I can't believe it, man."

Casey tugs on his sleeve. "C'mon, Riley. It's good! *He's* really good." She starts dancing, trying to get Riley to join her, but he's not moving. Not even when that old Chumbawamba song comes on and everyone starts hopping again, shouting along—*I get knocked down!*

"Nah, I don't feel like it right now."

"Hey—I'm sorry," I say. "How's your shoulder?"

He doesn't answer.

"Aw." Casey pouts as Riley walks off the patio. "But I wanted to dance!"

Now there's whispering and nudging and eyes looking my way. I'm the party gossip. The noise and the crowd feel unbearable, so I excuse myself and tell the girls I'm going to make my own way home. Up top, I see Riley and Casey sitting on the front steps. I want to go talk to him, sort this out— but do I go after him now? While he's trying to have a good time on his first real date ever?

No. I've wrecked it enough. He'll see. Riley will change his mind when he sees us swim together, sees how good Erika and I look. Then he'll real- ize that joining an all-girls synchro team doesn't make me any less of a guy.

THIRTEEN

After being at Chelsea's, it feels like I'm coming home to a kid's playhouse—especially with Dad's large frame sitting on our mini-porch. "It hopes to grow up to be a real porch one day," Mom likes to joke, 'cause there's room enough for two people to stand and wait for the door to open, but that's it.

I'm always surprised by how young Dad looks—Mom's older than he is, so I guess when Dad visits I expect him to have aged just as much as she has. But an even bigger surprise is how I get weirded out by his curls, every time. Because with his height, his hair, and his big grey eyes, *all the better to stare you down with, my pretty* ... it's like a beefier *me* sitting on the steps waiting for me.

I get a feeling in the pit of my stomach that's not exactly dread but close enough—'cause it'll be hard work to make conversation after we're done talking about my training. I tend to ask all the questions. (*Hey, how's work? Anything new going on at the station? Seeing anyone?*) His answers never give me a lot to go on. (*Fine. Nothing new. Nope.*)

And, of course, what I have to say now is harder than any awkward conversation.

"Is Mom inside?"

"Yeah, she's gone to bed."

"Are you staying here?"

"No, I've got a room at the HoJo. I just stayed up to see you. So you were out at a party?"

"For a while."

"I was gonna watch your practice on Sunday, but your Mom tells me you might not be there."

"Well, I'll be at the pool. But ... Dad?"

"I heard."

No way! Did Mom tell him already? Why's he so calm? He must be so angry. My heart starts thumping hard.

"Cragg told me about the suspension. But you're back now, and I know you'll get back into it." Dad shakes his head. "He told me you threw some kid on the deck?"

"No, I didn't—" I sigh. So that's all—he still has no idea about synchro ... "Dad," I start, trying to think of the best way to put this out there, to let him know.

He shuffles over to make room for me on the step, and I sit down, smell the cigarette smoke on his clothes. At least now we don't have to look at each other. We can just stare off at the street and the empty park across the road. It's better this way.

"I'm ... changing sports."

"What?"

"You know synchronized swimming, right? The coach thinks I have a lot of potential in the sport. Guys are just getting started in it, and it looks like—"

Dad laughs. "You're joking, right?"

"No! Dad, I'm serious. This is really big. There's, like, no guys in the sport at my age. They *want* guys to join because there's a new event. And with so few guys doing it ... Well, chances are really good for me. If I work really hard, I can position myself to compete ... like, at worlds. The *Olympics,* even. This is a *huge* opportunity."

Dad shakes his head. "I guess this is why your mom couldn't look me in the eye all night."

"Come on! This is a good thing. I'm still going to train, and I'll work really hard."

"Did you stop and think why there aren't any other guys? Hasn't it occurred to you that there aren't enough people who would show up to watch a guy doing synchronized swimming?"

"No. Why? Seriously. It's way more interesting than watching racing."

Dad lets out a deep sigh.

"C'mon, think about this. You're smarter than me."

"No, I'm not."

Dad looks at me long and hard. "If you can't see that, you're blind. So don't give me that."

I wish he didn't beat up on himself. I wish he were stronger. Would it make a difference? I think so. Maybe if *he* felt stronger, he could leave me alone.

"And you're better than I was. I've watched you swim."

"So that's it. You don't think I can do this."

"Look, don't get me wrong. I still love you."

"Um, good?"

"I just can't understand what you're *doing*. I don't know what else to give you, Bart. You know I can't give you brains. If you're getting any of those, you're getting them from your mother. Are you doing okay in school?"

"I do okay."

"Just okay?"

"Look, why does everything have to be about whether I'm successful at school? Or sports? Why can't I just *be,* and just do something that I love? Isn't that enough?"

"Why should it be enough? Would that be enough for *you?*"

He has a point. This drive to succeed at stuff, it's not just coming from Mom and Dad.

"No."

"Yeah, I didn't think so. Look, in just a couple of years from now—hell, less than that—you're going to be out on your own. If your mom and me weren't concerned about your future, what sort of parents would we be?"

"Fine. Okay. But Dad, if you're covering coaching and SI fees, that's all I want. I don't need anything else right now."

"Well, your mother takes it from here. If you're going to drop out of the Sports Institute, she'll figure out where you're going next."

"I don't have to drop out of the SI. As long as I'm enrolled in a competitive program, I can keep going."

"I'm not going to pay for it."

"What? Why? Just because I'm not racing?"

"I'm not rewarding you for dropping out."

"This isn't dropping out! It's just ... changing course."

"Bart, you were headed to nationals this year. You were on track for a university scholarship. You already have university coaches scouting you, asking you to apply. They're not going to do that if you're a synchronized swimmer. You're not just changing course, your sinking your damned ship!"

"This is about me doing something you think is girly, isn't it? You think I'm—"

"Cut the crap. I don't care if you swim in a goddamned tutu. I just don't want you to throw away what I've given you. And what you've worked for. I never had your chances."

"I never wanted to wear a damned tutu! God. Look, I have a chance at this, Dad. *Please*. I don't want to put all the pressure on Mom."

"You think your mother's going to pay for the Sports Institute now? And coaching? Travel?"

"No. Of course not."

"So how—"

"I don't know! I'll figure it out. But seriously, what's the difference, Dad? You say you didn't have a chance to pursue something you were good at. You loved swimming, you could have gone places. But you're saying I can't have that chance with synchro? The coach told me I have a real chance at this. I could be the first guy in *Canada* to swim nationally at my age!"

Dad scoffs, "Sure, big fish, small pool."

"No. It's more than that."

"You know Cragg said if you keep your focus you could make it to the Olympics one day. He believes you can do it."

"I can do it with synchro!"

"Oh, guys compete at the Olympics in synchro?"

"Not yet."

"Yeah, it's a women's sport." He shakes his head. "I don't want you doing this."

"It's not just women! Guys swim synchro at the world championships. But that doesn't matter to you, does it?" Oh, great. First coach, then Riley, now Dad. How come every guy I have to tell can't get this? Why do I have to explain it every time? "Okay, so if they changed the rules and this became an Olympic sport, and I made it to the Olympics, you'd buy it that I can be a boy and do this?"

"Sure. But it's going to take a lot of change in the world for that to happen."

"Why? Why should it have to?"

Dad looks at me like I'm an idiot for asking. But seriously, why should being a boy doing a sport that's traditionally female mean I'm any less of a boy? 'Cause that's what he's worried about. I know it.

"You're just doing this because you can't control anything else about my life. Otherwise, why would you care what the money goes toward if it's still for sport costs? If it's still for my school program?"

"That's not it. You don't get it."

"Yeah, I don't get why you even come here anymore!" I step off the porch. "I see you twice a year. It's not like you're involved in my life or anything. Seriously. Why?"

"Why what?"

"Why bother coming to see me? Why give us money for anything?" I shout. Our neighbour directly across from us opens her curtain and looks out from her townhouse.

"I made Melanie a deal."

"Oh, so you made Mom a deal? Well, how is this not breaking that deal?"

"Bart, you don't even know what it was about."

"Hmm. Let me guess. It went like this." I start putting on exaggerated voices for Mom and Dad. "'Gee, Mike. Now that you've got a job, think you could help out a little?' 'Oh, sure, Melanie, but do I actually have to see the kid?' 'You could at least pretend you want to. How about twice a year?'"

Dad steps down off the porch toward me.

"Bart, shut up. You don't know what you're talking about."

I push him. "You wouldn't be so upset if I didn't."

"Hey!" He grabs my forearm. "Don't you dare push me around. You don't push anybody, you hear me? I don't like what I'm hearing from Cragg, or what I'm seeing now."

"I don't care!" I rip my arm away.

"Well, I do! Say what you like, but I'm trying here!" he shouts back. "I'm doing what I can. I am still your father, like it or not, and I'm not going to see you throw away a sure thing." He sighs. "This has nothing to do with you and me."

Sure. Nothing to do with our relationship. But as far as I can see, my sport is all our relationship is. "Whatever. Look, why don't you make a deal with me? If I make it to nationals in synchro, will you pay for it then?"

"In one year?"

"Yeah. In one year. If I get good enough to swim at nationals in synchro in one year."

"Yeah, okay." He shakes his head. "Do me proud. I'm sure you can rise to stardom in a year." He pulls his keys out of his pocket.

"So that's a deal?"

"Whatever," he says, mimicking me.

"Is it a deal?"

"Okay. You have a deal, Bart. Get to nationals, and I'll cover it."

I watch him get in his car and pull away. I didn't even get a chance to tell him I swam my last triple-A time. Not that *that* matters anymore. But he always used to be happy when I made my times. And I used to be happy when I could tell him that I'd made them. Now, I'm just ready to smash something, but I guess I can settle for beating my pillow.

Inside, Mom's sitting right by the door. She looks mad too.

"Oh. How much did you hear?"

"Everything."

I sigh. "I'm sorry, Mom."

"Hey, I'm sorry too." She hugs me. "But like you said, we'll figure it out."

So she's not mad at me—she's mad at Dad. I don't have the heart to ask her if I was right about him. I can't bring myself to find out if he only comes to see me because she asks.

FOURTEEN

All through October and November, I train just as hard with the synchro club as I have the past year with the Rosa Waves—I put in the same hours and give it everything I've got. It's just that everything's new. And so much harder! If I'm going to make it to nationals and show Dad exactly what I'm capable of ... Well, let's just say I've got a big wall to scale.

What's great is that, for the most part, the Rosa Pacific synch girls want me in the pool with them now. I feel more connected to their team in just one month than I ever felt connected to the Rosa Waves, aside from Riley.

Speaking of Riley, he's technically still talking to me, but he's pretty distant.

"Have you asked her out yet?" he asked me after school again this week.

"I can't. It ... would be weird. We're working together now, and it's like ... I don't know. A professional relationship."

"Huh. Well, good luck with that."

"What does that mean?"

"It means ... just what it means."

"Well, I can't date my duet partner!"

"If you say so."

Erika and I have a technical routine now, swimming to spooky Halloween music. It's cool. But I *love* the "Breathing Underwater" routine, and it just keeps getting better.

I've worked hard to learn not only the patterns of the routines with Erika but also the patterns of the relationships on the team. There's Erika and Julia: good friends. Chelsea seems to know them really well, though you couldn't call them *friends*. Casey is super friendly and seems okay with everyone. Kyoka turns out to be an exceptional coach herself—she's given me tons of pointers, so she's definitely over her first shyness about having me on her team. Not Huiyan, though—she just sticks with Kyoka.

The first Friday in December, Mom and I catch the ferry to the mainland and drive to Surrey for regionals. All the national stream swimmers in the province come to this meet, and our results are broken down by region. We stop at Timmie's for dinner with the team before heading to Aquamania, the host pool, for the figures event. I get my chili and a sour cream glazed and a large peach juice, and grab a seat. The next thing I know, Erika and Julia drop their trays onto my table. Mom takes a few steps toward me and the girls, balancing a chili and a small carton of milk on a tray. Then she stops, and half smiles. I smile back. She takes a step back and looks around before making for an empty chair at the end of the row of synchro mothers.

The other moms huddle around Amanda, their backs to my mom. Do they even know she's trying to sit with them? I feel like I should get up and sit with Mom, but I just want to keep talking to the girls.

"Aw. Tell your mom not to take that personally, 'kay, Bart?" Julia says.

"Yeah, okay."

After we eat, the girls get more donuts for the road. I offer Mom the last bit of my sour cream glazed. "Hey, I'm done. You want this?"

She shakes her head.

"But you didn't even get a donut."

"It's okay, Bart. I'm not actually hungry."

I put the plate down on the tray trolley next to us. "Yeah, me neither."

On their way out, Julia waves her donut bag at us. "Last call!" she shouts.

Mom smiles. "The girls seem nice."

"Yeah." I wave at Erika and Julia as they make for the van. "I like them a lot."

Mom gives me a funny look.

"If you're wondering if one of them's my girlfriend, then the answer is no."

"It looks like you're pretty close with a couple of them."

"Well, no girlfriend yet, Mom." *No boyfriend either.* I don't say it—but I know she's wondering.

It's been two months of swimming with the girls and watching Dive Boy and the other perfect bodies plummet from the tower—and I haven't a clue what's going on. I'm physically closer to all of them, but all that's given me is a yearning to get even closer. Okay, I'll admit it. It's given me a stronger yearning for sex.

Breaking the awkwardness, I get up to leave and Mom follows. I flip up my hood for the dash through the rain to the car, but Mom hangs onto the open door.

"Wait—" she says.

"What?"

"Do you need to be at the pool so early? I think you still have an hour before the event. We could stay and chat for a bit."

But my nerves mixed with the smell of sweet fried dough has started to make me feel a little sick. I just want a moment of peace before we get to the pool for the event.

"I dunno. We can talk in the car, right?"

"How about after your event?"

"Well ... I think we have to land drill tonight before bed. Sunny said something about meeting her in the lobby once we're checked in."

"You sure? I could take you out for a hot chocolate."

A guy in line glares at Mom for letting in all the cold air. I just slow-shake my head at him.

"Okay. I just don't get to see you much anymore." She smiles weakly, and heads through the door. I follow her out and we sprint across the parking lot, half-soaked by the time we get in the car and Mom starts the heater. When she pulls out of the lot and onto the highway, the empty water jugs slide around in the back.

I turn on the radio, and neither of us talks. We drive through the rain straight to Aquamania.

• • •

We snap our caps on and get in the water with swimmers from about ten other clubs to warm up our ballet legs. At one point, I ask Chelsea if she thinks there's any chance that junior worlds—the international competition for our age—will have a mixed duet event this year.

She boosts herself up on the deck and pulls off her cap. Her long blonde ponytail flops down on her shoulder, half-wet.

"Why?"

"I wanna go. Do you think Erika and I will? If they open up the mixed duet at junior worlds?"

"Well, Bart, synchro takes a *lot* of work. Figures are hard," Chelsea says, scooping water up with her cap and dumping it back in the pool.

"It's not that bad," Erika says to me.

"What do you mean?" Chelsea asks. "You just told me you weren't sure you'd nail your figures for your age group this year."

I look at Erika. "For real? Seriously, if *you're* not sure you'll nail them, what hope do I have?"

"I was just worrying—I didn't really mean it. We have *lots* of time to practise."

"If you had as many hours in as me," Chelsea says, "you'd already be getting really high figure scores. You used to."

Erika pushes off the side and swims away from us.

"Touchy," Chelsea says.

"What's this about?" I whisper to Julia.

She blows out her breath. "Okay. Erika and Chelsea have both been invited to trial for the national squad. They've been through the second phase of trials, which is a figures event. At the next one they swim a routine. It's a lot of pressure."

"Yeah, and I kicked Erika's ass at the figures," Chelsea says, overhearing us.

"So what happens if you make it?" I ask Chelsea.

"We represent Canada in international meets. See? This is a serious sport," Chelsea says. "Don't think you can just come over here and play at it."

"For real, I'm *not playing*, Chels. Do I look like I've been playing for the past month?" I've been busting my butt, working on my figures before my duet routine practice, and after, while the girls are in team practice. She's *seen* me. How can she think I'm just playing around after watching me train with them?

"Okay, so tell me what I have to do to be serious."

Chelsea just shakes her head.

"Your figures have to get *really* good," Julia says. "You'll have to nail those. That's where girls who've been doing it all along drop out, because they get into higher categories of figures and then can't do them. They're just too hard."

Erika swims back over and gives me a look like, *Hey, want to go warm up without these guys?*

"And it doesn't matter how good Erika's figures are," Chelsea says. "If *your* figures suck, Bart, then you'll bring down your duet score."

"What do you mean?"

"They get averaged," Erika says. "It's the same for team or duet. All the figure scores of the swimmers in the routine get added together and divided by the number of swimmers."

"So you share *my* crappy score that I got on my own?"

"That's right."

"My score will bring down your ranking? That's so not fair!"

Chelsea shakes her head. "Oh, you're such a racer, Bart."

But I'm not anymore. And it's not like I'm new to the concept of making a team effort, but, man, this is hardcore.

The girls have all had years of training and know the figures by heart, while I don't know my heron from my ariana. Lucky for me, Sunny knows ballet—so she can translate a lot of the movements into something I understand.

But still. If I can't swim the figures for my age group, I'm not getting anywhere near provincials—let alone nationals.

• • •

At the figures event, a judges' panel is set up at each corner of the dive tank. Each panel has the name of the figure they will judge on a piece of paper taped to the table. And behind each table, three judges sit waiting to scrutinize every position of every limb of every swimmer. No pressure.

Aquamania's dive tank's colder than ours. Waiting in line to swim out one at a time in front of the first panel, I'm shivering like mad. Some of the girls, the lean, small ones, are also trying to conceal their chattering teeth. It's one thing to keep moving all the time, but to wait here like this is torture. I just hope my muscles don't totally seize up.

My first two figures are okay. It's not like I can expect a score of nine out of ten—only Olympic-level athletes get scores that high. On one, I get just over six points, which is decent for my age group—but then I get a five point three on the next. I know the judges aren't supposed to compare me to all the girls who swam before me, but how can they not?

The next figure is manta ray. I'm okay through the first part—sailboat, ballet leg, then into surface flamingo. But as my body unrolls, I lose my centre and feel myself wobble out of alignment. I just hope the figure's recognizable.

I catch the announcer say a five point something. I look at the judges' cards, but they've flipped them back and put them in their laps so fast I can't see the scores.

Still, Sunny smiles at me when I come for my debrief. "Bart, you tried really hard."

"What was my score?"

"Well, one judge had you at five."

"But that's dropped, right? If it was highest?"

Sunny sighed. "Yes. They'll drop the highest and lowest scores, then take the average of the other three."

"So what's my average?"

"Four point seven."

Deficient. Not a pass. Damn. I look at Erika, waiting in line—but her eyes are focused ahead of her. She's in the zone. She's not even shivering.

I really, really hope I didn't just screw up our competition score.

The last figure's butterfly, which starts with a pike pulldown—one of the hardest things to swim in synchro, but I nail it. And once that figure's over, I am *so* relieved. Even if my scores are less than great, tomorrow morning will be the first time anyone outside our club sees our full duet routine. I can't wait. It'll make up for all of this.

FIFTEEN

"You're pretty quiet," Erika says.

We're sitting around Erika and Jules's hotel room, eating the breakfast sandwiches we grabbed from across the street. The girls have to get ready, and I want to at least watch the ritual, even if I'm not taking part in all the hair and makeup prep.

"Just ... trying to identify the hotel smell."

"Well?" Erika balls up her sandwich wrapper and aims it into the trash can.

I flop back on one of the double beds. "Eighty percent newish carpet. Ten percent pool chlorine. Ten percent bathroom cleaner."

Erika drops her head. "Seriously, what's eating you?"

I sigh. "Scores. Meet nerves." *Chelsea,* I don't say. But I'm wondering ... What would she do to get back at me for stealing Erika away as her duet partner? Or, what would her *mom* do? Amanda still really doesn't want me here. She makes that obvious—the way she looks at me, then looks at the other mothers ...

I roll over toward Julia. "Do you think Amanda Gates is against me swimming for the club because she thinks I'm gay?"

"For real? I think she'd be *relieved* if you were gay."

"Yeah?" I bounce off the bed and stand up tall, looking at my reflection in the big mirror over the dresser.

"Bart, she's a prude," Erika says. "She doesn't think we should be wearing bathing suits and swimming this close to each other under water." She slides her hip along mine. I laugh. "Okay, forget Amanda. It's time for business."

The moment has come. We have to gel our hair before competition. At least, the girls do. We don't know if *I* have to yet. Sunny hasn't said anything about my curls. I'm assuming I'm just going to wear a cap.

"Hey," Erika asks, "what's the name of the guy who swam for Canada at worlds last summer?"

"Robert Prévost," I say.

Erika turns around and looks at me, impressed. Then she pulls out her phone and finds the CBC sports coverage.

Julia says, "Oh, what about the Russian kid! Take a look at his video. He had some hair."

The girls watch. Finally, Julia speaks: "Well, look, his do's totally fallen out of place."

Erika shakes her head. "It's just a crap gelling job. He probably didn't pin properly."

"You guys. Do I have to gel or not?"

Erika ignores me and passes Julia the phone, who holds it up close. "Oh, yeah," she says. "I see what you're saying. But I'm not going overboard with eyeshadow like that kid."

Erika says, "You'll have to do some. Go back to Prévost. There's definitely some eyeliner going on there."

I take the phone and bring up the US duet. "Look, Bill May doesn't wear makeup."

Erika takes the phone back. "Ha! If those are his natural eyelashes, I'm Snow White." Then she looks up at me and flashes a huge smile. "Get ready to shine, Synchro Boy!"

I lean my head back and groan. But secretly, I'm glad. I'm just playing along, the reluctant guy ... It's expected, right? But I've seen the glam makeup and the shiny hair and wondered what it would be like.

"You can't make me do this!"

"Oh, yes I can! I don't want you losing us presentation points."

Erika grabs the box of gelatin and opens up a package. When the water boils, she mixes the contents with a little hot water. She puts a towel over my shoulders, then paints the hot, wet gel on. It goes on slowly.

"Ugh, this smells like ... wet dog." So much for glam. It might look cool when it's done, but, man, gelling is gross!

Julia says, "This makes it a bit better." She puts a couple of drops of vanilla extract in, then dips her brush to start gelling her black twists, which she's pulled up into a high bun. "Hey, slow down!" she says, dipping her brush again. "Stop hogging the gel, you white kids with no itty-bitty edges. You don't need all that."

"Hey, I have little edges," Erika says.

Julia scoffs, "Like hell ya do."

"Those flyaway hairs totally plaster to my forehead if I'm not gelled enough. And, uh ... I'm not *all* white."

"Japanese-slash-white girls do not have to worry about their edges, and do not need all the gel," Julia proclaims. "Neither do boys with short hair who are ..." Julia turns and looks at me. "What are you?"

"Um ... Irish? Maybe?"

"Okay, boys who think they might be Irish but who aren't sure do not need all the gel either."

The laugh helps me relax. But then Erika starts the hair dryer to set my gel, tapping my head every now and then to test it. The smell from the gel mingles with the fluttery feeling I already have from Erika touching my head, and I feel sick with nerves again.

"I can't believe you guys have to do this every time you compete."

"And don't forget makeuuuuup!" Julia singsongs as she opens up a makeup kit filled with brushes and pots and lipstick tubes. "What, you never had to do your makeup when you were a dancer?"

"Uh ... I guess I was too young."

Erika switches off the dryer and holds her hand out for the kit, ready to take over. I stay absolutely still, waiting to see what this feels like. I let her sweep shadow into my brows with a little brush. I try to keep my eyes shut but not squeezed so she can line my lids with waterproof black liquid eyeliner. Her fingers pull my skin taut, and her hand brushes up against my cheek. The liner brush feels like a tiny, cool, wet tongue.

My eyes flash wide open.

"Yeah, that's the idea, Bart," Jules says. "Show 'em your peepers, and don't forget to smile pretty for the judges!"

I give her a weak smile.

"What's this?" I pull a tube out of the kit and unscrew the cap. "Oh, mascara." I lean in close to the mirror and touch the little brush to my eye-lashes, sweeping it out to the tips.

"Nice. You sure you've never done this before?" Julia asks, and she gives me a look.

"I swear!" I say, laughing.

Jules takes a lipstick out of her kit and holds it up to Erika.

"No," Erika says. "Not that one. Too warm." I get uncomfortable under her gaze while she studies my complexion. My eye colour. "Yeah, and too dark. Bart should wear something lighter."

"So, the synchro guys—do they actually wear *lipstick?*"

Erika grabs something else out of the kit, not listening.

"I don't know about *lipstick.*" But a voice within me says, *Please say yes. This is fun.*

"'Back to the Fuchsia.' Perfect." Erika opens the tube and twists up a tip of the most obscene pink I've ever seen.

"Say, 'wish!'"

"Wish."

"No!" She laughs, and squishes my cheeks. "You have to hold it. Say wish."

"Wish."

She smooths it over my top, then bottom, lip. "Oops. Let's fix that."

I feel her thumb brush my bottom lip. My whole body lights up. Sheesh. It was just one touch! This is nuts. It's not like I've never touched Erika. I mean, this is synchro. I've had my legs wrapped around her hips. I've held her head in my hand. We've been intertwined for hours at a time, getting our choreography down—but I've never felt like this. What's with this one touch?

Erika looks up from my lips to my eyes. She inhales like she's just come up from an inversion she's been holding for ages. Julia notices, and whistles.

Then Erika turns away, rifling through her kit for the next instrument of my transformation.

But she's blushing. And when Julia looks back at herself in the mirror, I take Erika's fingers in my own, place them back on my lips, and kiss them.

Oh, man.

SIXTEEN

Erika laugh-snorts and pushes me out the door of the hotel, my team jacket up over my gelled head. "Run! Don't let anyone see!"

I dash for Mom's car waiting in the drop-off zone and open the door. Julia pushes my head down like she's sticking me in the back of a cop car. Erika takes shotgun and slams the door, and Jules slides into the back next to me.

"All set?" Mom asks. "Everyone's got everything?" Then she spots me in the rear-view mirror. "Bart? What the ...?" she trails off. "Do you have to wear makeup?"

"No, Mrs Lively," Julia answers for me. "We convinced Bart to try it. We thought if he came in gel and makeup, the other girls would ... well, relax a little."

"It's like an icebreaker," Erika says. "If they felt intimidated by coming to a meet with a guy—" Erika turns in her seat so she can see me for a second. "Well, seeing him gelled and in makeup will help, right? How could they be intimidated by those pretty brown eyes?"

"They really pop with that liner," Julia adds.

Mom loops around the parking lot at Aquamania three times before deciding to bail and try to find a spot somewhere else—but not before passing Amanda Gates in her van with other girls from the team. Mom holds up a hand to wave hello as we pass, but Amanda doesn't wave back.

"Rude!" Erika says.

"She's just trying to park," Mom says.

Whatever—she's deliberately ignoring Mom. I lean over and honk the horn, and when Amanda looks, I wave.

"Bart! You know I hate it when you do that."

"Do what?"

"Honk the horn for me!"

"Well, you're so afraid to use it!"

"You know, I'm just going to let you guys out." Mom pulls up at the roundabout in front of the pool's entrance, and we grab our massive backpacks, stuffed to bursting with extra towels, snacks, and water. Erika tries to throw a towel over my head to hide me, but I tell her no. She and Jules get out.

Mom says, "Bart, wait a sec. Can I tell you something?"

"Yeah, what?"

"They're treating you like a mascot. Dolling you up like that." Her eyes look sad for me, but I'm anything but sad.

"No! No, it's not like that ..." I watch the girls walking up the stairs. "They like me, Mom. And ... I wanted to do the makeup."

"You did?"

I sigh. The girls are getting swallowed up by the crowd, and I'll lose them if I don't go now.

"Yeah. I gotta go."

• • •

When we go through the doors to the pool, we're hit with the wave of warm, humid air, the sound of hundreds of voices echoing off the tile and the glass walls, and the splashing of the waterfalls and the waterslide emptying into the play pool. We go straight to where the official figures scores are posted from last night. The figures for everyone on our team are listed together, and I'm last—not a surprise. Chelsea's in first, and Erika second. Also not a surprise.

"Is that bad?"

Julia puts her arm around my shoulders. "It's your first real meet."

"But will they keep our duet out of provincials because of my score?"

"We need to swim the routine, and then we'll see how that scores. Then we'll know where we stand," Erika says.

"Even if I failed the figures?"

"I don't think you failed ..." Erika looks back at the score sheet. "It's okay, Bart. You're going to get better! They *can't* hold you back just because your first meet wasn't as stellar as you hoped."

Man, I hope she's right.

A gaggle of Rosa Pacific synch girls in our midnight-blue jackets spot us and wave. When we get on the pool deck, Sunny's with them, wearing a big grin. But she doesn't say anything about my hair. Or my face. Or my figures.

Chelsea arrives and spots me. "You're serious? This is for real?" She looks up through her brows, her index finger with a perfectly manicured nail pointing at my head.

"Yeah, why not?" Erika's eyes sparkle. "It's for the routines. He's got to be gelled."

"He's wearing *makeup*."

"What's the matter with that?"

I feel the temperature drop.

Sunny says, "Looking good, Bart. Put your cap on for warm-up, though, 'kay? Then your gel won't come out before your event." She doesn't bat an eye. She goes over to the pool where Kyoka and Huiyan are egg beatering, waiting for her instructions to warm up for their duet. They spot me, and Kyoka waves. She points to her head and laughs. Huiyan just sinks so only her eyes are above water.

Eight girls wearing bow ties and pink suits walk past, their high buns glistening with hard gel, their bubble gum–pink lips smiling at me.

Chelsea says, "You're making people stare."

"No way. I haven't even taken off my pants yet."

The girls are all in the most severely cut suits for their team routine, bright green with shiny lizard scales and red rhinestones. They all wear starkly dark lips, and blush, and green and gold eyeshadow. I'm pretty sure their costumes draw more eyes than my hair and makeup.

"Look, Chels, I know I didn't have to get done up for today, but we just thought that it would ... break the ice."

"What ice?" she asks. Chelsea's practically vibrating. She looks behind her into the pool, then back at me. "All the water here looks melted to me." Then she turns and dives in, leaving me alone.

So it still doesn't matter to her that I'm all in? I can't believe she still thinks I'm just mocking her.

I take off my jacket and warm-up pants. Immediately, I feel 500 or so eyes on me, on the shimmery swimming briefs that match Erika's suit for our technical routine. The fabric on this suit is not as thick and sturdy as spandex. I've never swum in front of the girls without my long swim jammer shorts. I've never exposed so much flesh before. And they've never laid eyes on the pale skin of my upper legs.

I break out into goosebumps.

When we got fitted, Erika said, "Deal with it. Think we don't feel ridiculous in the sequinned suits we wear?" But there's very little surface area to decorate a guy's swim briefs. So this glittery appliqué of a spiderweb's going to draw all the attention to my ass and my junk.

I shake it off and dive in after Chelsea. Time for warm-up.

• • •

When our technical is over and it's time for the mixed free event, I walk across the bulkhead in a shiny, bubbly suit, following Erika. Erika's suit has a kite on the front, bursting out of a wave, with bubbles running up the back, like the back's under water.

In the stands, someone whistles, and I look up. Lots, *lots,* of people are whispering to each other.

The news about *a guy swimming* has made the rounds between the technical event and this one, and more people are here to watch. Some girls waiting at the bulkhead point at us.

I lean down and whisper to Erika before we walk out.

"You know what I like?"

She turns and gives me a funny look.

"That you haven't asked me if I'm nervous."

She rolls her eyes, and when the whistle goes, we walk.

We haven't really figured out the deck work yet, so when the music starts, we just dive. Our music switches to its fast, upbeat tempo, and we execute the set of quick, precise arm movements that starts our routine. Erika's shorter than a lot of the girls I've watched swim so far today. She doesn't have those long, lean legs like Chelsea or Julia. But she's got something else altogether—strength, speed, and precision like you wouldn't believe. And it's not just that. She's better. I just can't say exactly *how*.

We're synchronizing with a rhythm, together, expressing ourselves without words, but with every cell in our bodies. We slice past each other's bodies, surface, and make eye contact, connect again.

Erika's passion and energy surround me, and I'm in it, inside her energy, wrapped up in it and part of it as my body mirrors her movements. And then the music bridges into a chorus, and we switch out of that pattern into a give-and-take sequence that feels like a wordless conversation.

We end with our arms straight and sharp, taking this pop song about breathing under water as far as we know how to go. And when it ends, the judges are clapping for us. *Clapping*. And if I'm not mistaken, it looks a little like the meet host might have been tearing up.

I don't notice that Erika's nail has grazed a spot just under my eye until I feel a tickle on my cheek, and when I reach up to touch it, I come away with blood on my finger.

"Bart? Are you okay?" Erika grabs my wrist. "You're—"

"I know."

Blood and sweat, so far. Now all that's left to give is tears, and if my figures this morning bring us down, that won't be hard.

"I'm okay."

"Be careful." Erika licks her thumb, and then, before I can even register what she's doing, she swipes at the cut. "Don't let them see. They'll have to drain the pool."

"What?"

"If they have to drain the pool, or treat it ... they'll rebook us."

"For real? They'd drain the whole pool for something the size of a paper cut?" I hold the heel of my hand onto my cheekbone and press while we wait for our scores. Normally, we'd have to wait until the next competitor swims before we could hear our scores announced. But we're the only competitors.

"Difficulty, nineteen. Artistic impression, twenty-three. Execution, twenty-one."

"Sixty-three!" I smile at Erika. "Sixty-three's good, right?" A world champion might score in the high eighties and nineties out of a hundred, but for our level, this is good.

"Yeah," Erika says. "It's good."

"Is it high enough? To go to provincials?"

Erika smiles, but just with her lips. Her eyes aren't in it. I know her mind's busy factoring in my figures score and trying to decide how much that will bring our routine down.

"It might be."

"But it might not."

Erika grabs my wrists. "Listen, you can't freak out, okay?"

I nod.

"You'll get better. You're already awesome."

But awesome enough?

When the official dismisses us, we walk back to the bleachers where our club is camped out. I'm still panting like mad, but Erika's fine. "How have you caught your breath already? I'm so wiped!"

Amanda shakes her head at me. "You don't float, Bart. In case you hadn't noticed ... You're not a girl. You can't change that."

"I float a little." I look at Chelsea, sitting next to her mom—but she just looks away from both of us, pretending she didn't hear.

Then Amanda mutters to the mom next to her, "Not to mention the hairy legs sticking out of the water. Who wants to see *that?*"

Good grief, I don't even *have* hairy legs. I'm a swimmer. I've been waxing them for years.

"Bart?"

I turn and see Mom—and she looks frozen in place. She heard. Mom stares at Amanda for a moment, then turns to me. "The café's open. How about we go get some lunch?"

"Okay, I'll meet you up there."

Mom walks off the deck. I start walking toward the showers, but before I get out of earshot, I hear Amanda say to her daughter that I won't be competing at provincials. Chelsea asks her mom, "Why not?"

"His figures aren't good enough. Sunny will have to pull him."

"That's not true," Erika says as she and Julia catch up to me. "Amanda's just trying to scare you off."

The girls steer me toward the warm kiddie pool by the hot tubs.

"Come on. Come with us!" Erika looks around, making sure no one's watching. Julia hops in, then Erika. They sink their heads back, under the water. "Come on, quick ... Before someone sees."

"What are you doing?"

"It loosens up the gel," Julia says.

"But we're not supposed to," says Erika. "If we get caught, the club'll catch hell, so make it quick."

I hop in the warm water and dunk my head back. It's pretty shallow, so we have to lie down to get our heads in. Three little kids playing at the other end pour water over each other and screech. I sit up.

"Wait. Is it warm water that's getting the gel out, or is it baby pee?"

The girls laugh.

• • •

I meet Mom upstairs in the echoing lobby of Aquamania. She immediately grabs my chin and turns my face to better see the scratch under my eye.

"What happened to you?"

"Aw, it's okay, Mom. I just got nicked in the pool."

She sighs. "Took you long enough to get changed."

"Yeah, well ... That stuff is hell to get out of your hair."

We line up and order sandwiches, and when Mom's waiting for the payment to go through, she squints and brings her fingertips to her temple.

"You okay?"

"I have a headache already. I don't know how you can stand it." Pools are noisy. It's never bothered me—but maybe Mom's talking about more than the noise.

"Here, I got it." I take her tray over to a table by the windows so we can look down into the pool, then come back for my own. We sit down, but she doesn't pick up her sandwich.

"You look tired."

"I'll be okay. It's just been a really busy time at work. But on the bright side, the overtime's paying for some of your synchro fees."

"But now you don't get a weekend off."

"It's not like—"

I shake my head. "No, it's not okay. If Dad kept his end of the bargain—"

"Your dad is free to do whatever he wants." Mom opens her hands, like giving up. Like she's just resigned to whatever he decides to do—support us, or not.

"That's bullshit. That arrangement is bullshit. Aren't you mad at him?" She looks like she might cry. "Oh, no, Mom. I'm sorry." I sigh deeply. We're quiet for a bit, neither of us eating. "You know, I can at least get myself to meets now, Mom. You don't need to do this anymore."

"You're retiring me from pool duty?"

"I just don't want you to feel like you *have* to be here. I like that you come, but you should have some downtime. It's not fair."

There's a flicker of something like relief on her face, but then she takes my hand. "No, Bart, I want to be here for you. And those other parents look at you like—"

"I'll be fine. Go home. You know I can get a ride back with Sunny. She's got the van."

She pulls her hand away and takes a sip of tea, then puts the mug down on the table. For a while, we just watch the swimmers below.

Mom pushes the other half of her sandwich toward me. "Okay, then. Go ahead."

"So it's okay?" I ask her. "I'll ride back with them?"

"Yeah, it's okay. You know, I think I'll catch an earlier ferry. It would be nice to have some of the afternoon at home."

"Yeah. For sure." I pick up Mom's sandwich and take a bite, chewing self-consciously with her eyes on me.

She gives me a weak smile. "You know, it's nice to see you point your toes again."

●　●　●

At the end of the day, Casey rides back with Kyoka, so it's just Chelsea, Jules, Erika, and me in Sunny's van. We pile in, tired and a little giddy. Chelsea plugs her phone into the car's stereo, and we sing along to the music we're swimming to—not the cut versions but a playlist that Chelsea made of everybody's full songs.

The mixed duet music comes on, and I look at Erika and start hamming it up, all exaggerated expressions and hand motions. "Is this my life?"

"Ahh-ah-ahhhh-ah," she sings back, all fake earnest.

"Am I breathing ..."

Then everyone joins in, even Sunny: "*Under water?*"

Well, I can tell you one thing. This meet? It was a lot more fun than any racing meet I've ever gone to. Even that one time Riley and I rubbed Icy Hot in the crotches of the other guys' suits.

By the time we're off the ferry, the evening light's gone, the playlist is done, and we're calm in the darkness along the highway. Erika's leaning her head against my shoulder. I feel the warmth of her through my sweatshirt, and it's quiet and still, Chelsea and Jules plugged into their headphones now. I'm not listening to anything—just the sound of Erika's breathing, and cars going by outside. As the van navigates through the streets toward home, I match my breathing to hers. Inhale, exhale, in sync.

SEVENTEEN

It wasn't enough.

That's what we learned when the competition scores were posted at regionals. If my figure scores bring our duet down again at the next meet, that's it—we won't get to compete again. I'll be damned if that happens.

Sunny gave us Monday off after the event. On Tuesday, I skip my last block and get to the pool early because I know Sunny comes to have her own lane swim before practice. I head out on deck and see Dive Boy stand up from the water fountain.

"Hey!" he says. "It's like we never left."

"Right?"

"So, are you skipping class?"

"No, I've got a comp coming up next week. The whole dive club's training extra. You?"

"Skipping."

Dive Boy laughs. "See you around, bad boy."

He walks a few steps away, but then I shout, "Good luck next week!"

He turns back around. Smiles. "Thanks."

I walk over to the dive tank, where Sunny's doing laps. When I look up at the dive tower, Dive Boy waves at me from the steps.

I wave back.

I don't know what's going on. It's been a while since I've made a new friend who isn't a girl ... And whatever this is with Dive Boy, it feels different from just making friends. Something about the look on his face. Like he *knew* I'd be looking up to the tower.

It's more like flirting.

I take the steps down into the dive tank, and wait for Sunny to lap back this way.

"Bart! What are you doing here so early?"

"Are you finished? I don't want to cut your workout short."

Sunny swims up to the wide staircase and sits on an upper step. "No, it's fine. I'm close enough to done. What's up?"

"Sunny, I know I need more practice time with you. I ... wonder if I couldn't set up some one-on-one coaching?"

Sunny thinks, stretching out legs that are still strong and lean after retiring from synchro herself a few years ago.

"Well, I could at a cost. When are you thinking?"

"How much time do you have?"

"We could try an extra half hour before your weekday practices, and just focus on figures. Can you get here at two?"

"Yes! For sure. I'm here now and it's one thirty, right?"

Sunny frowns at me. "I mean, can you get here at two without skipping your last block?"

"Oh, yeah. Yeah, no problem."

"The coaching fees would be for two additional hours then, weekly. Is that okay?"

"Yeah, I can swing that." Not sure how, but I'll find a way.

"You know there's a chance there aren't any other mixed pairs entering the competition?" Sunny asks. "So far, I haven't heard of any others from our province. So you probably won't have anyone else at provincials."

"Then what about the qualifier for the national championships?"

"Who knows? If at least one other province has mixed pairs, then they'll compete it. If not ..."

"Automatic blue ribbon?"

"That would be a nice way to start off your synchro career, right?" Sunny teases.

But I don't think it's a good way to start off. "There's no point in automatically getting on the podium if I suck," I tell her. "I don't think it accomplishes anything to just win because you're the only guy who showed up."

"But entering this event that's never been included before? There's a lot of winning in showing up for that."

I swish my feet around in the water. "Thanks, Sunny. So you can get me good enough to make it to provincials?"

"I'll do my best. Listen, why don't you warm up with laps while you're waiting for the girls to get here?"

When Sunny goes, I look up. Divers were leaping in front of us the whole time we were talking. Through my mirrored goggles, I can't see who's on the platform now—but I hold my breath, and when the next figure leaps into the air, rotates, and plummets hands first into the tank, it's Dive Boy. I sink under the water and swim underneath him as he kicks upward. It's silent under the surface. Silent and suspended. And Dive Boy's body is floating above me, his legs kicking him toward the stairs.

I hold my breath all the way to the other side of the tank.

After twenty minutes of laps, I'm good and warmed up. I figure I'll go get the jugs now and practise some basic positions before Sunny gets started with me. Before leaving the storage room, I check the window—Sunny and Amanda Gates are right outside, talking. I lean on the door and open it, just a little, but they don't see me behind them.

"Well, when Elizabeth wasn't passing the figures at her age group level, *she* wasn't allowed to compete," Amanda says.

"She was an alternate on the team for part of the season, yes."

"Then have *Bart* be an alternate. This is not fair to the girls! What are they supposed to think when one of their team members gets suspended from competition for not keeping up, but you bend over backwards to have this boy in the pool with them? Why would you send him to a competition when he can't even score passing figures!"

"Bart can't swim team. And he passed *some* of his figures. He's close to getting the rest."

"Well, for Pete's sake, Sunny, you just told Chelsea you can't work with her before practice starts anymore. Because now you're coaching *him*."

"That was an informal arrangement with Chelsea. I've made a formal arrangement with Bart. You know, if Chelsea wants to start early, she's welcome to work on her own. And I'll still be here. I can still keep an eye on her practice—it's just not one-on-one."

An informal arrangement? So Sunny was essentially coaching Chelsea extra, and for free. I guess I can see why she would. Why wouldn't a coach throw everything into a swimmer who's obviously going to succeed? She'll bring home medals for the club. Others will notice and be attracted to that. More good swimmers will join the club.

Now I'm getting in the way of that for Chelsea and Sunny.

Amanda won't let go. She keeps harping on Elizabeth's suspension.

"You told Elizabeth she was removed after she failed the category figures. You have to tell Bart the same thing. You have to remember that there are girls watching what you do. You don't even know if he's serious! He could just be in it for kicks, you know? Then you're wasting your time—and the girls."

"I happen to know he's very serious."

"We could go to a bigger club, Sunny. We're very mobile."

It's hard enough to listen to Amanda try to get me booted from the competition, but something about her threatening Sunny like this pushes me over the edge. I can't just eavesdrop anymore. I push the door open, and it squeaks. Amanda turns and sees. She and Sunny step out of the way to let me out.

"Did you just threaten to leave the club?" I ask, but I'm speechless after that. Because Chelsea is standing right there, behind her mother. I didn't see her through the window, but she was there all along, just letting her mother go on without saying a word.

"Bart, Chelsea, go warm up."

"I am warmed up."

Sunny just gives us a death stare until we clear out of there. We get to the water and stop before we get in.

"Chelsea, what's going on?

"What? Nothing."

"You just let your mom try to cancel our mixed duet competition! I can't even ... You know if I don't participate in the next competition, that's it for *Erika's* duet too. I know how you feel about her, but you can't sabotage her duet for your revenge. She's working so hard on it."

"Sure." Chelsea shrugs. "You both are."

"Then what the hell?"

"It's just ..." She looks at me. "It's just that fair's fair, Bart."

I shake my head. "No way. That is not what this is."

"Whatever," Chelsea says, and snaps on her cap.

I'm so mad I pick my own lane outside the club's roped-off area so I can go as fast as I can and not run into anyone.

At the break, Sunny asks me to stay back as the girls grab their snacks and sit on the deck. "Bart, I'm sorry, just as sorry as you are," she says, her deep brown eyes so open and her brow furrowed. "But Ms Gates is right. We normally don't enter a swimmer into a competition without them having passed their age group figures. If I am to follow our precedent, I can't send you to provincials."

Oh, for fuck's sake.

Immediately, I feel all my anger at Chelsea that I'd burned out at practice come flooding back. Blood-boiling anger.

Erika comes up, and Sunny and I both look at each other, like—*Are you going to tell her?*

Sunny sighs, and spills.

"You can't do this to us, Sunny. *Please,*" Erika begs.

"Bart will still compete his figures at provincials. And if they're good enough, you will compete in the mixed duet event at the qualifier. Okay?"

Erika goes over to tear a strip off Chelsea. Chelsea just stands there, her face growing red.

"Erika ..." I go over and put a hand on her shoulder.

"She doesn't even care," she says, turning to me.

"I didn't say that!" Chelsea snaps.

"You don't have to!"

"Come on." I manage to pull Erika back. "Getting angry doesn't change anything." I learned that after all the times I reacted to shitheads over in the Rosa Waves.

But what is this? Is Chelsea saying: *No duet for me—then no duet for you*? Are we fighting over Erika? Is that what's going on?

Whatever. Chelsea's just another wall. Her mother is a wall. I can scale walls.

EIGHTEEN

What happens to you when your parent is convinced you're gay—or at least, what happens to me is that I tend to overdo it with the training.

Today, I'm totally getting a chance to do that. Sunny's devoting Wednesday's practice to strength. We start outside, with evil plyometrics with hundreds of jump squats, jump kicks ... then into the pool. Sunny pushes me through a full scull rotation—front layout, back layout, reverse propeller, split sculls, alligator, foot first, barrel, dog, double overhead, you name it. Then splits with resistance cords attached to our ankles.

Onto the deck for the torture that is flexibility training. Julia and I pair up, and Erika and Chelsea pair off. Normally duet partners pair off together during any land training, but they're so used to doing the stretch routine with each other, they just naturally start together.

Erika winces and Chelsea asks her if she wants to go further on her stretch. Erika nods. Chelsea pushes, and I wonder if I could do that without being afraid of hurting her. Those girls are not afraid to inflict a little pain in the name of better splits, or a deeper stretch, or stronger arches.

I watch them move from stretch to stretch, pulling each other's arms and pressing each others' backs—without even discussing what they're going to do next. *Those two could get better scores together than Erika can with me.* I need to try harder.

God, I hate toe curls. Nothing makes endless foot flexibility training tolerable. Especially when Julia's pushing my pointed feet toward the ground with all her upper body strength while I try to flex my toes upward. Ow.

Then the ab exercises. Lying on the wet deck because I forgot my mat. I just want to go to the locker room and puke. Really. If there was any undigested lunch in my body, I would. I just hope all this training makes me strong enough to match Erika in the water.

I've got about two months. Two months to pull my skill up, which is really just forty practices, maybe fewer if there's time off for winter break. Julia, Erika, and I sit on the edge of the pool when the torture is over, and Sunny comes over to talk to us. Julia slaps the tiles next to her. "Have a seat," she jokes, but of course Sunny stands—she's always dressed in her yoga wear, with long shorts or cropped pants so the bottoms don't get wet. Never in a suit herself.

"You three are always together now. I should give you a trio," Sunny says. Erika and Julia laugh. "Bart, you going to stay later to practice your ibis? Might as well, since there's still another thirty minutes of pool time."

"Sure. Whatever you think I should do."

"See, girls? This is the attitude you should be aiming for," Sunny jokes, and Jules pushes me off the ledge, into the water.

"Hey!"

"Stop getting us in trouble, newb," Erika jokes.

"Be nice. You don't want to scare away our first boy," Sunny says, then leaves to wheel the speaker back into the cabinet.

"Weeell?" Julia says. "Anyone want to hit the hot tub before we leave?"

I keep egg beatering in place, thinking about the next nine weeks. "Will you guys help me get my figures up to where they should be?"

"Yes, of course." Erika slips into the water next to me. "It's in my best interests," she says, smiling.

With Julia on deck and Erika swimming next to me, they take me through the evil ibis. I screw it up the first time. Then I go into a back layout again, to start over. Stupid ibis. My figure doesn't look anything like the long-beaked water bird it's named after.

Erika swims up next to me. "Okay, don't freak out, but I'm going to touch your hips."

"Um, okay."

She holds me in position and I try again, then come up and lift my goggles.

Julia laughs. "Your ibis is a drowning bird. Your bird needs a floatation device."

Erika sighs. "No, Bart. You just need to focus your power a little more. More power in your sculling. Don't get discouraged. Transitions are hard!"

Julia stands up. "Okay, you crazy kids. I'm done for tonight. Bart, you're doing great. Keep it up."

So then it's just us.

"Hey, do you have anything left in the tank?" I ask her. "Want to run through our duet routine once before we go?"

"Yeah, sure," Erika says, but I can tell she's tired by the way she says it.

"You're sure?"

"Sure, I'm sure. One more."

We go through our routine just with the count, no music. We come up and she pops her goggles off, shaking her head. "You have to stop being afraid of getting kicked."

"Who said I'm afraid of getting kicked?"

Erika looks confused.

"I'm afraid of kicking *you*."

She laughs. "Oh, don't be. I'm so used to it."

"Well, I'm not. I don't want to hurt you."

"Oh, Bart, you won't. Just get closer—it'll help you stay in the pattern when we're syncing."

"Okay."

"And then when we're making those intertwined forms, don't stretch away from me. Stay close."

"We're pretty close!" At one point, Erika wraps a leg around my hips and we're vertical, and we kick two legs together, back and forth. Then we have the formation where we swim back to back, sculling in circles with our legs bent like the petals of a flower on the surface. And then there's the lift.

"But when you come out of those forms, it's like you can't get away fast enough."

I laugh. "Well, that's not true."

"So swim like it. You're not going to hurt me."

"Okay." I put a hand on Erika's. "Hey, thanks for staying extra tonight."

"I'm glad I could." She smiles at me, then gives my hand a squeeze. "You're going to get better."

"I promise I will."

• • •

For the next week, I practise every day. And every practice ends with Erika and Jules coaching me, doing the best they can to get me closer to perfect. But by the last practice before winter break, Erika's had enough of my perfectionism.

"What did I do? How can I fix it?" I stop and rewind the video, pointing out the place where something doesn't look right.

"It's not bad, Bart," Erika says.

"I need more than 'not bad' if we're going to swim this duet all the way to nationals. That's not straight," I tell her, pointing at my vertical, toes pointing off to the left a little instead of straight up.

"Bart, the number of people in the world with a perfect vertical? Is exactly ..." she holds up her fingers in a circle.

"Zero?"

"Yes. So you've got to stop stressing about that."

"You can't tell me nobody's got a perfectly straight vertical."

"Not reliably. Not every time."

"Well," I smile, "can't I aim for an accidentally perfect vertical?"

"I'd expect nothing less. But—on your own today. I'm done with the repetition for now."

I try to back off and stop being so needy, at least until after the Christmas break. I can't make Erika want to stop coaching me.

By the time I leave the pool, there's nobody else in the showers except me and Dive Boy. He says, "You're at it late tonight."

"Yeah, you too."

"Trying a new dive. So you're going to a competition soon?"

"Yeah. We're going to take our mixed duet all the way to nationals or bust."

"Awesome. So a mixed duet?"

"Yeah, it's a new event."

"But no *unmixed* boys' duet."

I smile. "Yeah ... just unmixed girls, and the mixed, for now. I guess they want the mixed duet to be like ice dancing. You know, powerful guy, graceful girl ... It's not all matchy-matchy like the girls' duets."

"But you could have an event like that for two guys, couldn't you? Don't you think there's potential for two guys swimming like you do?"

"Okay, so you're not actually interested in swimming synchro, are you?"

"Not for myself. I'm just imagining it. Don't you think two guys swimming ... has potential?"

"Well, sure."

"Do you think it would be hot?"

"Oh, well ..." I look up at the ceiling. An image of two guys swimming a duet flashes into my brain, and it's not ... unappealing. Actually, picturing, say ... me and Dive Boy, swimming some of the sequences that I swim with Erika ... Well, yes ... *Hot.*

Yeah, so much for getting clear.

Crap. So what do I say? It's not like my answer's no. But if I say yes, does that mean Dive Boy will assume he knows my sexuality and ... I don't know. Ask me out? What if that's not even remotely what I want? What if I just get attracted to guys sometimes, but ... that's all it is? Passing attraction—that doesn't mean anything?

"I don't think the swimming world's ready for that yet."

"They should be." Dive Boy grins. "Are you?"

I turn off my taps. "Well ... sure. Whatever people want to do." I grab my towel and go into the change room without looking at him.

Outside, I run into Erika coming up the stairs from the change rooms, and I put an arm around her shoulders. She puts an arm around my waist, and we walk up the steps like that. I hope Dive Boy sees us, because maybe he'll make an assumption about *this*. And maybe he won't ask me any more questions I can't answer.

Of course, I'm sure that *this* is just because Erika and I touch constantly now, right? It has to be part of getting connected as duet partners—the duet's led to a physical friendship. My body's accessible to her now. We're just accessible to each other.

●　●　●

Christmas comes fast. Sunny gives us a week off of practice. Well ... almost a week. I think about the two weeks we'd take off from the Rosa Waves and laugh. The synchro team is there after the lane racers go home, and we'll be there days before they get back.

For the first two days, I sit around watching duets on YouTube and eating really bad food. After the third day, I'm itching to get back in the water, so I text Erika to join me at the pool. I do some laps and practise the junior category figures.

Tonight's Christmas Eve. Dad often comes down and spends Christmas Eve with me before Mom and I drive up Island to Grandma's for Christmas Day. Either that or he comes after, before New Year's. This year, he's taking overtime at the plant. Now that he's not backing my swimming, though, I don't know why he needs the holiday pay. But I can guess why he doesn't want to come down and visit.

Whatever. Mom and I will be headed to Grandma's tonight, and there's her pie to look forward to. I always like to get a big workout in before two days away with Mom and Grandma. If I don't go, I'll be bouncing off the ceiling by the end of Boxing Day, after all that sitting around. "I'm getting better, though, right?" I ask Erika after we've swum the end of our duet. I'm trying to get used to the part of the routine at the end that's all vertical, that requires a lot of really quick movement, and I can't come up to breathe—but

I can't quite make it the whole way yet. I feel these little convulsions, my body begging for air.

"For sure, you're getting better. But let's just swim it through once without analyzing it, okay?"

So we run through our routine in the nearly empty dive tank during a public swim, trying to hear the music in our heads while the sound system plays "Rudolph the Red-Nosed Reindeer" and "Santa Claus Is Coming to Town."

I come up and gasp just before the last figure in the sequence.

"Oh, man. I'm sorry."

"Almost!" Erika says. "Nearly there."

We get out and head to the hot tub. "Hey, we've got six more weeks 'til provincials! That's a ton of time to get you through to the end." She doesn't say *if you're going*. Just like I don't. We're giving no room for failure. No room for maybe.

"Yeah, six, but more like five with holidays … Do you think I'll be ready?"

"Yeah, I do."

I wish we could sit here side by side a little longer, but the pool's closing announcement comes on. And in an hour I've got to be packed and in Mom's car, ready for the drive. I spend so much time with my synchro teammates now, it feels weird to go away for Christmas. Like … instead of going *to* family, it's like I'm leaving family for the holiday. I think about what it would be like to have Christmas with the team, and just about follow Erika right into her change room.

"Whoops. Wrong room."

She stops and laughs. "I'll see you upstairs?"

"You bet."

Up in the lobby, I wait while they're turning the lights off in the café and a janitor pushes a mop down the hall. Erika comes up the stairs, her wet hair combed back and tucked into the hood of her jacket. She's holding a wrapped present, with a bow.

"Hey. Gotcha something."

I open the gift tag. It says, *To my partner in breathlessness. xo Airika.*

"Air-ika ... I like it. Should I open it now?"

She nods. I pull off the wrapping and unwrap the tissue inside. It's a *Breathing is for the weak* T-shirt, just like hers.

"Ha! Thanks. Hey, shouldn't that tag read no-Air-ika?"

We've been swimming like twins, so connected. So why didn't I even get that she was going to give me something for Christmas? "Aw, I didn't get you anything."

"Hey, you swimming with me is my gift."

"Well. I'll do my best." I lean over and give her a kiss on the forehead. She looks up at the ceiling. "What?"

"I was looking for the mistletoe."

"Oh. Yeah, no mistletoe."

"Too bad."

"Too bad?"

Airika, or Erika, smiles and backs away toward the front doors. "Merry Christmas, Bart. Text me if you get bored."

"Wait—"

"Gotta go. My ride's here—"

"Okay. Merry Christmas, Erika."

I watch her wave and back-slam the door open. When she turns to go, I let all my breath out.

NINETEEN

I'm back at practice on the first Monday of the year. And I have something to look forward to—I may not have gotten Erika a Christmas gift, but I figured out something better. While we were off, Sunny contacted the organizers to see if Erika and I could demo our free mixed duet as part of the watershow on the second day of provincials. We may not be able to enter our routine in the competitive event—but at least this way people will get to *see* it.

"So it's a go?" I ask Sunny.

"It's a go!"

"Yes!" I can't wait to tell Erika when she gets here. I hop in the pool, excited to warm up.

Looks like Chelsea's excited to get back to it too, since she's here swimming laps while I warm up for my first half hour with Sunny.

What I really want to work on now, though, is breath work. I need to get my oxygen efficiency up, and the way to do that is unders—swimming lengths of the pool under water, without coming up for a breath.

I touch the wall at the same time Chelsea does.

"Hey, Chelsea."

"Hi, Bart."

"Happy New Year."

"What do you want?"

I laugh. "Let's do an under challenge."

"Now?"

"Yeah. You ready?"

She starts drawing in a deep breath, so I do too, making sure I push off at the same time. We glide below the surface. I keep looking to the side, and Chelsea's there, looking over to see where I am. There's pressure in my chest at the end, but I don't surface. I pop up at the wall just ahead of her.

"Twenty-five's too short. We should do fifty. Do you do fifties?"

"All the time, Bart. Why don't we just see how far you can go? See who can last the farthest."

Obviously, that would be Chels. But I have to start pushing this hypoxic training if I'm going to get the oxygen efficiency I need to last through the final sequence in the mixed duet.

"What's the farthest you've gone?" I ask her. "Have you ever done a seventy-five?"

Chelsea just pushes off the side of the pool, so I follow. I bet she's done a seventy-five. I bet she'll do one right now. And I'll be toast, and she'll gloat.

I dolphin kick to start, and then switch over to underwater breast stroke. It's slower, but I won't expend as much energy. I make the twenty-five. Halfway across the next lap my throat threatens to open in search of air, but I make the fifty.

The second turn is brutal. But I keep going, keep telling my lungs no, even though I feel like my chest will implode and suck in the pool water. The hum of the filter sounds like it's getting louder in my head. I look over and see Chelsea still kicking through the deep.

Keep going, I tell myself. *Don't let her win.* But I feel dizzy. A swarm of white dots eclipses the dark blue pool tiles. I try pulling harder—I'm not going to let Chelsea beat me to the seventy-five. *You can beat her. You were the star long course swimmer. Breath is for the weak.*

But the dots join, and then everything goes dark.

For a minute, I hear my duet music. Just for a few seconds. I feel warm, and still, but that's just for a moment too, because someone's pushing me above the surface, arms wrapped around my hips. Erika? My turn to be flyer?

I come to out of the water. Her arms boost me farther, all the way out now, and I turn and see the beige tiles of the pool deck. I cough.

"Thank God!" Chelsea shouts. My lungs burn, and I feel like I could cough more deeply. I start, then spew up water onto the deck.

"Shit, Bart. What were you trying to prove?"

I blink, and take in Chelsea's face.

Sunny runs down the deck with a lifeguard.

"Bart, are you okay?" she asks.

"My head's killing me. My chest hurts."

"We're going to call an ambulance."

"No! Don't do that. I can—I'm okay."

"You fainted under water," Chels scolds me. "You could have died!"

"Chelsea," Sunny scolds, "we don't need the drama right now."

I almost laugh at Chelsea's exasperated frown.

"It's okay. I shouldn't have kept going."

Sunny's face is close to mine. "I don't know if the girls have told you, Bart. But I was a competitive synchro swimmer too."

"Yeah. You swam for China?"

"And got a world trophy. So I know what pushing yourself is like. And I know you can get stupid."

"Are you calling me stupid?" I whisper, and she cracks a smile.

The lifeguard straps on a blood pressure cuff and checks the gauge. He listens to my breathing. I wish I could just get up and go change, get the hell out of here, but my body feels like lead.

And Chelsea's holding my hand.

"You'll be okay," the lifeguard says. "But you should get checked out."

"I'm going to text your mother," says Sunny. "She can pick you up?"

"If ... she's home. I can wait if she's not."

"You sure you're okay?" Chelsea asks.

"Sorry, Chels. Is this stressing you out?"

"What, you almost dying?" She frowns.

"No, me *not* dying. Now you still have me in the club."

"Oh, for Pete's ..." Chelsea stands up, shaking her head.

"For Pete's sake?" I cough, but it sounds like the bark from a seal. "Be careful, Chelsea, you're starting to sound like your mother."

She whips around. "I just saved your ass. You should be a little more grateful."

She's right. She actually seems more upset than me. "Okay. Hey, Chels ... Thanks for pushing me."

She looks at me with her arms crossed, and her frown loosens up into a look of recognition. "Yeah, you're welcome."

The other girls from our team come out onto the deck for practice. Erika and Jules nearly run down to reach us.

"Oh my God, what happened to you?" Erika says as Chelsea walks away.

"I'll be okay. Just inhaled a little water." I cough.

"Shit. We've got five weeks 'til provincials. You better not get sick on me," Erika says.

I shake my head. "I won't."

Sunny rubs my back as I sit up, smiling.

"What?" Erika asks.

"Speaking of provincials," I say. "I've got something to tell you."

TWENTY

Our first day at provincials back at Aquamania, I grab the program from Erika and flip through the schedule. "Whoa ..."

"What?"

I point to the event. Sunny already told us it was on day two of the provincial competition, and although I believed her, I still wanted to see our names on paper, to have it feel real.

But it's not just us.

Erika snatches the program from me. "Who are ... Nikki and Josh? From Kelowna Dolphins? Oh my God, there are *three* more mixed pairs!"

"Where do they come from?"

"Yukon."

"Yukon comes to our provincials?"

"Yeah, they come to ours since there aren't enough Yukon teams to hold their own event. And there's a pair from ... Oh no."

I grab the program back from Erika. "Oh, Sunny ... why didn't you tell us?"

"Tell you what?" Sunny says, walking into the pool lobby wheeling our cooler.

"*Freaking Aquastellars?!*"

Sunny chuckles. "I didn't know, Erika. I don't know everything about every other club."

"Yeah ..." Erika narrows her eyes, "but you'd know about *this*."

"Sunny! You told me it was an automatic blue ribbon at the qualifier if I passed my figures here." But it won't be if Aquastellars are in the competition. They're one of the best clubs in the province.

"I thought you didn't want an automatic win anyway. This is good, right?"

"Yeah, but ... some preparation might have been nice." Okay, don't panic, don't panic. You're okay.

Sunny comes up close to us and drops her voice. "Look, I didn't know until about a week ago. And I didn't want this to throw you. But come on, it's good! Having some competition will keep you guys on your toes."

"You know what this means, though, right?" I say. "If these guys are here ... there will be more guys. Like, in other provinces. At qualifiers." I go quiet, imagining what it might be like, a bunch of mixed duets there.

"Okay, don't lose your focus," Erika says, clapping her hands in front of my face.

I laugh and pull her hands down. "I'm not."

"You looked like you were gapping out there. And we still have to perform tomorrow."

Sure. In front of guys who are all swimming better than me. Who all passed their figures, no doubt. But still ... if these guys are here, then guys from across the country might come out of the woodwork to enter our first junior synchro mixed duet event at qualifiers. Like there's actually a place for us. I feel scared and comforted all at once.

●●●

For the first time since leaving racing, I see another competitor in the pool with a Y chromosome.

As usual, we have the figure event first. I spot one of the other guys in the lineup at the judge's station straight across from me. He looks younger, like they're probably having him swim up into a higher age group to do the event. Then there's a guy I saw in the hall earlier with red hair and bleached streaks. He's in the lineup at the other corner on our end. They're both wearing swim jammers, so I silently curse Sunny for telling me I had to wear the swim briefs back at regionals. I look around, but I don't see the third guy.

And get this—I pass. I more than pass! I get scores in the sixes. I'm so excited I just want to scream.

I wait in the lobby, wearing our Rosa Waves Synchro jacket. I see Josh, the guy from the Dolphins, and he gives me a nod before leaving with his duet partner. Then the Aquastellars guy comes out in a pair of sweats. He's got a shaved head. He comes up to me and extends a hand.

"Hey, I'm Kim."

I can't picture him wearing makeup and a sparkly suit, but I guess synchro guys don't *all* swim like that. And who knows? Maybe he will. Maybe I won't be the only guy fully glammed up for the swim tomorrow. I wonder if Erika's going to do my makeup again for the routine, and I feel my skin tingle at the thought.

"Bart." We shake hands.

"My coach told me you guys have a mixed duet you're going to do tomorrow."

"Yeah, just at the watershow. Still trying to get good enough to compete it."

"Ah. How long have you been swimming?"

I smile sheepishly. "Aw, not long, if you mean synchro. Just since October."

"Before that?"

"Racing long course."

"Cool."

"You?"

"Gymnastics before this. This is my second synchro season. First competitive year."

"Oh, wow."

"Still doing racing?"

I laugh. "Not enough time. Still doing any gymnastics?"

Kim laughs too. "No way. Hey, you met any other guys doing this?"

I shake my head. "It's just me back home."

"Yeah, I didn't think I was going to see another guy here."

"There you are," Erika says, looping her arm through mine. I introduce her to Kim. We talk about the #MixedDuetOlympics movement and exchange contact info. After we talk a bit, we say our goodbyes and good lucks for tomorrow.

On the way out to Sunny's van, Erika says, "I think he's into you."

"Well, then I think your gaydar's broken."

"Is it?"

She's digging. She's basically asking me if I'm gay, and I don't know if that's because she wants to ask me if I'm into her.

We're the first ones to the van. We'll have to wait for Sunny.

"Yeah, he wasn't into me."

So we can both talk around this. Apparently, I have no problem with that.

TWENTY-ONE

I'm back in my hotel room for ten minutes before my phone buzzes. I pick it up, expecting a text from the girls about what we're doing tonight. Instead, it's my dad.

> How'd your comp go?

Oh. Mom must have told him about the meet. It's not like I've been keeping him up to date so far this year—and I have no desire to now. It's not like he actually cares.

> Hey you there?

The phone rings. I let it go to voice mail, but he doesn't leave a message.

> I don't come see you just because your Mom told me to. She didn't make a deal to get money. I could have disappeared. She gave me that option

> should have taken it while u had the chance

> Dammit pick up the phone

It rings again, but there's a knock on the door, so I tap Ignore and throw my phone on the bed. Erika, Casey, and Jules come into my room bearing Girl Guide cookies, salt and vinegar chips, and a caddy full of nail polish. Good distractions.

"Hey, there." I try to shake off the stress and look welcoming.

"This okay?" Erika asks after the others have come in and taken up residence on the double beds.

"*Mi casa es su casa.*"

Erika flops down on one bed and stretches her feet out to Julia, who shakes up a bottle of polish.

"Ugh. I just can't believe how early we have to get up tomorrow."

"Maybe we should just go to bed now?" I ask.

"And do away with first night competition tradition? No way."

Julia says, "We'll end up collapsing at nine tomorrow night, so it's not like we'll get another chance to have some fun."

I reach over and grab some chips from Casey, who's holding out the bag. "Where's everybody else?"

"Kyoka and Huiyan aren't up for it. They're turning in early," she says. "Well, Huiyan isn't. But they're sharing a room, and Kyoka doesn't want to wake her up when she goes back later, so ..."

"What about Chels?"

Erika pipes up. "I asked her. She's got some visualization practice or something. She said she might be up later."

"Which is a no," Jules says.

Erika holds out her palms. "But I asked."

Not a surprise. Chelsea's been keeping her distance from us since I nearly drowned during our unders race. I go to the sink and rinse the salt off my hands, then run my fingers through my curls. "What time's that gelling call?"

Julia groans. "Five freaking a.m."

It would be so much easier if we didn't have to do that part. More pleasant too. The makeup's fun. Putting the gelatin in my hair? Is just ... ick.

I finger-comb my curls away from my forehead, looking in the mirror, while the girls chatter behind me. Then I flatten my hair down completely, looking at my face without its usual blond, curly frame. It's what I look like with a cap. Or wet or gelled hair ... or no hair. And I look less like my dad that way.

Bill May shaves his head.

I pick up the clippers I use to trim the back and sides, and fish out the guard from my kit. I clip on the guard, plug it in, and turn it on—it starts to hum. A two—the one I use for the back.

Sighing, I raise the clippers and shave off the first strip, right from my forehead to the back of my head. Shave it right off. Curls fall onto the counter, onto my shoulders. Erika shrieks, and then covers her mouth. I smile at her in the mirror, and take off another strip.

Casey pauses with a chip halfway to her lips. "Uh, what are you doing?"

I shave off another, and another. Jules screws the bottle of nail polish closed, gets up off the bed, and comes up behind me.

"Did I miss anything?" I ask her, holding the clippers out. She takes them and puts one hand on my shoulder, pushes me down on a chair, and then touches up some spots in the back.

"Turn around?"

I turn around to face Julia, and she clicks off the clippers. "Nice," she says.

I stand up and look in the mirror again. I smile. I'm all eyes and grin.

"I can't believe you just did that!" Erika says. For a second, I'm scared. What if it changes how I look too much? What if ... that makes me look wrong to her?

"I mean ... I love it." She gets off the bed to come fuzz my head. Behind us, the clippers are on again. I turn around and Julia's taken off a strip of her own hair. She laughs out loud. We watch as she does the rest, all of it gone, a much bigger pile than mine.

"Damn, Bart. You have some good ideas. I should have done this ages ago."

"You guys! You look awesome," Casey says.

Julia turns around with the clippers. "You next? C'mon, Casey."

"No way! I mean, *you* guys look awesome. I think I'd look like I had a beach ball for a head."

"You do have a big head," Erika says, and Casey pushes her.

"Okay, then. How about it?" Julia asks. "I'm gonna sleep in 'til six. *Six.* This rocks."

Erika stands in front of the mirror, and I watch her eyes. I can see her weighing it. I go stand between her and the mirror, stand right in front of her, toe to toe, face to face. That spark between us lights up, and I grin. "I dare you."

Erika takes the clippers off the counter. I knew she would if I dared, so it was kinda unfair of me.

The clippers start humming. She begins at the back, and her long, straight hair starts falling to the ground. There's a lot of it. She reaches her hand up and touches the back.

"It feels so cool!"

I brush the back of my hand gently over the back of her head. "Yup."

I give her a few touch-ups, and she turns around to face the girls. Julia's jaw drops. "Wow."

"Does it look weird?" Erika asks.

"No. It looks good!"

When I click off the clippers, Erika just stares at herself in the mirror, her eyes wide. One hand travels up to run from the back of her neck over the top of her head. She catches my eye in the mirror.

"Do I look like a boy?" she whispers.

I don't know what she wants the answer to be. She looks like she always does when I see her.

"You look like Erika."

She's going to start to cry. I pull her into a hug and tell her, "It's just hair. If you hate it, don't worry. It'll grow back."

"But ... I don't hate it. That's not it." Erika wipes her eye with the cuff of her hoodie, looking at us standing next to each other in the mirror. "It's just ... I feel so different."

I fuzz her head, then my own.

"Yeah, me too."

The girls finish their pedicures. I stay quiet, watching them, eating too many chocolatey mint cookies. Then I let Erika do my toes. The girls all leave by eleven, and I open the window to get the varnish smell out of the room. Then I go to the wastebasket and take out one lock of Erika's hair. I curl it up in a tissue with one of my blond curls.

When I look at my phone, there's still no voice mail.

TWENTY-TWO

Before provincials, Mom took me shopping for my own makeup.

"Things I didn't expect to be doing for my son," she said when we walked into the drugstore.

"Well, aren't you glad you get to share your arcane knowledge of water-proof makeup?"

"Of course." She chuckled, and fluffed my curls. She led me to the mascara first.

"This stuff's my favourite," I told her.

"I had an inkling."

"What? How?"

"You left mine in your bathroom!"

"Oh."

"And you should really use remover when you take it off. You came to breakfast all smudged."

We got two types of waterproof mascara—two very different brushes—so I could test them out and see what worked for me.

And the best was when we discovered a line of waterproof liquid cream eyeshadow. I could not *wait* to try that out.

In the morning, I let the girls sleep in, and do my own makeup. I open the little pot of glittery mousse-like stuff and brush a layer of aqua shimmer over my lids. Then contour and some black liner over my waterline. It's so freaking pretty.

When I get to the pool, I walk into the lobby and it's different from figures, when everyone's walking around in white caps. Today, everyone's sporting their glamour—hair done, spectacular makeup, and glittery suits everywhere. I have to kind of weave my way around pairs and groups land drilling in the halls.

I drop my stuff at our section of bleachers near the dive tank, then slip off my sweats and turn around—and Chelsea's face falls.

"Oh, God. Look at you again."

I hold my arms out and twirl in place. "I know. Fabulous, right?" Then I lean in and give her a nice hard kiss on the cheek, leaving my fuchsia lip prints.

"Ugh!" She wipes her cheek with the back of her hand. "Bart!"

But get this ... I catch her smiling! I laugh. People are staring at me, sure—just like they did at regionals. But look, there's Kim coming now, with his hair gelled and wearing eyeliner, and a shiny gold Speedo, and I know I'm not the only one getting stared at today. Instead, I don't feel a shred of self-consciousness. And that? That's the weirdest thing. Weird and wonderful.

Chelsea opens her mouth like she's going to say something, but then she stops.

"What?"

But Chels doesn't answer. She just stares past my shoulder.

I turn around, and the girls are coming up behind me.

"Oh. My. God." Chelsea says. "You *all* did this?"

"You buzzed it!" Kyoka squeals. "It looks great."

"Not what I was going to say," Chelsea mutters.

Erika puts a hand up and brushes the two centimetres of soft black hair she has left. "I love how it feels."

Jules grins. "And tell me you're not jealous when I get out of the shower in thirty seconds and y'all are still in there fifteen minutes later, getting that crap out of your hair."

"Ha! You're so right," Casey says. "I just couldn't bring myself to do it."

Sunny hasn't said anything yet. She comes up and stares at the girls, and I can't figure out what she's thinking. "Aw. Now you can't wear the bun covers I got to match your suits." She sighs. "Okay, duets—get in the pool now."

Erika and I take our seats on the bleachers and watch the girls get in the tank.

We cheer for Kyoka and Huiyan's duet, and then for Julia and Casey's. When they're done, we watch the masters group. Swimmers who have aged out of the competitions at nineteen can join masters and keep swimming. Some of them are so old, they're like moms and dads—but they're still so good. Toward the end, Erika and I hop in the warm-up pool curtained off from the performance pool.

We sink below the surface into back pike, ready for our vertical thrust. When we come back down, we link legs for the joined pattern that we added to the routine. Erika's leg skims against my bare upper thigh. This is different from in practice, when I'm wearing my swim jammers. Very different. It's good. Very good.

Oh, man.

I slip out of the connection and surface.

Erika pops up after me. "Bart? What's the matter?"

I laugh. "Nothing. I just ... need a minute." Right now, I need to think about the routine. Not about how Erika's bare skin feels sliding against mine.

"Bart?" Erika's brows knit together. "We only have, like, five minutes. We haven't even practised the lift yet."

"Yeah. Just a sec."

"Oh." A look of recognition comes over her face, and my insides do a flip-flop. "It's okay," she says, with a smug look. "Take your time."

We laugh. I back away and egg beater in place, powerfully enough to boost myself out of the water. Nobody can egg beater and stay hard—instant cure.

I shut my eyes and run through the routine in my head. I lift my hands up, hands becoming legs, representing the movement. I get through the section in my head, and then nod at Erika.

"Okay."

"Gonna be all right?" Erika asks.

"Yeah."

We connect again, make an S shape that spins in a circle, then separate. Albatross twirl. Then the lift.

Now, anytime our eyes meet, it's charged.

More people are in the stands now, more than watched the duet event this morning, and the energy's getting us pumped. We get out of the warm-up pool, shed our wraps and our caps, and get ready near the bulkhead. I jump up and down, shaking my limbs out. The other mixed duets in the stands wave and whistle at us. Chelsea is sitting in the stands right by the bulkhead, but she's not cheering. Is she waiting for us to screw up, so Sunny won't send us to the qualifier?

The first whistle goes, and it's our turn.

When our music comes on, I'm totally inside it. Erika and I dive under the water—and that's when I feel it—this is going to be the best performance we've done yet.

When the singer says, *Out of place all the time, in a world that wasn't mine ... to take*—I feel the slightest pang of regret that we're not doing this for real today. That the competition isn't mine to take. But after a couple of bars of just the guitars and the drums, she comes back and sings: *I'll wait.*

Yeah, me too. 'Cause this is worth it.

In the last two weeks, I've come close to swimming the end perfectly, without needing to break for air. Erika said we could change the choreography at the end, but I said no. I want to do it the way we planned, even though it's a risk.

Now we're swimming *so* close on our intertwined bits. My spins complete neatly, our transitions are as close to perfect as possible with me swimming hard and fast to keep up with Erika's natural buoyancy.

Something about the physical connection between us has shifted, and it's powerful. It's like it's lit us on fire.

I open my eyes under water. The lyrics, as clear down here as they are on the surface, sing out: *Is this my life?* Down here in the deep, I look up at Erika on the surface, and all I see is someone I can't get enough of.

Someone I'm compelled to touch. Right now? I feel like this world under water is my life. And I am totally fine with that.

I launch her up and out for our lift, and I know it's completely lit, because when I come out again, I hear the stands cheer. I take a giant breath. We go down again, and here come the quick vertical leg sequences that nearly kill me. Erika and I agreed we wouldn't push the hypoxic training until I was recovered from my fainting episode, so we've just shortened our routine ending. But I know the full sequence will someday score us serious difficulty points. Even the part we're doing now is more of a challenge than anything the other pairs tried today.

I've built up the stamina to power through this far, and I'll power through even further in the weeks to come.

Erika and I surface together and look right into each other's eyes. It's like that morning she did my makeup—erotic. And the stands whistle and clap as we freeze there, caught up in our intense connection.

We break away and swim to the side, still breathing heavily from the exertion. They're still cheering! It's great! I even see some judges who came to watch.

Erika and I climb up the ladder and turn to look at each other. That shift in our connection is still there.

Kim comes down from the stands, and his partner, and Josh.

"We'll have to watch out at the qualifier," Kim says. "That was awesome!"

"Thank you," I tell them. "We can't wait to see you guys swim tomorrow."

Sunny's so proud of us too. She comes to give us a quick hug and tell us we swam well. Our teammates also come down to hug us.

Then Chelsea looks at us like there's something she wants. She hugs me. "That was really good," she says.

"Thanks." I hug her back.

She doesn't hug Erika.

●　●　●

The next afternoon, when it's time for the mixed duet event, I sit in the stands with Erika on my right. Chelsea sits on my left and pulls out her phone, switching it to video.

"You're going to shoot their swims?"

"Yeah, I got one of you guys too."

Julia sits down on the other side of Erika and takes her hand. I know it's hard for her to watch these guys compete and get scored—it sure is for me. I want to be there so bad I'm aching for it. And when the first pair starts, I feel cheated.

The technical event is first, and the Aquastellars nail it.

It's great there are more guys here. I'm ecstatic. But at the same time, I'm worried. Especially about Kim and his partner. There are whistles and cheers as they stand at the edge of the bulkhead, ready for their free routine. Their club shouts their signature cheer, and they walk on in sync. Their music starts, and I give Erika's other hand a little squeeze.

"Oh, he should have a little more height," Chelsea says. She leans over to me. "See that? Watch the timing ..."

I glance at Erika. She looks past me, glaring at Chelsea, who keeps playing commentator.

"Pretty good difficulty," she says. The pair attempts a lift, but they don't finish cleanly. "Oh, too bad. That would have been excellent, right? They'll get high scores for artistic, but that's going to cost them some execution points."

I laugh. "You're good at this."

The pair finishes, and we go wild, cheering and clapping. They stand on deck, ready for the scores. Difficulty, eighteen. Artistic impression, twenty-two. Execution, sixteen. They smile and wave, but you can see the confused disappointment in their eyes.

"Huh. I would have thought they'd score higher," Chelsea says.

"I know!" I say, outraged. "They were pretty spectacular, just like their technical. Aside from that one, they *nailed* their lifts. Everything was so pulled together—their suits, their music, their choreography. I'm, like, jealous. Do you think the judges are biased?"

"Not sure yet. We'll see."

Erika shushes us as the next pair walks on. I can tell Josh isn't as experienced as Kim, but these two are working hard. Chelsea comments all the way through their routine too.

Nikki is obviously so much stronger than Josh, and I worry. The routine isn't as creative as the Aquastellars', and Josh isn't making it look effortless, like Kim did. "Did I look like that?"

Chelsea shakes her head. "Not even close."

"Oh. Cool." Kim and his partner looked well matched. And I certainly *felt* well matched with Erika—not like I was struggling to keep up with her.

The pair finishes and climbs out to wait for their score.

"You guys were way stronger," Chelsea says, and looks me right in the eye. Wow. I have to admit, I'm grateful for Chelsea's take on all this. I like knowing where I stand. If I just watched this in silence with Erika, I'd have no idea.

"Thanks."

The scores are announced: Difficulty, twenty-one. Artistic impression, twenty-three. Execution, seventeen. Chelsea's brows rise. "Well, now see that?" she asks. "The judges must want to see more synchronizing. They scored these guys higher than I would have thought."

"But it's the free routine!" Erika says.

"I *know* it's the free routine." Chelsea glares at Erika. "But let's face it, I know how to interpret scoring, and judges are used to what they're used to."

Erika shakes her head. "Well, what's the point if they're going to make us swim the same as two girls?"

"It's not the same," Chelsea tells her. Then she leans close and says quietly to me, "I saw you two. Even if you synchronize more, it's not going to be the same."

I watch Chelsea watch the pairs step up on the podium, and I wonder if she's suddenly so into the mixed event because *she* wants to do it now.

"Hey, can you send me the video you shot?" I ask.

"Sure."

When we walk back to the stands to get our stuff, Erika says, "Boy, she seems to have warmed up to you now."

"Well, you know. Maybe Chels saw the other guys and she got over me joining your club. Maybe she's turned it around."

Erika stops for a split second, then keeps walking. "Just don't trust that turn."

You know, if I could get over whatever part Chelsea played in us not competing today, I would have thought Erika could—but I don't know everything that's happened between them. Or maybe I just don't understand.

Before leaving the pool, I go into the gift shop. They've got mugs with different swimming sayings on them. *Eat my bubbles.* Another one with three stick figures in side fishtail pose, and *in sync.* And there's another one, which I think would be perfect for Erika. I get it for her, like a thank-you gift—because I may be grateful for Chelsea's perspective, but Erika's the one who's brought me this far.

That night, I write an email to FINA, the federation that holds the international water sport competitions, to tell them that the mixed duet should be competed at the FINA World Junior Synchronised Swimming Championships next year, the synchro-only event for swimmers fifteen to eighteen. I write that there are guys my age, in my province, starting out and doing well. I write that we—and the girls we swim with—want to see the event included. And I beg them to recommend the mixed duet event to the International Olympic Committee. If it were part of the Olympics, that would send a message of inclusion ten times as loud as when they accepted the event at worlds in Kazan—the championship for all aquatic sports. It would give boys in synchro cred with everyone around the world—not just people who are already inside their sport. They could take up the sport and dream of Olympic gold, instead of giving it up in favour of other water sports.

Josh from the Dolphins is going to send a letter too. So is Kim from Aquastellars. I talked to them after the events today.

And in my email, I ask them to watch the videos Chelsea shot of Erika and me swimming to "Breathing Underwater" and the other pairs swimming their free routines.

I sign it and send it to FINA's technical committee for synchronized swimming. Then I send a copy to Bill May with a private message. I tell him what we're doing, and I tell him I'll do anything else he can think of.

TWENTY-THREE

Erika stayed on the mainland after provincials for a big family wedding, so I'm looking forward to a whole practice of figures on Monday. Ugh. But before I get in the water, Sunny calls me and Chelsea over while everybody else goes to warm up.

"What's up?" I ask her.

"With Erika away today, I want to see you pair with another swimmer. We're going to try something with you and Chelsea."

I look at Chelsea, but she just looks away.

"Sunny, I already have my tech and my free routines. And guys can only enter those two events, right?" Qualifiers are just five weeks away. Why give me something else to work on now?

"We need a sense of how you swim with others in the club too. Don't worry. I get the girls to switch up now and then when I'm planning for the next year."

"For next year?" I look at Chelsea again. "But it's February."

"Yes, planning! Welcome to my life," Sunny says. "And it's not easy when you don't know who's going to keep swimming the next year."

What does that mean? Who does she think won't swim next year?

"I'll still be here."

"Good, I'm glad to hear it, Bart. Now you two get warmed up and we'll start."

I warm up with fast laps, like I'm back in speed racing. When I wait at the end for the girls to finish warming up, I look up at the tower, watching the divers at their practice. Trying to spot Dive Boy.

Chelsea swims up to me. "So, did you win?"

"Win what?"

"The race, dork. We must be racing, right? You were going a hundred miles an hour. Oh. You're mad. Are you mad at me?"

Yes. No. I don't really want to swim with Chelsea, but I know that's unfair. If this is what Sunny wants, I'll do it. And I *know* I could learn something from Chels. She's the best technical swimmer in the club, maybe even the province. Swimming with her would get me that much closer to a medal.

Of course, I wouldn't admit any of that to Chelsea.

Have you ever seen any of the swims from the Men's Cup?" Chelsea asks.

"Men's Cup? In synchro?"

"Yeah! You haven't heard of the Men's Cup?"

"I'm surprised you have. Since when did you get interested in men's synchro?"

Chelsea ignores me and pulls herself up out of the water. "They have it every two years. Look." Chelsea dries off her arms, grabs her iPad, and brings up a YouTube video. "This was Japan's entry a couple years ago." She kneels down so I can see the screen.

They're not super synchronized and their routine leaves me flat. But there's one guy who really brings it for the rest of the team.

"One of those swimmers is good, though, right?" she asks. "He swam the mixed duet for Japan this year. His solo's quite good too."

"Yeah, there's actually a Japanese movie ..." I blush, bringing it up. *Waterboys* mostly parodies men's synchro swimming. But I still watched it.

"That movie's what inspired him. Hilarious, right? Seriously, though— you're better than that routine, Bart. But you see how they're working so hard not to sink? You see how they could barely get that guy out of the water on that lift?"

"Yeah ... They don't make it look easy like you do."

"Girls are built for it. We have the body fat. Guys don't. But one guy swimming with one woman, I'm starting to see that can work."

"I could just eat more donuts."

"Yeah, and get a little pot belly. I'm sure that would be real pretty on your back layout."

I splash her, then duck under the water so she can't splash me back.

We hear the clang of Sunny's key on the ladder and pop up to see her beckoning us to the side.

"There's a routine sequence I want you to start practising," she says. "If this goes well, you two can work on this duet starting now, for next season. It's not too early, if we're talking about something for national competition."

Chelsea looks at me and smiles. No. No, no, no. This is not part of the plan. I'm supposed to be swimming with Erika. A lesson or two here and there, sure. But to commit to a routine with Chelsea?

"Uh, Sunny?"

"Yes, Bart?"

"I'm sorry, but ... am I going to have to practise this when Erika gets back? Because I'm a little worried about getting our routines ready for the qualifier."

"When Erika's back, you'll swim with her. But you can make use of your time with Chelsea now."

Chelsea gives me a little smile.

Sunny instructs us on the choreography, and we go through as much as we can remember before she adds a bit more. She's not critical of how we're swimming it yet. But it won't be long, I know.

"This is a good skill to have, Bart, if boys ever go to the national squad trials, like Chelsea and Erika will this weekend. If you ever want to swim for Canada, you would need to swim a routine that you get taught at the trials. You don't get to build up to it over weeks and weeks like you do with the routines you swim in the national championships."

Wow. Okay, then.

"Do you wish you were coming?" Chelsea asks me.

"Where? To the national squad trials?"

"Yeah."

I face her squarely. "No boys allowed."

"Not in the *team* event. But if they're going to include the mixed duet

.event at junior worlds and the Olympics, they'll need a guy on the national squad, right? And I thought that's what you wanted to happen one day?"

"Of course! Yes."

"So let's get to work."

She leads, I follow. And I barely keep up. Swimming with Chelsea's like swimming with a drill sergeant, and I don't wonder that Erika had finally had enough. But I figure I can take it for a while—it feels good to step up the challenge again, now that provincials are behind me, and there's nothing between now and the national qualifiers in Quebec City.

TWENTY-FOUR

A bolt of bubbles stabs the deep, and I watch Dive Boy's body hold still for a moment, before he kicks up to the surface.

I surface too, and watch him climb the tower again and walk out on the platform. Dive Boy—slapping his legs with a chamois. Winding up and kicking out his feet. Warming up to the idea of taking the next plunge into a pool we share, yet don't.

The dive tank's divided. He dives from the air, into his half. I sink from the surface

down

into the depths

of mine.

When he gets out the second time, I think I see him wave to me. But when I get in the hot tub, he's not there. It's probably for the best. I mean, I don't even really know what I'm doing here, looking for him.

When I get to the change room, I check my phone. The girls should have got home from trials today. There's a text from Erika. *Chelsea made Junior Squad Phase 4 trial.*

Just Chelsea?

I try texting back, but there's no reception down here. So I get changed quickly so I can get upstairs. While I'm drying off, the Rosa Waves guys come in, and some of the divers.

I head to the stairs, phone in hand, and run straight into Dive Boy.

"Whoa," he says, and puts a hand on my bicep.

"Sorry."

"It's okay."

Geoff, Andy, and a couple other guys come out into the hall, and Geoff half body-slams me as he passes by. My bag falls off my shoulder and I drop my phone.

"Asshole," I say.

Dive Boy passes me my bag. "Your phone's not busted, is it?"

I pick it up, and thank God, the glass isn't cracked.

"Hey, don't let them get to you."

I nod. Dive Boy has brown eyes, and they're warm and deep like his voice. I'm struck by his compassion—it's more than any guy I know has ever felt the slightest bit safe to express. Even Riley, when it's just us hanging out. Maybe *especially* Riley.

"You okay?"

I can't speak. I will not cry in front of him. I will not do it.

The change room door slams open again and Riley comes out, as if I just summoned him with my thoughts. He looks at us, then looks away immediately, like he doesn't see me.

"Yeah. I'm good. Thanks."

I give Dive Boy a quick smile and he chuckles, like he doesn't believe me. I watch him leave out the back entrance. That on-the-edge feeling, like I'm going to burst into tears, turns angry. I jog up to Riley, grab him, and put him in a headlock.

"Ugh, get off me."

"You're pretending like you don't know me anymore?" I let him go.

"What are you talking about, freak?"

We walk up the stairs and talk about training, like it's normal, and we're normal. Then we run into Geoff and Andy and the other guys at the top. Geoff's laughing about something. He turns and sees us, and makes kissy noises in the air. At Riley and me. I feel like all the stress just gets lit on fire, like Geoff's *mwah mwah* is a match. I lunge for him and throw him back against the wall. Riley just stands there. Andy just stands there. Geoff laughs.

"Oh, for fuck's sake," I say, and leave them all and walk out of the lobby.

I turn on my phone and text Erika back.

> R u back now? Can I come see u?

I wait a few seconds, and my phone buzzes.

Please

• • •

We turn down a path that opens out to a park lit by one streetlight and the light from people's back porches on the other side of a fence. Erika heads straight for the old metal merry-go-round, which makes a cool metallic echo when she jumps on it. I hop on too, and we take a few spins.

"Okay, gotta slow down." Erika drags her toes in the sand. "Too soon after dinner."

I help us stop, then hop over the bars to sit with her on the edge.

"So what did I miss while I was gone?" Erika asks.

"Well, did you hear about Sunny giving Chelsea a mixed duet?"

"With *who?*"

"While you were gone before trials ... She just wanted to see me pair with someone else from the club, I guess. She said it wouldn't be something for this year. Just next."

"With you?" Erika's eyes narrow. "You agreed?"

"I did what Sunny asked. But ... listen. I'm not going to let it get in the way of our practice, okay? We're going to make the most of the next four weeks."

Erika lets out a noise halfway between a growl and a sigh.

"Like she knew I wouldn't make the squad. You know what this is about, don't you?"

"No, what?"

"If the country's ever going to send a mixed duet to the junior world championships, they'd pair up the best guy they have with a girl from the national squad. And if the mixed duets are going to start happening at the Olympics ... Well, they're going to start competing the event with younger swimmers, Bart."

"Yeah, but I'm not the best junior guy. You saw Kim. And we don't know who else is out there. I'm totally not ready. And what about Prévost? Wouldn't *he* be the one swimming for Canada?"

She shrugs. "If he still wants to, I guess. But by then... well, he's older, right? Maybe he'll retire. And you could be ready. It wouldn't take long." Erika gives a little rueful smile. "And you know what they'll do? They'll send you with Chelsea. 'Cause she'll make the national squad."

I get a flash of involuntary excitement, wondering if that wouldn't get me closer to kissing a medal. Then I shake that question off. I take in a deep breath, and sigh it out.

"It sucks, Erika. You should have made it." I squeeze her hand.

"It *so* sucks," she chokes out. "I just hate Chels." Then softer, "Just tonight. I'm too jealous."

"Of course you are. It's okay to hate Chelsea, like, for a few minutes. We all do."

"Exactly." Erika laughs through her tears. "She makes it easy."

A little too easy. I hate Chelsea right now for making the squad when Erika didn't, because now I wonder if one of those other guys' duet partners from provincials made it to the squad. What if their routines go on to compete from our province, and not ours? Is my chance at nationals, and the medal, further away now?

For all my worry, Erika just looks sad. I lean over the bar between us and give her shoulder a squeeze.

"You made it to phase three! Don't just brush that off. You did awesome."

"I *could* have done awesome."

"Here ..." I reach into my bag and bring out the mug rolled in white tissue. "I'm sorry it's not wrapped for real."

"What? You got me a present?"

Erika unwraps the mug and smiles at the picture of three stick figures doing synchro, a fourth floating face down on the surface of the water.

"*If one synchronized swimmer drowns, do the rest drown too?* Oh, yeah. You're all going down with me!"

"Well, I was actually thinking the drowning one was more *me* than you. But if you're the one drowning, I'm totally going down with you."

Erika pushes my shoulder. "You shouldn't!"

"Well?" I look at her amused, like, *What do you want me to say?*

"Okay." Erika wipes her eyes with the cuff of sweater sleeve that's poking out of her raincoat. "What gets me is that Chelsea never seems to even *love* it, you know? She never seems to be inside it. It's like synchro's just some perfectionist horse for her to beat or something. Does that make sense?"

"Totally. But I can see how synchro would draw out anyone's perfectionism."

"Right? It's so rigorous. There's all the memory work. A gazillion figures that have a standard that's impossible to meet unless you're just gifted or something ..." Erika starts up the merry-go-round again, slowly pushing with her left foot.

"But routines are about expressing emotion. Physically."

Erika drags us to a stop and looks at me, her eyes wide. Recognizing that I get it.

"Yes! But Chels doesn't get that. And it drives me crazy."

"She's pretty athletic."

"Completely. And so freaking competitive." Erika starts us spinning again.

I look at her lips, the perfect skin on her cheek. Would it be weird to kiss her here on the merry-go-round? Does it wreck the duet if you start getting this close to your partner? Can you still work together?

"Do you know Chelsea once swapped out this other team's gel packets for ones she made herself with sugar?"

"What?"

"We were twelve. She steamed open the packets, dumped out half the powder, poured in sugar, and resealed them. Then she put them on the team's prep table at provincials. Their hair got all goopy and it didn't set. None of them could figure out why their gel wasn't hardening."

"Wow. That's ..."

"Shitty. I know. And I was too afraid to get her in trouble, so I didn't say anything. I never did."

Erika turns the mug over in her hands, and brushes her thumb over the picture.

"Is Chels sorry you didn't both make it on the junior squad?"

"She said she was. But ... it's like her swimming, right? Her heart wasn't in it." Erika drags us to a stop, then switches direction. "You can tell *your* heart is in it, Bart. The way you light up in the routine—you're so genuine. It's like, I can hardly believe it when I see you. You're so ... happy."

"I am happy. God, it makes me happy."

"Good. *You* should be able to go to the national squad trials."

"Maybe one day, if the rules change. But in the meantime, we're going to get our duets to the nationals, and we're going to show everyone how awesome we are, and then we'll be kicking ass next year. *I'll* be better, and you'll have another crack at the national squad. And when the first duet goes to the junior world championships ... it's going to be ours."

"Then the Olympics?"

"You bet. It's ours. Seriously, our duet's going to be the best, and I will work *so* hard."

"I know you will, Bart."

"I can swim Fridays too. I only need one day off a week. What do you say?"

"I'm in."

"Okay. It doesn't matter how many other mixed duets are at qualifiers this year, we're going to get on that podium."

Erika smiles at me and nods.

It feels overly bold, stating that right now, but I really, really want her to know that I believe in our routine. What we've been working for is so much more important to me than whatever might happen with Chelsea.

"Promise me?" I ask.

"I promise."

I look up at the streetlamp that lights the park with a murky, yellow glow. I'm starting to feel a little nauseous, so I drag us to a stop.

Erika looks thoughtful, her eyes watching my lips.

"You know, I think it was after she saw us swim the demo. I think seeing how far you've come ... she figured out that we're going to get a lot of attention. That we're going to get noticed for what we're doing."

"And she likes that?"

"She'd like it for herself. Because, attention? Well, that's even better than perfection. Best in combination, of course."

And with that, Erika pushes off the sand again at the same time I do, both of us leaning into it. She laughs. "Look, we're syncing out of the pool now."

"Is that bad?"

"No way! You know you're gelled as a duet pair when you start doing that."

We spin a final couple of times before getting up to walk back to her house. Someone's turned on the porch light.

"Thanks for the mug, Bart," Erika says, and opens the front door. She turns back to face me. "And for coming to see me."

"Hey, anytime." Normally, I wave bye when we part after practice, but now the gesture feels stupid, or wrong. Instead, I step forward and wrap her in a hug. "I'll see you tomorrow."

We part, and Erika's eyes sparkle, reflecting light from some distant streetlamp, or the stars. Her eyes are black and magic.

"Yeah, see you tomorrow."

TWENTY-FIVE

Today, I look for Erika all morning at school, but we don't have any classes together, and her path through school just doesn't cross mine.

I only have classes with Chelsea, and she tends to avoid me. But right now she's walking down the hall in my direction with her posse.

"Hey, Bart."

Talking to me outside of the pool? Yeah, this isn't the usual state of affairs.

"Uh, hey, Chels. Have you seen Erika today?"

"What, you're not going to congratulate me?"

Ugh, right. Now I feel like an idiot.

"Oh, yes—totally! I heard you rocked the national junior squad trial. Congratulations."

"Thanks, Bart. Here," she says, holding out a bag of candy. "Have some."

"What is it?" I ask, reaching in and reading the bag at the same time. Candied ginger. My hand hovers above the chunks covered in granulated sugar. "Oh."

"Come on." She shakes the bag. "Spice up your day."

I take one and pop it in my mouth, tasting the sharp and sweet lump while Chelsea introduces her friends.

"This is Emmie and Sadie. Emmie and Sadie, this is Bart."

Emmie's short and cute. Sadie? Tall, wearing an impatient fake smile. She asks, "Are you on your way to the meeting? I think it's already started."

"What meeting? Model UN?" Maybe I can find Erika after all. But Chelsea just knocks Sadie with her elbow to shut her up.

"Bart," Chels says, "I was telling them about how you can handstand for, like, half a minute without falling over. They don't think you can do it."

"What? Of course I can do it!" I laugh. "You need me to demonstrate?"

Chelsea looks up at me through her lashes thick with mascara. "Well? Come on, Bart, They don't believe you. What else are you going to do?" She pops a piece of ginger in her mouth.

I give her my big grin. "Okay, then. Step aside, ladies."

Emmie and Sadie look at each other like they don't know what's going on. Ugh. I don't know what's stupider—that I've just volunteered to do a handstand in the hallway, or that I let Chelsea flirt with me. I bet she never said anything to her friends about me before she saw me in the hall and decided she could mess with me.

Now there's nothing left to do but step into a handstand and prove myself. So I do. And I hang out there for a while in a split with one leg bent, then open up into a full split, then bring my legs up to straight and just stand there, with my T-shirt down around my neck.

"Oh, I am so tempted to tickle you right now," Chelsea says.

Emmie says, "Do it!"

I take that as a cue to step out, but not before Chelsea sneaks in one tickle of my ribs.

"Hey!" I pull my shirt down and stick my tongue out at her. All the blood rushes back out of my head, then Chels gives me a look that makes the blood rush into my cheeks. The sort of look you'd give someone if you were imagining what it's like to kiss them. That look.

Emmie and Sadie say they're going for a walk outside, and Chels tells them she'll catch up in a minute.

"So. You still looking for Erika?"

"Yeah. Yeah, I ... just thought ..." Great. Now my cheeks are redder. "You know, I'd see how she was doing."

"Girl's like a rubber band, you know."

"What?"

"She'll bounce back, Bart. You don't have to worry about her."

"I dunno. It seemed like a big deal yesterday."

Chelsea shrugs. "See you around." Another look. Then she's three steps away, and I swear I hear her say, "Nice abs."

What the hell just happened?

I head down the hall in the direction of the cafeteria, thinking I might catch Erika there. But instead, I pass an open door and spot her in a class-room being used for a lunch block meeting—of the Genders and Sexualities Alliance club. Erika's sitting next to Julia, who just then turns, sees me, and waves. I wave back. Then she tries to wave me in.

I pretend I don't see her wave, and just head on outside.

•   •   •

That afternoon, Julia grabs me at the start of practice before I can talk to Erika.

"Hey, where'd you go?"

"Uh, at school?"

"At the meeting, yeah. You took off. I thought you were going to join us."

"Oh, I was just looking for Erika. But it seemed like you guys were busy, so ..."

"Bart." Jules laughs. "What? Oh, come on. She's my best friend, but she's not my girlfriend."

I stare at Julia. "Oh, I didn't think—"

"You didn't think what? That Erika's gay like me?"

"No, I ... Geez, Jules. Okay, anything I say right now is going to be the wrong thing, isn't it?"

"Don't sweat it, Bart. Just ... if you see us again, maybe join us? You want to change some attitudes here in the pool, that's great. School could use it too."

u

TWENTY-SIX

The parking lot at the pool is completely empty at 4 a.m. I knock on the glass doors, but Erika's uncle is pushing a loud floor waxer back and forth. Finally, he shuts it off and I catch his attention. He lets me in when I tell him I'm Erika's duet partner and directs me to the side door. Then he watches through the glass wall on the second floor to make sure I am who I say I am.

I walk along the second level corridor, open to the pool below. It's so quiet that I can hear a mini speaker hooked up to Erika's phone way down in the corner of the dive tank, playing Sarah McLachlan's cover of "River." The pool is lit only by the lights under the water and the light filtering in through the windows to the lobby upstairs. The moon's still visible through the skylight.

This version of "River" sounds smooth and sharp, like the glassy surface of ice. It's like the water in the other pools this morning, still as a mirror.

Erika's continuous spins make me ashamed that I felt any pride at all in what I've accomplished since regionals. Her spins are the smoothest, straightest, most beautiful ones you'll ever see.

I drop my bag and lean on the railing above the stands. Erika's under for so long during her solo—so long, it's like her legs become all of her, straight and controlled, folding, bending, describing circles in the air. Then the music ends, and she comes up to breathe. I wave at her, but she doesn't see. Her music pauses only long enough for her to take a few breaths before it loops, and she begins again.

This time, I watch differently. I analyze the transitions, the elements and how they connect. When she runs it through again, I land drill along with her swimming. At the end of the song, she sits up on the deck, pushes her goggles off, and sees me. Her face lights up. She looks up at her uncle behind the glass and waves. He waves back and turns away, and I run down the stairs to the deck.

"What the heck are you doing here, you insane boy?"

"We need practice, don't we? We've got all those other guys to beat now. Besides, it's not fair that your solo gets to be so much better than our duet."

Erika's grinning. I'm grinning. I feel ridiculous, but there's an undeniable pull, a kind of energy that wasn't there before provincials.

Erika treads water, looking up at me. "Well, what are you waiting for? Get in the water."

"You got our music on there?" I nod at her phone.

"Yep. Different playlist. But you can pull it up."

I set the music to play and stand in front of her again. The pool is completely still, no one here, nothing but Erika's eyes on me.

The first bars start. "Does this one loop too?"

"Loop?" Erika frowns. "Oh man, were you here for a while before I saw you?"

"Just two run-throughs. I promise." I peel off my layers, dive in, and swim up beside her.

"You watched me. The whole time."

"And you were beautiful." The words come out, just like that. I blush. "You were. I'm sorry. I have to tell you ... I mean, of course I've seen you swim it before. But it's *so* good."

"You're sweet."

"So should we—"

"Yeah. From the start?"

We swim to the bulkhead and climb up, and wait for the pause. The music starts with a synthesizer crescendo and a beat that matches my elevated pulse. We dive and emerge, raising our arms up in poses inspired by martial arts—a knife hand, and a blade hand. Then we intertwine, separate, pike to vertical, then continuous spin. It's so different even now, so much *better* than when we performed it at provincials. It's like the energy that blew up in our faces there is only focused on each other, and it connects us in sync. And unlike swimming with Chelsea last week, there's something bigger than the technical perfection.

The tempo picks up, and we slice our legs through the quick series of vertical forms. Then I lift Erika at the line *I'm the weight, you're the kite*—and she spins off my shoulders, lands with one graceful arm extended. Another series of quick verticals, and we both boost up in sync, and we're done.

"You synced really well with Chelsea at practice yesterday."

"So you noticed."

"I'm not saying I liked it."

"Sunny's still got this idea we should be trying it out. She even wants Chels and me to come in Friday for some of my extra coaching time."

"I get it. She's seeing if you guys swim well together. And you do."

"Okay, but I'm not—" I shake my head. "Erika, I'm not going to swim any duets with Chelsea."

"You don't know that. You might get to."

"*What?* What do you mean *get* to? That's crazy! I already promised you. We're taking our duet to nationals. I'm not swimming a duet with Chelsea. Not for competition. Not this year."

"Bart, she's good. I've been thinking about it since we talked. She's *really* good. If she wants to swim a mixed duet now because she's changed her mind about boys in synchro ... and she wants to swim with you while she's on the national squad? Well, maybe you shouldn't pass it up."

I shake my head.

"Bart ... it might happen. Sunny might ask you."

"Well, I'm not swimming *this* with her. 'Breathing Underwater' is ours."

"Of course." She smiles.

The music loops again. Erika goes through the hand motions, counting, and then I join her. When she counts, "*One* two *three* four *five* six *seven* eight, *ONE*," I jump in mid-song, and we swim the routine together, to the end.

At five thirty, we get out of the pool. Erika pulls off her cap, pulls on her big sweatshirt, and flips the hood up over her buzzed head.

"Bart, let's go. Follow me."

"What?"

"Come on."

I gather up Erika's phone and speaker, and grab my bag.

"Where are we going?"

She doesn't answer, but when we head around the corner, I figure we're on our way to the hot tub. That would be nice. Except she turns abruptly and starts climbing the steps of the dive tower.

"Erika—"

She disappears up the next flight.

Damn. Okay, there's a really good reason I've never been interested in dive club. And it's not that I didn't want to wear the little Speedo briefs.

"Bart?"

Erika looks over the side of the second flight of stairs.

"Yeah. I'm here."

"Follow me!"

Fine. I take the steps up the first flight. Then the second. I make it up seven of the eight flights, and my heart's pounding. I swallow, and mount the last flight up to the top—where Erika sits on the edge of the platform, ten metres above the pool. I don't dare look over the sides.

She turns and smiles at me. Pats the spot beside her. "Come have a seat."

I'm fixed in place. If I thought I could get away with it, I'd just lie down here at the back of the platform. I swallow hard. Then I force myself to take a step. But I stop. I can't make myself go past the spot where the railing ends and it's just an open platform. I don't want to see the deep blue water of the dive tank below.

"Hey," I say. It comes out like a squeak. "Maybe, Erika, I'll just bring your stuff back down ... I don't want it to get knocked off or something ..." I turn and retreat down one flight of stairs, crouch down, and wait.

"Bart?"

When she comes around the corner, I grab her sleeve and pull her down beside me.

"Hi."

"Hi. Uh, are you ... scared of heights?"

I take in a deep breath. "Terrified." But now we're sitting on a landing protected by a nice thick wall. I sit with my back against it, totally relieved.

"You're okay." Erika pats the back of my hand.

Sure. Okay *now*.

"What do you like about the tower?"

"Sometimes, I watch the pool kind of come to life from up here. All the lights come on, and people start arriving for early practice. It feels like I'm—I dunno—an eagle surveying my territory, I guess."

"Nice image."

Erika starts to get up, but I pull her back down. "Stay here a while." I take Erika's phone and speaker from the top of my bag and set them up. "Play us something."

Erika finds a playlist that isn't one of her routine songs on a loop, and a song starts to play, too loud at first, but I turn the volume down. It's slow, with a low-fi guitar and a hazy melody—it would be hard to swim to, but it's soothing.

"Isn't this awesome?" she asks. "It sounds like it was recorded in a pool."

I laugh until I cough. "You classify that as awesome?"

"Totally. Everything awesome happens in a pool. Or maybe it's just because I spend pretty much all my waking hours in one."

"So the law of averages would have it ..."

"Yeah, something like that."

We listen to the singer praising the moon's beauty.

"Just like this morning," I say, looking up at the moon through the giant skylight. "But it's got nothing on you."

Those dimples of hers pop up as she smiles at me. I don't think anyone could look as adorable at five in the morning in a giant hoodie and a bathing suit.

My fear's quiet now. Now, I'm just aware of Erika sitting close. I've pulled her right beside me, and our hips touch. I look at her, and she looks back, unblinking. I stare into her warm brown eyes like it's a contest, then it turns into something more. Neither of us talks. We just listen to the slow, lazy guitar, and to the things unspoken between us. Until I take her face in my hands and plant a kiss on her cheek, and then I put my lips to hers. There's the smell of chlorine, the taste of coffee.

She kisses me back.

I pull her onto my lap, her smooth legs sliding against mine. We stay there, kissing, for an hour.

Or, it feels like an hour. Breath is for the weak.

Her music runs out. Eventually, the lights come up, and I gasp. She laughs.

"Should we get out of here?" I ask.

"No. Just give it a few minutes, and we'll go down and blend in."

"Divers?"

"It's Wednesday. No diving until seven. Come here." She pulls me close, her hand on the back of my head, and kisses me again. Deeper.

I pull off her hood and run my hand over the stubble of her hair. One way, smooth. The other, an even prickle.

"Your hair's awesome. Like velvet."

"You know how to flatter a girl."

I put my hand on her thigh and squeeze.

"It's not flattery, Er." I slide my hand down to her knee. Erika's elegant knees. "Your legs are so perfect."

"So are yours. Your legs are beautiful."

"No. You don't even know."

She laughs again.

"I'm serious. Right side up, upside down." I run my hand back up to her thigh—and the rush of that moment when we warmed up at provincials comes back to me, when her leg slid across my upper thigh. The memory amps me up now until it's too much, and I have to pull her hips closer to mine. And there's no hiding the effect she's having on me. Erika meets my eyes and her expression goes serious too.

We torture each other until the sound of voices below announces the divers' arrival. Erika groans, and we disentangle.

"You'll come practise tomorrow?" she asks.

"Is this practice?"

She just smiles. Oh, man. Why can't we stay here in this stairwell for the rest of the day? I don't care how high up it is. Or how scared I am.

TWENTY-SEVEN

> Bart? It's been ages since I've seen you.

Mom's making me feel guilty.

> You've been leaving so early every morning. Are you home for supper tonight?

Yes

> Good. It'll be special.

Erika and I practised together every morning the rest of the week. Well, for a portion of the mornings, anyway. We spent a good deal of time in the stairwell of the dive tower. I wanted to see her at school too, but she had a makeup math test on Wednesday at lunch. Thursday, she'd already promised the social committee that she'd help plan the winter banquet.

I put my head down and round the corner. Riley's coming my way. I wish I was walking down the hallway holding Erika's hand. I want him to see us, and make some joke with me that I was in "hot pursuit" all along and just keeping sly about it. I want to tell him about what's going on—about the duet going to qualifiers, even.

"Hey, man," I say when I reach him.

Riley gives me the smallest of nods. Turns away, like he's got someone else to talk to, even though he's walking down the hallway as alone as I am.

"Riley, come on. Wait a minute."

He turns back to give me a look, like I'm taking up his precious time.

"Let's ... do something together. You and me, and Erika and Casey? We could even see *90210 Shark Attack*."

"No, I don't think so."

"What, Casey doesn't like monster flicks?"

"I already saw it. You were right. It was lame."

"Oh. Well, we can do something else. Pick up a cake? Go to Western Speedway and catch a race, then do the go-karts?"

"No, you hate the go-karts."

"Well, it could be fun with the girls."

I watch a couple of Rosa Waves guys come out of class and nod at Riley.

"Yeah, I gotta go," he says. "Look, I'll talk to you later."

Riley falls in line with the Rosa Waves guys. He laughs at something Geoff says as they head down the hall.

I keep walking. Pretend like it's nothing. It *is* nothing. I'm making out with Erika. Our duet is amazing. We're on top of the world.

But then I hear the familiar whisper.

Fag.

I spin around. None of those guys are looking my way. I don't know who said it. Something doesn't feel right. My heart starts beating faster—'cause it's different when you can't see where it's coming from. If someone jumps me, I won't know whether to fight back or run. I see the girls Chelsea was talking to that day. What's her name—Sadie? And Emmie. They're looking my way. But it couldn't have been them—it sounded like a guy's whisper. I turn back, but now everyone's just walking past, the bell gone, all classes dismissed.

Someone grabs me from behind. My heart shoots into my throat. Julia spins me around.

"Jesus, Jules. You ... Jesus."

"Ha! I scared you." She backs off and looks at me. "You need a minute?"

"No! I'm fine. I just thought—" I sigh. What should I tell her? That I thought I was going to get jumped? "Never mind."

"Okay, then you're coming with me."

"Where?"

Jules pulls me down the hall and around the corner to the classroom where the GSA meetings are held. Oh, right. That's what Erika does on Fridays—I should have remembered.

"Jules, I love you and support you a hundred percent. But I'm not really a joiner."

"Like hell. You joined *synchro*, man."

She pushes me inside. Erika's there already, her head bare. I've seen her wear a toque everywhere outside of the pool since she buzzed her hair, so that's different. There's about another half dozen kids, mostly our grade and the grade above. And Dive Boy.

Dive Boy. I hesitate before stepping farther into the room, but Erika waves me over. Jules sits on top of a desk facing everyone, so I guess she leads the meetings.

Before Julia can say a word, Dive Boy breaks into a grin. I nod at him.

"Welcome," he says. "I *so* knew you were queer."

I get up to leave.

"Dave! Way to make Bart feel comfortable," Erika says. "I don't think that's in the spirit of the club, mister."

"I'm not ... I'm not queer," I tell them.

Erika looks back and forth between Jules and Dave. So his name's Dave.

"Excuse me," I say.

In the hall outside, I try to calm down. This is not the day I planned.

"Bart." Julia steps out, pulls me into the next empty classroom, and shuts the door behind her. It's the bio lab and smells faintly like formaldehyde from a recent dissection. "Look, I am so sorry. Dave told me he's been talking to you after practice sometimes, and he thought ..."

I shake my head. "I don't really care what he thought."

"Are you mad at me? Just because someone made an assumption about you?"

"No. I'm sorry." I lean my forehead on the wall. "I guess—I guess he's got a reason to think what he thought."

"Okay."

"I might have ... checked him out. He's ... he has a stellar body. But ... I dunno, Jules."

She laughs. "Bart, don't sweat it."

"I hooked up with Erika." I say it, and then I wonder if Julia doesn't know yet. "Did she tell you? Okay, I sure hope she told you. I don't think she'd mind me telling you ..." Crap. Maybe she was keeping it under wraps so the other girls in the club wouldn't feel weird about it. Not that I think it should matter.

"Well, Bart, maybe you're bi. That's okay."

I slam my fist on the wall and push off.

"Or ... not. But Bart, this group's here for anyone who gets flack about their sexuality. Or their gender identity. Don't you think Erika and I have been putting up with mass bullshit since we came to school with our heads shaved? Yeah. And don't pretend you don't put up with shit because you're swimming with us."

I sigh out a deep breath.

"Right?"

"Yes, and I shouldn't *have* to. Wanting to swim synchro has nothing to do with my sexuality! Why should doing synchro mean I'm queer any more than ..." I look around, and land on a poster showing the kinds of marine life with exoskeletons. "Than liking lobster?"

Jules shrugs. "I honestly don't know."

"Well ... that's why I'm not saying ... that I'm queer. Because if I'm just another queer boy joining a synchro club, it doesn't mean anything, does it? Then everyone can say, 'Yup, that's a sport for girls or gays or boys who want to be girls.' And that's bullshit. I'm a *boy*. I'm all boy." I shake my head. "And it shouldn't matter if a queer guy wanted to do synchro either. Like, it shouldn't be about any of that! It's just a sport."

"With sequins. And makeup." Jules laughs.

"So what?" I sigh. "That's exactly my point. It just ... feels like it stands for something way bigger. If a girl wants to go do a thing that's always been a guy thing, she gets cheered on. Guys can't make those kinds of choices without people making a call on their sexuality."

"Yeah, it's bullshit."

"I just want people to be okay with it, you know?"

"Are *you* okay with it?"

"Yes!"

"Okay, then what's the problem?"

"The problem? People telling me who I am when *I* don't even know. I walk in here and the first person who lays eyes on me wants to define me."

"Bart, he's just hopeful." Jules laughs. "David's got the biggest crush on you right now."

David. Like the sculpture. "Well ... that's great."

"Is it?"

I don't say anything. Jules just pins me under her stare for a bit, until I sigh.

"Jules, anyone who's ever called me queer's been someone I can't stand."

"I get it. But don't you think you're trying a little too hard?"

"Trying too hard not to be gay? Because I'm not *trying* to be gay or trying *not* to be gay, Julia. I'm just being me, and letting my dick lead me to who it wants. And right now, that's *Erika*."

Jules goes quiet and looks down at her hands.

"Hey, I'm sorry. I didn't mean to be crass."

She shakes her head. "No, it's fine."

"No, I'm awful." I run my hands over my face. "I meant my heart too. My heart's leading me to her. I'm sorry. But ... I got together with *Erika*, Jules. And not just this morning, but ... for the past three days. We've been going to the pool early to practise and end up messing around—and it's *awesome*. And not one moment have I worried about not being guy enough. Not one split second with Erika have I worried that maybe I'm too feminine to be with her. She likes the boy I am, you know?"

"Yeah, Bart. I know."

"You know? Well, what's this about?"

"It's about Erika *and* Dave. He's my friend too. They both stand to get their emotions a little trampled on if this goes badly."

"But Julia, I barely know Dave! We just ... chatted a few times after practice. I didn't even know his *name*. I'm sorry he's got a crush on me, but ..."

Jules looks at me hard.

"You don't believe me? Fine." I push back my chair so it scrapes along the shitty linoleum tiles. Jules winces.

"I'll see you at practice," I tell her. I have my hand on the doorknob when she stops me.

"It's just that Erika's worried about you. She doesn't want you to feel ... trapped."

"What?" I turn and look at her.

"You've got a lot of energy. It's going in a lot of different directions. She doesn't want you to decide you can't be with her because ... you know. If you were interested in him too."

So Julia knew that Erika and I were together. And she *still* told Erika about Dave? Or Erika already knew. How did she know? Can she tell just by looking at me, looking at him?

"I'm going."

"All right," she says.

I walk down the hall, furious. I turn and Julia's standing outside the meeting, watching me go. "I'm not angry at you, Jules," I shout back down the hall. "I love you, okay?"

"I know," she shouts back. "Love you too."

TWENTY-EIGHT

It feels like I came out to Julia. But I didn't come out to Julia. I didn't even need to. To her, I was already out—she just assumed. Dave assumed. My *mom* assumes.

Is it still an assumption if it's also the truth?

Is it also the truth?

Synchro's hard enough. I don't need the rest of my life to be hard too.

I carry my anger around the rest of the day, about being rejected by Riley, about being called queer. Riley used to be the only guy who accepted me as I am. Now I don't even have *one* other guy I can talk to. Sure, I've got all these girls as friends now. And I know that doesn't make me any less of a guy—but I can't help but feel like maybe everyone else thinks it does.

I just need a good workout, so I'm glad for the extra practice today after school. When I dive in, I breaststroke down deep, feeling the pressure on me as I get close to the bottom of the tank. Feel the pressure squeezing my head, my chest. My underwater world, keeping me together.

When I come up to the surface to swim laps, I go hard, wanting to exhaust myself. Wanting not to think.

After warm-up, Chelsea and I stand on the little ledge at the side of the pool and drill the arm movements to the count.

"*One* two *three* four, *five* six *seven* eight ..." Sunny grabs my upheld hand and brings it forward. "Here." Then she pushes it back to where I held it before. "Not here. Okay, start again. *One* two *three* four, *five* six *seven* eight ..."

Then we're back in the water. But Sunny's on me every other minute.

"Bart, I want your leg to strike the water like lightning hitting the ground."

"Bart, if there's a splash, it should be one splash—I shouldn't hear two. You're down on the same count, come down together."

There's one movement I really like. I sweep my arm around in a circle so it looks like my arm's making my leg disappear into my body. But I'm not doing it well enough for Sunny.

"Bart, you have to swim sharper!"

"You're all over the place today." Chelsea pops up and blinks the water out of her eyes. She's practising sans goggles, just because she can. "What's this?" She takes my arm and wiggles it around. "You're a floppy fish."

"Well, it's supposed to be looser, right?"

"Not like that, it's not."

I bite my bottom lip. Mom came and watched us practise the other night. "Chelsea's tolerating you now," she said. "It's different from before. Just make sure you let her know how much you appreciate her working with you—she didn't always want to, right?"

Right.

So I let Chelsea flop my arm around and insult my form, and I take it.

Chels sighs. "Let's just try from the lift again."

We submerge, and I take her hips and power whip kick, getting her out of the water to her knees. We submerge again for a quick leg sequence, then surface—and there's a grin on Chelsea's face. And there's no performance. No one watching us. She's just smiling because ... something's making her happy.

"What?"

"That was better," she says. "I forget your power every time, until you've got me launched."

Wow. Okay.

"Let's keep going."

We finish up our practice with figures using the jugs and ankle weights.

"Do you have to be anywhere?" Chels asks. "Stay if you can. I can help."

Something at the back of my mind says I should be home. But hell, it's Friday night. No practice again until Sunday morning. And the more time in the pool before qualifiers, the better ... So staying and getting some coaching from Chels feels like a good idea.

"Yeah, I can stay."

The pool's quieted down. The water polo team's left, and there are just a few public swimmers in the lane pool, some kids in the teaching pool. A couple of seniors are practising their water walking in our section now, but there's still lots of room. We run through the beginning choreography of this new routine and Chelsea stops, comes out of position.

"Okay, roll back should be with a scull by your hips, then a support scull."

"Hips first?" I wouldn't have thought. Still, I come out of the figure better than I have before. And after Chelsea shows me swordfish straight leg, she goes under and watches me try it.

"No, no. You're scooping." She shows me her scull, and it looks totally different from mine. "Like this."

I lift one leg, then go into splits, sculling this new way. It's better.

"It's always in the sculling, Bart. If you don't have your sculls down, you won't swim as sharp."

"Have you thought about coaching?"

"Oh, yeah ..." She nods. "When I'm done competing. That won't be for a few years, though. You know, we don't peak until we're, like, in our twenties. It's not like gymnastics."

"I guess that's good news for me."

We get out and land drill through a sequence of movements.

"Okay, stop. The movements have to *stop* at the end. If you kind of smoothly go through each movement, it's like you're mumbling."

"Mumbling?"

"They've got to be defined. Okay, close your eyes."

I shut them, and Chelsea counts, "*One* two *three* four, *five* six *seven* ... Whoa, whoa, whoa. Stop."

"What?" I open my eyes.

"You're out of sync with me."

Chelsea arches her back and runs her fingers through her hair, her chest sticks out. I try not to look.

"But Chels, with my eyes closed I can't see you!"

"That's not supposed to matter! You have to synchronize to the music. If you go *precisely* on the count, we'll be in sync. Think about the movement happening at the very *start* of the count. Snap it. Sharp."

Chelsea runs through her movements again, counting. I keep my eyes open this time, but just pay attention to her voice, not what her arms are doing.

"Okay, better."

"Hey. Why are you doing this, anyway?"

"Doing what?"

"Helping me. What's changed?"

"Um, you're doing a duet with me now." Chelsea looks up at me through her lashes. "And besides, it takes a lot of guts to do what you're doing."

I grin. "So I'm gutsy?"

"And you're dedicated. You know, we're not that different, you and me. You're just as much a perfectionist."

I laugh.

Chelsea just lifts her eyebrows and stares me down.

"Okay. Maybe." She's right. There's a thread of competitive perfectionism that runs in both of us, and I know we could go far if we competed together. Oh, man, and then wouldn't people have to swallow everything they've ever whispered about me in the halls.

"Now close your eyes." She counts through the sequence again.

"How was that?"

"Good." She studies my face, and I stare right back at the complete symmetry of hers.

"Hey," she says. "Your lips are chapped. Come here."

Chelsea drags me by the arm to where we dropped our stuff on the other side of a giant stack of mats. She leans over, digging around in her bag with her head down. Her suit's cut low enough I see a little cleavage. Riley is not wrong—*nobody* is wrong about Chelsea. She's gorgeous.

Especially the way she's a little standoffish. A little removed ... like you're just not good enough for her. Because then, when she does start to look at you—it's like you've levelled up.

She's found what she's looking for and stands up, holding a little tub of lip balm.

She stares at my lips while she puts a little on her finger, then rubs my bottom lip. Man, what is it with the lip stuff? Is this just the way synchro girls flirt? What if she's setting me up to mock me?

"Hey, Chels. Do you remember the grade seven dance?"

"Yeah ..."

"Yeah, but do you remember when I asked you to dance?"

Chelsea's smile falls. So I guess she does remember laughing at me, at the idea that she would have anything to do with Bart Lively, the skinny kid everyone thought was gay.

"That was a long time ago," she says. "Do you still think I'm awful?"

"What? No, geez. I don't think you're awful."

"So do you like me now?"

She dips her finger back in the lip balm. I'm confused.

"Chels, you didn't even want me in the club. *I* should be asking *you* if you like me."

"What do you think? I saved your life, didn't I?"

"Well. Touché."

Chelsea finishes my bottom lip, then screws the cap back on, staring into my eyes like she's saying, *Now you're good*. She takes my hand to give it a squeeze, and I squeeze back—but then she doesn't let go.

So I take a step toward her. She brushes her fingers over my short, wet hair. And then she presses her lips to mine.

Wow. What would Riley think? What would the Rosa Waves guys do if they could see *this*?

It's kind of surreal. *Chelsea Gates!* my brain shouts. Chelsea Gates and me, surrounded by some kind of lust haze.

Ha, my brain says. So there. So there, everyone in grade seven! *So there,* Chelsea's judgy friends. If they could see her now.

"It tastes good, right?" she asks.

"Mmm-hmm." I put Chelsea's finger in my mouth. She doesn't pull it away. She doesn't smack sense into me. She doesn't tell me to get lost. And oh, I'm not good. I've spent the past few mornings with Erika, playing with the distance between neutral and turned on, and it's an awfully short trip. I figure Chelsea and I will snap out of this. But I should know better by now—I've had to tear myself out of the same haze every morning this week. I don't snap. I wrench.

I manage to pull away. "Thanks for the balm."

"Your lips feel better now?"

"Mmm. I think so."

"Let me check again."

A wave of desire ripples out through my whole body as Chelsea reaches for me. I press my hips against her.

She chuckles.

"Oh, don't look so proud, Chels." I nuzzle into her neck and close my eyes. I taste the chlorine and salt on her skin. My lips trail back up her neck again to her lips, and when I open my eyes, I'm thinking, *Erika.* Oh my God. What's going on?

It takes a moment to drag myself out of the haze. It takes that moment for my brain to get through, screaming at me, *Erika.* Erika. Erika.

Yeah, I don't want to be doing this with Chelsea. Not actually. And I feel panic, my heart racing, but not with desire now.

Then my brain finally gets into full gear and I'm feeling the panic completely and I don't know why my brain is still screaming, *Erika! Erika!* when I've finally figured it out.

Yeah, brain. Got it.

And then I realize—Erika is staring back at us from behind the glass in the lobby. I see the flash of her red toque on the stairs, heading up. Heading away.

No. No. *No.*

All the *Ha,* all the *So there,* turns to shame. The shame burns into the wrinkles of my waterlogged skin.

"Chelsea, stop," I whisper. I push her shoulders away from me. For a flash, she looks hurt. But I haven't got a spare second, because Erika is gone.

I run away from Chelsea. It's an awkward, slow run across wet tiles with half a hard-on, trying to be careful not to wipe out. I run up the back stairs, past the divers' land training practice, and slam into the heavy doors to outside. A wave of cool air hits my hot cheeks.

"Erika!" I shout. I run, barefoot and wet, out into the parking lot. I scan the cars, trying to spot her little silver sedan. She's leaving—barely slowing down for the speed bump before the crosswalk. We lock eyes, but she presses on the gas and keeps going.

Shit.

When I get back on deck, Chelsea's gone. Her bag's gone. I grab mine and get changed fast.

I ride my bike into Erika's neighbourhood. There's no porch light on for me tonight, but I ring the doorbell and hear arguing from inside, up the stairs. Then thumping. Then Erika opens the door.

"I made a mistake," I say, too loud.

"God! Shhh."

"Please, listen. Please."

She steps out onto the porch and closes the door behind her. That soft orange streetlamp lights up her face, and I see she's been crying.

"I'm so, so sorry."

"I was just going to the pool because I thought I'd meet you after practice. We talked about Fridays." She wipes her eyes with her sleeve. "I ... I know it's not like we said we wouldn't see anyone else or anything. I thought ... maybe you were interested in *Dave.* But ..." She shakes her head.

"Bart, this just hurts." She shakes her head again, and her voice comes out angry now. "I mean, what was that? A revenge make-out session? Were you hate-kissing her?"

"No! It was just an accident. It was just something that happened, and I don't know why, but I'm *so* sorry that it did."

I reach out for her hand, but she pulls it away.

"No."

"Please?"

She starts crying again. "Chelsea gets everything she wants. She'll get you. She'll get you for the duet too. Just wait."

"*No*, Erika. It was just a stupid mistake. She doesn't really want me."

"You don't know that."

"Well ... it's irrelevant. Erika, I just want you. Do you want me?"

"Yes."

"Then *have* me. *Please*." I step toward her, but she crosses her arms and takes a step away.

"I'm too *mad*, Bart. You think it's that easy?"

"No. Of course not."

"You're going to have to give me some time."

I nod, because I will, I'll give her anything.

● ● ●

When I get home, the lights are all off except one in the kitchen. Mom's not in the living room. I look at my watch—nine fifteen. Did she go to bed already? I walk into the kitchen, go straight to the fridge, and pour myself a glass of milk. The table's set. Two place settings, in silver. The nice napkins. And a note on my plate.

Hello Bart,
I guess you ate elsewhere, but if you're still hungry, your lasagna's

in the fridge. Three minutes on high should do it.
Maybe see you tomorrow, then.

xo Mom

I put my empty glass on the table, sit down, and put my head in my hands. It's been a long time since Mom's made lasagna. But I can't eat anything. I didn't think I could feel any worse than I already do.

I start to cry before I hear Mom's footsteps coming down the stairs. She pulls a chair over right beside me.

"I'm so sorry," I wail, and lean into her as she gathers me into a hug.

"Hey, hey."

"You're gonna be so mad at me, Mom." I sink into her hug, and breathe in the rose-scented face cream she always puts on at night. She squeezes me tight.

"It's just dinner. Your teenage brain is supposed to forget stuff like this, you know."

"No! I suck. I'm so mad at myself."

She rubs my back. "What's going on?"

I look up at her face. She's not mad at all.

"Mom ... how can you kiss someone you don't even really care for, deep down?" As soon as I say that, though, I know it's not fair. I care for Chelsea now. "Or ... how can you just make out with a friend?"

"Oh, honey. It's okay. Did you ... did you kiss Riley?"

"God! No. Mom, no."

"Well, I don't know! You said a friend. You've always been a one-close-friend kind of guy. I don't know who ..." I can tell she's just as confused as I am.

"Would you be surprised if I told you it was a girl?"

"Oh." Mom's hand goes still on my back. "No, actually. Now that you say it." She puts her hand up to my head and kisses my temple. "So this is about Erika?"

"Yeah. Uh, and Chelsea." I pull out of her hug. "Chelsea and Erika. They're both gonna hate me now. And with Chelsea, well ... I'm fine with that. She can go ahead and hate me. It won't feel any different than before, right?"

Mom laughs. "Oh, I don't think she hated you."

"She will now."

"So what happened?"

I think for a minute about telling her an abridged version. I can't face telling her. Saying it out loud.

"Erika saw me kissing Chelsea."

"Ah. And you love Erika."

"Yeah ..."

"It doesn't surprise me. I don't think it would surprise anyone who's watched you practise together."

Oh.

"And Erika loves you?"

"Maybe she did. I don't know. But now she's so hurt, and she's so mad. Mom, what do I do?"

She sighs. "I wish I knew." She gets up and fills the kettle for tea. "Hey, speaking of Riley, how's he doing? Maybe you want to talk to a friend about this?"

TWENTY-NINE

> Ur probably busy making out with Casey but can you stop for 2 secs and meet me at Mickey Dee's?

> And why should I do that?

> I need advice. Just screwed things up with E

> Pls?

Half an hour later, Riley meets me at the McDonald's that's open until 2 a.m.

"I'm so glad I don't have practice tomorrow, because there's no way I could sleep tonight."

"Yeah, me too." Riley yawns, and takes a pull from his straw. "Looks like you can still eat, though."

I shrug. Yes, I may have ordered my usual two cheeseburgers no onions, vanilla shake, and side of nuggets, but it's purely for comfort.

"So you're saying you actually kissed Chelsea Gates." He sounds like he's impressed, just like I thought he would be. I don't feel any of that rush of pride I did on the deck. I just feel sick.

"It wasn't on purpose."

"What?"

"I didn't kiss her on purpose. And I'm not telling you to, like, brag or something."

"Yeah, I get it."

"What should I do, Riley?"

"How should I know? Not exactly an expert over here on how to stay together with a girl."

"Well, you and Casey are ..."

"Not anymore."

"You broke up? You didn't tell me!"

"Why should I?" Riley leans back in his chair, looks at me with his arms crossed.

"Uh, because I'm your *friend?*"

He looks toward the door, like he's more interested in people coming and going than what I have to say.

"Seriously, Riley. Why aren't you telling me stuff? You even asked her out back in September without saying a word to me."

"You were busy."

"Oh, come on."

"Okay, you want to know? You don't tell me shit. Why should I tell you anything?"

"I'm telling you something now!"

"Before."

Did I keep stuff from him? I really didn't mean to. Synchro happened so fast, but ...

"You knew how I felt. Was it a surprise to you that I joined synchro?"

"It was a surprise that you left the Rosa Waves."

"Well ... I didn't have a choice!"

"Yeah ... you did. You could have stayed. Or you could have told me yourself, instead of waiting for your fellow girls to spread the gossip."

"What the hell? Fellow girls?" Riley swallows and stares at the floor in front of him. But he doesn't take it back. Anyway, even if he did, it's too late. It's out there. "Jesus. Sound like Geoff, much?"

Riley shakes his head. "Yeah, sorry."

I wrap the last of my burger up and launch it from our table into the trash.

"It's not easy, doing what I'm doing."

"Yeah, I figured."

"It would just be good if my best friend could understand."

Riley sighs. "Okay. I'm no expert, but if you want to show Erika you care about her, you can't keep swimming a duet with Chelsea."

I know he's right. But I also know the more Chelsea works with me, the better chance I have of getting on that podium. Showing the world.

"You think Chelsea would even want to work with me again after this?" I twist back and forth on the swivel chair.

Riley laughs. "Dude, if you think I have her figured out, you've over-estimated me. But seriously, you can't. You can't swim with her, Bart. Not if you want to be with Erika."

When I get home, I go to bed with my headphones on. When "Breathing Underwater" comes on, I feel hot tears fall into my ears and go cold. I play it over and over until I fall asleep.

THIRTY

Walking down the stairs to the pool, I'm dreading going to the dive tank. I get on the deck and ask Sunny if she has a minute to talk.

"Just let me get my coat off, Bart."

I tried calling Erika all weekend. Every time, it went to voice mail. So I texted her, but I guess she just ignored that too. She should be here already. She's usually twenty minutes early for the weekday practices. But she's not. Neither's Chelsea, which I guess is good. Maybe Erika will get here before Chels, and I could get another chance to beg for mercy.

"Okay, what is it?"

"Sunny, it's the new duet. I just want to tell you that it's, uh, great to practise with Chelsea. She's ... like, I can really learn a lot from her. I just ... I don't think I need an extra duet. But thank you."

"Thank you? You think I gave you the duet as a favour?"

"Well—I thought so ... yeah. To give me more experience? And ... more variety for next year, or something?"

Sunny nods at someone behind me. I turn my head in time to see Chelsea snap on her cap. "Nope." Sunny shakes her head. "You don't want this, you better go talk to Chelsea."

Erika's words ring in my ear. *She gets everything she wants.* Crap.

"So it was Chelsea who asked for this."

"I thought it was a good idea too."

"Especially after she passed the last national team trials."

Sunny nods.

Nothing to do but suck it up and tell Chelsea I can't do it, I guess. All day today, I've been running it through in my head how I'll tell Chels that I made a mistake. Just ... how? She already knows I messed up. She knew the moment I pushed her away.

I approach her like she's an unpredictable wild animal. She zips up her backpack and throws it past me to the space behind the mats where we stood and kissed yesterday.

"Chels. About Friday ..."

"Forget it, Bart. Just put it behind you. I already did."

"I just want to say I'm sorry. I made a mistake."

"Yeah," she scoffs. "Obviously."

"*I'm sorry*. Really."

"Good. So let's get started."

"Uh, you don't have to. You know. Go through with this duet ..."

"Oh, come on, Bart. Just because you made a mistake, doesn't mean we're going to stop practising."

"You actually *want* to swim with me?"

"We're swimming this duet at qualifiers."

"What? *How?*"

"Sunny's submitted it. You can enter a technical and a free with different partners. So you and Erika are going to swim the free, and you're swimming your technical with me now. Sunny thinks we'll be ready by then." Chels stops and swallows back what I would swear are ... tears, if I thought that she cried, ever. "Bart, we're going to get noticed." Her voice goes quiet. "Don't take that away from me."

"Chels, I'm not—"

"If we swim this at nationals, it *will* get attention."

"And attention never hurts."

"Yeah." She smiles, and blinks away the tears that have formed in her eyes.

I can't say no. I feel like crap. I don't want to hurt her more than I already have. "Okay, then."

We get in the water and it's like I've forgotten all the choreography for technical. Sunny comes and gives us tips, but I get that, really, it's Chelsea who's running this routine now.

Sunny goes to coach Julia's solo, and we're on our own again. Erika's still not here.

"Bart, you're off the count. Try again," Chelsea orders.

I slam my hand down on the surface of the water. It makes a satisfying *smack* and stings my palm.

"*What* is the matter?" Chelsea asks. "Can you not just focus?"

"It's four thirty. Where is Erika?"

"I don't know, Bart. She's not at the pool. She's just—she's not here."

I look at the pace clock that nobody ever uses over here and watch the four coloured hands spinning around. We have four weeks before qualifiers. I have to get all the practice in that I can. So for now, I just spin next to Chels, and pretend I'm dancing in the deep.

THIRTY-ONE

Bill May's message back to me is on my phone. In my hand. He *for real* just wrote me back.

I text Erika immediately.

> Bill May wants to wish us well at qualifiers. We should practise.

> Shut the front door

I send her a screen grab of Bill's message.

> Looks 'shopped

> It's the real thing! r u coming back? pretty please? and u know i'm pretty

Nothing.
Nothing.

> pretty awful

> :'(

> btw, Sunny says if u miss any more practices she's going to make me swim w Chelsea for both duets at the qualifier

> Fine. See you next practice

I sit in a deck chair that I've set up at our end of the pool, facing the doors at the opposite end, where I know Erika will come in. When she comes onto the deck, I'm waiting for her. I'm the first thing she sees.

I hold my phone up.

She shakes her head at me, but she's still walking toward me. It's been four days since I've seen her. Her freckles look darker than I remember, which makes me feel like crying—how could I have forgotten a detail I loved so much?

"What are you doing?"

"Showing you this. Look." I pass her my phone.

She reads out loud. "'Erika and Bart, thank you so much for sending me the video of your free routine. You're doing great.' It's really him. Writing to us."

"Told you so."

"'Thanks for your support for mixed duets at the next Olympics. I look forward to seeing you there!' What? Is it a go? I thought—"

"No, no. They still have to meet with the Olympic committee next year. But the hashtag's gaining momentum. Have you checked it out lately?"

"No." Erika looks sad. "I haven't."

I switch over to my browser, search #MixedDuetOlympics, and pass my phone back to her. She scrolls and clicks, and I wait.

"Wow. There's so much support out there."

"Right? So, we should practise."

Erika passes my phone back and frowns. "Okay, I'll swim. But ... I really haven't had enough time to process."

"I know. I'm sorry."

Julia looks at us, and I get the feeling she's watching me to make sure I don't make any wrong moves.

After warm-up, we get in and work on the start of the routine. Erika's quiet, and she doesn't pop her goggles up on her forehead to look at me when we're talking like she used to. She stays behind the mirrored lenses.

Then we work on the end of the routine—the heart-thumping endless vertical sequence that makes my diaphragm convulse as I run out of air. But still, I don't come up until we're supposed to, and I manage to sync sharply with Erika.

"You're better."

"That's great! Wait, why aren't you happy? It's awesome, isn't it? We'll give the Aquastellars a run for their money."

Erika's shaking her head, fighting tears again.

"Hey. Hey, hey ... I *needed* to get better!"

"*She* made you better. It was her."

Chelsea. Again. She may be swimming way on the other side of the dive tank, but she's still right here between us.

"You're so much better technically. But it's like Chelsea's sucked something out of you. You're better, but ... now you're swimming like she swims."

"Hey."

"Oh, it's a compliment."

"Bullshit. You said she misses the point. You're saying I'm all precision, no feeling. Synchro automaton."

"No, but ... When you started, do you remember what it felt like?"

"Yes! Of course I do."

"Well." Erika shakes her head. "Whatever. Let's just start again from the beginning."

"I'd like that."

"I mean the *routine*, Bart."

I sigh. "It was worth a shot."

We get up on the bulkhead and start the deck work. We pause, waiting for the synthesizer to dive, but I hold my arm out to stop Erika.

"What?"

"I've got an idea." I go stop the music. We've never been satisfied with the deck work. It's never felt really integrated with the rest of the swim. "We should do something bigger, more dramatic. This song's about breathing under water—like, something that's not even possible, but it turns out to be your life, right?"

"Yeah."

"So the other time you're breathing under water, and it's your life ... is when you're in the womb."

Erika looks confused.

"We should start out like this, like ... fetal position."

"That's dramatic?"

"If we do this." I crouch down and curl up into a ball. "Everyone will be like ... what are they doing? It's a bit mysterious, right? Then when the music starts, we uncurl." And I unfold my limbs and stand tall. "And tumble dive in."

"Oh, yeah. Okay. That looks pretty cool."

We give it a shot, and Sunny agrees it looks better, then dismisses us for our break. Erika and I take our snack into the stands.

"Thank you for coming, seriously. I was started to get really worried yesterday when you weren't here."

Erika just bites into her sandwich and chews, staying quiet, until she finally breaks the silence. "You're pretty competitive now, huh? I mean, if you're ready to go to the qualifier with Chelsea."

"*And* you. Sunny says the club will have a better showing if Chelsea and I swim too ..."

Erika smiles ruefully. "Right, if Sunny says. Well. I guess you guys have that all sorted then. Bart, why *don't* you just swim both duets at qualifiers with Chelsea? Seriously, if you'd have a better chance."

"Hey—don't even suggest that."

Sunny waves us back down, so Erika balls up her lunch bag, shoves it in her backpack, and storms down the bleachers. And I follow her to the deck.

We start off in the pool now, picking up elements from the middle of the routine. The legs entwining. The push and pull movements that slide our legs across each other's.

Erika pulls away.

"What?" I ask.

"Maybe if we could swim in armour or something."

"Erika." I laugh. "We'd sink to the bottom of the pool."

She pushes up her goggles. Finally. But she's on the verge of tears.

"I can't be this close to you," she whispers. "It's too hard."

"No, please. *Please.*" Erika's brown eyes bore into me. They rim with tears and I reach out and touch her arm—but it's no use. She won't touch me back. "*Don't.* Erika, you back out, then what? No one will see 'Breathing Underwater.' Come on, we're in this together, remember?"

"I'm not in any shape to do this. You have to go to the qualifier."

"With you."

"*I can't do it,* Bart."

"But *please.*"

"No."

"You can't quit our duet! It's only three weeks away. Erika?" I try to take her hand in mine, but she rips it away. "Erika, *please.*"

"No."

She gets out, grabs her towel and her bag, and makes her way down the deck toward the change rooms.

I let her go and walk back to the dive tank. Everyone's staring at me. Chelsea motions for me to swim over to her. She sees me about to crack and shakes her head. "Look, just swim. Just go. I'll race you. Fifty-metre sprint."

I nod, slip my goggles down, and Chels and I take off from the wall.

My tears recede as I race Chelsea, and after practice, I get out and go to the hot tub. But when I see the girls all walk past on the way to their change room—all except Erika—the tears come back. I duck under the hot water for a second to shock them away.

Dive Boy comes by with a couple other guys from his team. The guys get in, but he sees me and holds back, like he's not going to join them.

"Dave," I say. I nod my head like, *Come on, you don't have to avoid me.*

He gets in and sits across the tub with his guys, and I give him a sad smile. He smiles back. It's a heart-melting smile—something else that makes my tears recede.

THIRTY-TWO

Chelsea and I make it to March. We make it to Quebec City.

The morning of the mixed duet event, I wake up early in my hotel room and plug in the kettle I borrowed from Sunny. My hair's grown out a little since provincials and I don't want the sides to look a mess when I swim. I hesitate, just for a second, then I mix up the gel, stirring it with a paintbrush.

It's my first synchro meet with clubs from all across the country. And I need to do it right.

•••

I wish the guys from the Rosa Waves could be at the qualifier. I wish they could see it, all of us at a huge university pool with the lights so bright they're like spotlights on a football field.

"What's the matter with you? You're so jumpy," Chelsea scolds. She's scary with her gelled head, black-rimmed eyes, and yellow and blue eyeshadow extending in two points beyond her brows. I can't decide what she's madder at—that I chose to wear makeup this morning to match her blue and yellow flame eyes, or that I borrowed her eyeshadow without asking.

"Sure, there are just five hundred other swimmers here," Julia says. "Nothin' to get too excited about."

But I *am* excited. I'm standing on the deck in a glittery Speedo that matches Chelsea's blue-and-yellow suit. There's just one problem. On the program, there are three other pairs aside from ours. The Aquastellars, one pair from Quebec, and one from New Brunswick. There's a chance we won't make the podium at all.

But it's not just that. I can't spot a single boy who's *on* the program. And I'd notice if they were here. Bare chests stand out in a sea of one-pieces. So I think … I think they're just not here.

If they don't show, that's it. This won't be a competition to see if we qualify for the national championship. It'll just be the end. *Don't think about that,* I tell myself. *Not before you swim.*

Erika comes up behind us. "Chelsea, you could send Bart up the dive tower to give him something to actually be scared about."

"Hey." I whip around. Was that comment supposed to be mean or flirting?

She does a double take. "Nice eyes," she says. But then she turns to walk away. So I follow.

Chelsea calls, "Bart, where are you going? Warm-up's in, like, ten minutes." I hold up a finger—just a minute.

"Hey. Erika. Do you notice something?" She turns around.

"You're ... wearing Chelsea's makeup?"

"No. I mean, yes. But no, that's not what I notice. I notice that there aren't any other guys here yet. And the mixed duet routine warm-up is in—"

"Ten minutes. I know." Erika's eyes soften. "I'm sorry."

"Like, where *are* they? I feel like I'm being stood up."

"Maybe they're just late."

I cross my hands over my head and slip them down around the back of my neck, arching my back, feeling the stretch. Trying to work out the tension.

"I wish it was us, Erika. Sunny does too."

"Sunny's got her eye on the prize. This is working out great for her. If she has a guy swimming with someone who's more than likely on the junior national squad ..."

"You don't know that."

"Well, come on. Chances are good."

"No, you don't know that Sunny *feels* that way."

After Erika quit the duets with me, Sunny mobilized. She got Erika replaced with Chelsea for our mixed duet entry for qualifiers. And she started working us *hard*. She made up a free routine, different from "Breathing Underwater." Not as difficult. Not as many risks. And I know that must have been hard for Erika to watch—because it's been hard for me to swim.

Erika looks away at the stands, and then back at me. "Well, good luck. I'll be watching."

When the event begins, the first duet, from New Brunswick, is called. They do not come.

The second duet, from Quebec, is called. They do not come.

They call us, the third duet. Chelsea and I assume our first pose on the deck together in front of hundreds of people in the stands, and I have to tell myself: *You're in a national competition. You've made it. Just seven months after leaving the racing pool ... you're here.*

The whistle sounds. We dive, and I boost Chels for our impressive first lift. We fall in sync, our patterns tighter than ever, our movements crisp. We keep our still, frozen smiles on, and the judges stare back impassively. For three minutes, I give the routine my complete concentration. And when we're done, egg beatering in place and smiling to a crowd that's cheering us, I wait to feel happy.

Competitor four, from Aquastellars, is called. But Kim and his partner aren't here.

When Chelsea and I take our place on the top podium, and they give us our ribbons and our automatic gold medals, I wait. But the satisfaction doesn't come then, either. It doesn't matter that the stands are clapping and cheering and getting loud. I remember what it was like at provincials. Even if we weren't competing, it felt so much better to have Erika next to me, squeezing my hand. Looking me in the eye, our connection sparked.

I want that back.

Instead, Chelsea and I have the podium to ourselves. Chels grins out at the crowd. She's smiling away, but I can't. Because even though we qualified, it's just us. No other province has a pair in the competition. With no one to compete against, there won't be a mixed duet event at the Canadian national championship.

Chelsea will go to swim her solo. Erika will go to swim hers. If the team event does well here, all the girls from our club will go.

But not me.

On the way out, while Chelsea and I are squeezing through the crowds coming out of the stands, a reporter and a guy with a camera and light stop us.

"Hi, I'm Michelle Stark from *Sports This Week*. Do you guys have five minutes? We just have a few questions."

"No." I keep walking, but Chelsea grabs my hand and pulls me back.

"Bart! Don't be cheeky. Just answer a few questions. It's good for the club!"

"Great, thanks for doing this, guys," Michelle says.

"I know what you're going to ask already."

"Oh? What's that?" The reporter's eyes sparkle, like it's some kind of fun guessing game. She knows, and I know. But now I have to say it. "Why are you guys in a girl's sport? Why are you competing with girls?"

"Well, I wasn't going to ask *exactly* that. But now that the question's out there, why *are* you in synchro?"

"I'm in it because I love it."

"Bart, you just qualified for the national competition by default. Now that there's no one to compete against, how far do you think you will you go in this sport?"

"Ah, now you're talking about the Olympics, right? And why guys can't go?"

An older couple come up and the woman pokes her head in between Chelsea and me. "You people make me sick," she says, looking right at me.

"Who? Synchronized swimmers?" I ask. "You're at the wrong event if that's the case ..."

The woman continues, "Synchronized swimming isn't for gays. Why can't you just leave synchro for our girls?"

"I'm not *taking it away* from them," I say.

Michelle doesn't drop her smile, but she looks at her cameraman and thinks before asking her next question.

"I know you and your duet partner were hoping to swim the first national mixed duet at the junior age group level. Do you have Olympic dreams?"

"Sure I do."

Michelle's smile persists, but she knows it's pointless to ask any more questions. But Chelsea prods me, not wanting to lose the moment. The attention. "Just tell her what you like about it. As a new swimmer. As someone who was a racing swimmer."

"It's using a whole different dimension in the water. You're not just moving horizontally. You have more space, it's more expressive. I like the routines, and moving to music."

"That's great, thank you."

The cameraman turns off the light, and Michelle tells us when we can expect to see our bit if it hits the news. In the lobby, Sunny stops Chelsea and me and confirms what we suspected: the mixed duet routine will not be competed at nationals.

"Fuck that shit."

Chelsea shushes me.

Sunny just stays quiet, lets it sink in, until I speak again.

"This is garbage."

"I wish the other pairs had shown up," she says. "I really do. I heard the girl from the Aquastellars pair got a concussion."

"Well, shit. But still ... I can't *accept* this, Sunny! Kim should have had an alternate! They should find out where the other guys were and hold a separate qualifier or something. Maybe they can make it more central, easier for the eastern guys to get to if that was the problem ..."

"It's not the end, Bart. You'll only be better next year," Chelsea says softly.

"Yeah, doing what, exactly, if nobody else shows up? A solo? They won't let me compete that either."

I walk out of the lobby while Sunny and Chelsea call me back.

•   •   •

On the way back to the hotel, I check my phone. There's a voice mail from Mom. *I saw you on the live stream, and you guys were so good! Call me back!* It feels weird to be at this big meet without her. We pass a Dairy Queen, and it reminds me of all the times Mom and I stopped for cones after a meet. I miss her so much. I wish we'd had the money for her to fly out too. But like Dad said, in just a couple of years I'll be on my own, so I guess I might as well get used to it.

That night, while the girls start the snacks and nails ritual, I watch the news from the local sports desk. Our bit appears and everybody goes quiet to watch. My answer about what I like about synchro comes first. Then it neatly cuts to Michelle asking about our plan for swimming the first national mixed duet event at the junior age group, to my Olympic dreams, and then my "Sure I do" is where they end it. They've neatly snipped out the harassment, but they couldn't edit out the angry look on my face afterward, so I look like a jerk.

I throw the clicker on the bed. "That's bullshit."

Chelsea glares at me. "Well thanks, Bart."

"No, I didn't mean you."

Erika looks at me, and for a split second, I see that she feels sympathetic, before she goes back to painting a coat of bright pink on Casey's toenails.

"Forget it. I'm going for a walk."

Out in the fresh air, I start to think clearly. But after I get a couple blocks away from the hotel, I hear footsteps running up behind me. I turn around, and it's Erika, her breath blowing out in clouds in the cold air.

"Hey. You want to talk about it?" she asks.

"You want to talk to me?"

"As a teammate."

A teammate.

"Come on. What's eating you?"

We start walking together, aiming for an unknown destination.

"Well, for starters, Chelsea and I swam a free routine that would have made Aquastellars freak—if they'd even shown up. I may not have loved it like I love swimming with *you*, but we were really good. And that woman couldn't even see that? She was so hung up on her own stupid ideas about gender roles that she couldn't even *see* what we did. And now that nationals are off? Nobody else will see it, either ... and that stupid sports reporter didn't even say a word when that homophobic woman cut in! And the news didn't even show it. They should've shown *that*."

"Well, you know they wouldn't, Bart."

"I know. But I've worked so hard, and the idiots are still there, ready to take stabs at me." I shake my head and swallow. Why do I have to cry so easily? I swallow, and try biting my cheek to stop the tears like Erika does. "It makes me wonder if that's why the other guys didn't show, Er. If they just know what we're up against, maybe they figure it's not worth it."

"I don't think that's it. And I don't think that's what's bothering you."

"You don't?"

"No. You're all mad, but you don't *get* mad, Bart. Not for more than five minutes, anyway." She laughs. "Not like I do. I think this means you're sad about something."

I stop and look at her. We've come as far as a city park, just a patch of grass with some benches. Nothing fun. No merry-go-rounds.

"Come here," she says, and heads to a bench. She sits down, and I slump down next to her.

"It just doesn't feel like I thought it would. I just ... technically succeeded in the first mixed duet at a national age group meet. First one. Ever.

But I feel like crap. Maybe I should have just stayed with racing."

"Bullshit. You don't mean that. You don't *feel* what you wanted to at the end of this meet because you're going at this all wrong. You've got to stop trying to be someone you're not."

"What, I'm not a synchro swimmer? You think I'm not good enough?"

"No! That's just it. You're more than good enough—when you let yourself be in it. Just ... let yourself be who you *are*, Bart, and you'll feel that same joy you felt at the beginning. You've been so hung up on swimming like perfect Chelsea, and you're so ... I don't know."

"What?"

"Okay, I'm just gonna say it. You're hell bent on showing everyone you can be a straight synchro boy. That's why you kissed Chelsea, isn't it?"

"That's what this is about? You don't think I'm—what, that I'm into girls? Well, excuse me, but everything up on the dive tower with you was real, Erika."

"I believe you."

"So?"

"So that's not all that's going on! You're so mad at that idiot at the pool tonight, but who cares? Like, I know you want to challenge everybody's idea of the image of boys in this sport. I get it. But the people who count don't *care* about that shit. They just won't. Seriously, Bart, you give the best performance when you just let yourself swim. I know you're happiest when you're not fighting anyone's idea of who you are too."

"So what am I supposed to do?" I press the heels of my hands to my eyes. I can't stop the tears now.

"Stop caring what everyone thinks. Just give it up, and swim."

I nod. Erika sits with me until I get my breathing under control. But she starts shivering, her parka no match for this cold.

"You want me to stay?"

"No. You're cold. You should go."

I watch her walk back down the sidewalk toward the hotel.

Later that evening, I get ahold of video that Sunny took and watch it on repeat. Chelsea and me, crisp and precise, making all the adjustments a guy and a girl need to in order to be in sync. I watch it again and again, looking for something—something that's missing. But we're near perfect. The slight misses that only judges would see? They're not it.

I keep watching it, trying to see if anyone else could tell what's missing, or if it's something only I can spot. Because I know what it is—it's the joyful spark between Erika and me when we swam—that was the *something* that made our routine special. The expression, the feeling I had when I started out in synchro, like I was dancing again. Then all that drive I had to get to nationals, to kiss a medal and make Dad, and Riley, and Coach all see this wasn't for nothing—that killed it. I lost my connection with Erika, and I lost the connection I felt to myself.

And I need it back.

I wipe tears away with the back of my hand. Before I plug my phone in to charge, I slip over to Twitter and tweet:

> Where are my synchro guys at? You were good
> enough to be here.
> #SynchroCanadaQualifiers #MixedDuetOlympics

I turn out the light, and my phone buzzes. I pick it up off the nightstand, and there on the lock screen is a reply:

> **Bill May** @BillMaySynchro
> **@Synchroboy2000** Don't give up!

THIRTY-THREE

Before I call Dad, I coach myself. I'm just going to talk about the deal, right? It's just about the money. I don't have to tell him anything else. I don't have to talk to him about what it means to me. We had a deal, and I'm just calling in on that promise.

"Hello?"

"Hey, Dad."

"Bart. So you decided you'd call me back?"

My hand holding the phone shakes. I stop breathing. This is stupid. I should just hang up.

Dad sighs on the other end of the line.

"So you're in Quebec City, eh? Pretty cold, I guess."

"You kept track?" I want to ask if Mom told him, but I stop myself.

"Of course I kept track. Bart? Are you still there?"

"Yeah," I say, low and beat.

"Doesn't sound like it's going too well."

"I made it through the qualifier."

"Oh." Dad breathes on the other end of the line. "Well, good for you. So on to nationals after all?"

"My events aren't going to be in nationals this year." .

"Sorry to hear that. But you can't say I didn't tell you—"

"You don't know anything about synchro! You haven't even watched me swim. You can't tell me anything about this."

I lie back and put my hand over my eyes, like I don't want to see myself screw up my whole plan for calling. But something in me just needs him to understand.

"There were other *guys*, Dad. Guys were at provincials, and there were guys who just didn't show up at nationals, but they were supposed to be there."

"Scratched?"

"Yeah. But next year, you know, there'll be more of us. Did you watch the world finals stuff I sent you?"

"Yeah, I did."

"Okay, so you saw then—guys all over the world are doing this. And I want to *keep* doing this."

"Well, looks like I can't stop you."

I open my mouth to tell him that he can, that he is—not paying for the training anymore has stretched Mom. It's why she couldn't be here to see me. And I hate him for it.

"Dad, if you could still keep your end of the deal to cover some costs, even though I technically won't be swimming at nationals ... We had a deal, right? It's not my fault they won't let me swim. Can you at least just cover the travel to this meet?"

He does that big inhale thing he does when he's uncomfortable. Or when someone's asked him something he doesn't want to say yes to.

"Look, your mother didn't make me a deal for money." My heart sinks. Does this mean he won't help? "I told Melanie ... After I left you guys, I wanted to come back. I kept trying. I told her I wanted to be in your life, but I was a screw-up, Bart. Your mom said I could only see you if I was going to be a proper dad to you—stop screwing up and help you grow up. So that's what I'm trying to do. Trying to help you make the right decisions."

"I think I am, Dad."

"Yeah. Well, Cragg told me how good you're doing."

"What?"

"He's seen how hard you're working. Said you're working harder for this synchro coach than you ever did for him."

I'm hit with a sudden urge to cry. He said that to Dad? Why hasn't Cragg said two words to me since I left? Still, he's noticed.

Don't cry on the phone with Dad, I tell myself. *Just don't.*

"So you'll cover it? Please?"

"I think you should get a summer job this year, okay?"

I sigh. "Okay."

"But, yeah, I'll cover this. At least you're still in the water."

"I'm not going back to racing, though. You get that, right?"

"We'll see. But I'll come see you swim synchro, kid. Just tell me when."

That's the question, though, isn't it? Still, he's watched the stuff I sent him. And he'll come see me swim.

And he wanted to come back for me.

"Thanks, Dad."

I click off the phone and lie motionless on the bed. I got the money. But if Dad expects me to go back to racing? I'm not sure if I won that one or not.

THIRTY-FOUR

The next day, Chelsea swims her last phase of the junior squad trials. When it's over, she cheers—she's made it on. Then our whole club cheers—even Erika.

Chelsea's one of the newest members of the junior national squad.

The girls run down on deck and hug her. I follow, and give her a hug too. It's a weepy, melty moment, one I know the girls have looked forward to for years—and with Julia's and Erika's arms around me and Chelsea, and mine around them—I'm part of it. There's no question about that.

I think back to how I hoped *so* hard that being in the middle of the girls would show me, one way or the other, which way I'm leaning. Who I would want.

But it hasn't. All it's shown me is that I have some pretty great friends who are girls, and sometimes, I'm pretty damned attracted to them.

Even the infuriating ones.

I head back to the hotel, stop at the gift shop in the lobby, and pick out the only treat I know Chelsea likes—a small box of chocolate-covered ginger. At least I won't be tempted to eat any of them.

"Oh, hi," Chelsea says, a little confused to see me at her hotel door. "Come on in."

I pop my head in. "Your mom isn't here?"

Amanda Gates hasn't been in my face since Chelsea started swimming duets with me, but she hasn't exactly been a cheerleader, either.

"Moms don't stay with us. They have their own block of rooms where they stay up and drink wine and strategize fundraising or something. I don't know what they do."

"You sound a little tired of the moms."

"Well," she says, and exhales loudly as she sits down at her laptop, "whatever I feel, it doesn't matter. I wouldn't be here without them."

"True." I get that. I wouldn't be here without mine, either.

Chelsea presses the space bar and I hear the sounds of the pool, and the start of our music.

"That's the video for our free routine?"

"Yup."

I come around to watch, and see her click a share link.

"Where ... Who are you sending this to?"

"To my new coach!"

"You're sending them our video? Why?"

"You want a chance to swim in worlds someday?"

"Sure."

"Maybe the Olympics?"

"If I turn into a girl, sure."

She sighs. "No, Bart. Seriously. If the Olympic committee accepts the mixed duet."

"Well, yes, of course!"

"So, I thought you could come out to Montreal in May, while I'm at the national squad camp, and we could keep training."

"Oh? While you're getting ready for junior worlds in July?"

"Well, I just don't think we want to lose momentum. Not if we want to make it to the Olympics." She smiles.

I smile back. I'm better now, sure. And give me another year of working this hard, I will be *amazing*. And if the Olympics mixed duet is on? You bet I'm going to give it all I've got. But Chelsea can't take me with her to Montreal, and she knows it. There is no national coach scoping clubs for guys to pair up with their junior swimmers yet. If there were, they would have been at this meet.

"Chels, thank you. I mean it. But I can't go with you."

"But isn't this what you wanted?" She frowns. "I thought when I made the squad ... You wanted to go all the way to international competition, right?"

"I do. But ..." But my heart's not in our routines. She sees that, and I see it in her face.

"I guess this is about Erika. When I saw her leave the hotel room last night, after you left ..."

"She's not swimming with me. And it's not just her ... It's about me too."

"Well, if you change your mind about Montreal, I can be very persuasive, Bart. I could make it happen."

"Thanks, Chelsea. Thanks for swimming with me, okay?" I say. "And for everything you put into getting me here. I know things weren't easy for you this year, and I know that I was part of the reason for that."

Chelsea starts waving off what I'm saying.

"No, really. And you took over from Erika as my second coach too." I put the box of ginger on the table by her laptop. "I've got a debt way bigger than can be paid off with a stupid box of ginger."

"Oh," she says, putting a finger on the box. She sighs. "You don't owe me anything." She sits up straight and takes a deep breath. "Well, just your life."

We laugh. I get up and give her a kiss on the cheek. "I'm ... I guess I'll just see you at the airport tomorrow."

"Yeah, tomorrow."

Dear Bill May:

Everyone's saying, "See you at #MixedDuetOlympics." But everyone knows that's just what people are saying because they're not giving up. They're keeping the faith.

Well, my faith is slipping. None of the other mixed duets showed up to qualifiers, and get this ... even though we qualified for the national championships? Chelsea and I won't be going, because there isn't another pair who will enter the mixed event. There's no competition now in my age group.

Not enough interest.

You probably got told that a fair bit. But you probably also never screwed things up with your duet partners. You probably never spent so many hours with a partner and got so connected that you started moving in sync outside the pool—and then screwed that up.

I did. The first routine I sent you was with my partner Erika, and I wish so much that people got to see that one. Chelsea's a great swimmer, and I have so much respect for her—but you should see Erika and me swim.

Well, it's done now. She's not my partner anymore.

Chelsea—my current duet partner—made the junior national squad after the qualifier. That's awesome. But she's moving across the country to train, so my ride ends here.

Bill, I'm not ready to stop.

—Bart

THIRTY-FIVE

"Bart, why did you stop ballet?" Sunny asks, after a crappy first practice back at our home pool.

"Oh, you know. I was turning twelve." That's the average age when kids' interests change—they call it the twelve-year-old cliff. It's usually explanation enough.

"Did you stop liking dance?"

"No, I loved it."

Sunny looks up at where my eyes are fixed, on the divers overhead. Then she looks hard at me again.

"In Russia, lots of boys dance ballet. You should have grown up in Russia."

There's a thought. Then I laugh, thinking about Alexandr Maltsev, the guy from the Russian mixed pair that won the mixed duet free routine at the debut of the event at worlds last year, the competition where Bill May and his partner took gold for the technical. When Maltsev joined the all-girls national synchro team in Russia, I guess people were worried he wouldn't have enough opportunities to compete. So they tried to get him to join water polo. He refused. And last year, he made history.

I stay in the water a while, after everyone's gone home. I kick off the wall and practise a solo routine—Erika's solo. She'll swim it at nationals, and she doesn't know I've been watching her so closely that I can replicate her movements, her control, her perfect patterns, right down to the way she rolls her wrist, or flicks her fingers up when she extends a hand out to the audience. Totally feminine movements that somehow look right on me, that *feel* right.

Nothing's going to be enough to make me just one of the guys, or impress the Rosa Waves, or my dad—not hooking up with Erika, not winning a medal at this sport. All that effort to fit into the straight box? It feels like the effort to get to a certain level of perfection in synchro. That perfect score. I wanted the perfect scores for so long, I lost track of what the scores were *for*. All they were for was access—access to this amazing, beautiful sport that speaks to my soul in a way racing never could.

Now, I know it doesn't matter how hard I try, no one's ever going to hold up a six-point-anything on how Boy I am.

And I have stopped giving a fuck.

In my head, I swim to Erika's music. And I'm thinking about Bill May's strength and skill. I wonder if he ever got my message. I wonder if he ever watched the video of Erika and me doing our free routine. I wonder if he can see what I see.

When the music talks about teaching my feet to fly, I execute a perfect vertical spin, and it's the best I've ever done. I can feel it.

When I get out, Dave is standing on deck, clapping.

"Hey." I kinda laugh, despite myself.

"Hey, yourself. I'm just headed to the hot tub."

I look off to where the Rosa Waves practise. No one's there. The rest of the divers have gone to the locker room. Team practice prime time is over, and it's just the leisure swim crowd taking over the pool.

"Yeah, me too."

We walk under the waterslide and get in.

"Bart, I'm sorry if I made you uncomfortable that time at school. But you should know, the word 'queer' isn't name-calling. Not from me. Look," Dave moves over to sit next to me and lowers his voice, "I saw a guy who's been checking me out, a guy who swims with the fucking *synchronized swimming* team, and *forgive me* if I made an error."

I squeeze my eyes shut, like I'm at the top of a roller coaster. "It's not ... it's not an error."

"Whoa. Okay, then. Hey, are you okay?"

I'm not. I'm definitely not. But I am. I'm not dissolving. I'm not imploding. Nothing is going wrong in this moment.

"Yeah." I shake my head. "Why wouldn't I be? Maybe ... let's just change the topic."

Dave takes a deep breath, and lets it out. "Okay. Let's see. Did you ever think about diving?"

"No. Definitely not."

He grins. "Scared of heights?"

I just splash the bubble buildup at him. He splashes it back.

"Your spins? If that's what you call them ... they're like rotations in diving. You could do arm stands ... I've seen you."

"Yeah? I dunno. You're doing a lot more gravity work than we do in swimming or synchro. I don't think I've got half your strength—the way you launch off your arms into a rotation like that?"

Dave smiles, and those eyes still pin me in place. So now he knows I've been watching him. Now he knows I've assessed, exactly, the strength of his arms. That I've watched him that closely.

"Well, we've all got our strengths," he says.

A guy gets out of the steam room, and Dave's eyes follow him.

"Hey, don't pretend I'm not here," I joke.

"I'm just having a look ... Just like you do, right?"

I laugh, and grin.

"Okay, so how's the love life, Bart?"

"Oh, man. I don't know."

"What don't you know?"

I open up, telling him more than I've told anyone about what I've felt—and thought—for years. His brown eyes never leave mine once. It's like he's so focused on talking to me, I have to look away at something else.

"And it's not just Erika. I've always had crushes on girls. Ever since I was, like, five. I think my first crush was Kimberly, in kindergarten. I think I was in love with her ringlets."

"Or did you just *want* her ringlets?"

"No." I laugh. "Had my own. Don't you remember? Before I shaved my head?"

Dave gives me a dead serious look. "I mourned the day you shaved your head, Bart."

I laugh.

"You didn't see the tears, but ..."

"Oh, shut up." I push Dave off the bench and he dunks his head under the water. And then I feel his hand run up my leg, up between my thighs. When he pops up and brushes his hair out of his face, he looks for my reaction.

I'm shocked still.

Dave sighs. "I always dreamed I'd get to touch those curls. So ... not always girls, then?"

"What?"

"Your crushes. You said you always had crushes on girls. But ..."

My heart's pounding hard. I want to tell him the truth that he already knows—that *his* crush isn't one-way. I want to tell him that the way I always want someone else to pull me onto the roller coaster—because I can never bring myself to face those heights.

But no one else is going to get me on this ride.

"No. Not always girls."

Under the water, Dave grabs hold of my hand.

"It's okay," he says. Then he whispers in my ear, "My crushes aren't always on guys."

I take a deep breath. And I know what he's telling me. That it doesn't have to be one way or the other.

The change room's empty. Dave and I watch each other get dressed, and when he leaves, it's unspoken but decided. I follow him. He walks past his car, keeps walking along the path that runs behind the aquatic centre to a little neighbourhood park. He pulls me with him into the bushes where it's private but lit slightly by the streetlamp. I put my hands behind his head and pull him to me, and *I* kiss *him*. There are shadows of leaves on his face. He kisses me back. I'm hard instantly.

And I think about Erika.

"I'm sorry," I say.

"For what?"

Dave runs his hands up under my shirt and pulls me close. I'm not the only one who's hard.

"I'm going to be a jerk to you."

Dave kisses my jawline, and I gap out for a bit, overcome with want. *Need.* My hand travels down his back, grabs the perfect ass that I've watched get out of the hot tub on more than one occasion.

Dave runs a hand over my abs. Even as I'm responding to his touch, I tell myself I won't do this again. Not because I'm scared. Not because I won't want to.

"Dave, listen. Seriously. I'm a jerk. I want to get back together with Erika. I'm ... I can't ..."

"Shhh."

Then my Dive Boy does this little thing—he takes my bottom lip between his teeth—such a small thing, but I nearly collapse in a puddle of longing.

We make out until we're too tired to keep standing.

•••

Last night, I dreamt that Erika and I swam naked. She got me out of the pool and laid me down beneath her. She held my wrists up above my head, and we had sex there on the pool deck. People were walking by. They didn't say anything or even really look, and we didn't care.

When I woke up, my heart was pounding. I had to toss the sheets in the laundry, and have a shower.

Last night, I made out with a guy for the first time. And this morning, when I left for school, the sky was so blue—it was so clear, and I was just filled with all this desire for Erika. I walked to school in the sunshine, dreaming about touching her.

Last night, I made out with Dave.

The world didn't implode.

I'm clear as the sky—I love Erika. I'm also attracted to boys. I *could* fall in love with a guy, someday. I feel that now.

But right now? It's all her.

THIRTY-SIX

"Woo, look at me, I'm a water ballerina," Geoff says, spinning in place, off balance.

I try to ignore him.

I peel off my swim jammers and towel off. They want to make a big deal of it? Make me uncomfortable? Fine. I'll just leisurely dry off my junk right in front of them and watch them avert their eyes. Ha.

Riley catches my eye and looks away. Geoff sees Riley's discomfort, grabs him, and tries to spin him around. Andy laughs.

"Guys, your form is off," I deadpan. Then, naked, I go over and put a hand on Andy's bare back. My other hand gently pulls his shoulder back. "Stand up straight."

"Fuck off," Andy says, twisting away.

I turn to Geoff, who's just standing there, stunned now. "Geoff, you need to tighten your glutes." I give his backside a pat before he even knows how to react. "It's like you guys know *nothing* about dance."

Riley looks at me like he's scared I'm going to get the crap beat out of me, but nothing happens. I just pull on my sweats, and the other guys keep their heads down, get changed, and get the hell out of there as fast as they possibly can.

Dave looks at me from the shower and smiles. I smile back. And behind me, Riley laughs.

"Hey, are you around this weekend?" I ask him.

"Yeah, last free weekend before we ramp up the training for the next meet."

"You up for Sombrio?" The last couple of summers, Riley and I have camped overnight on this amazing beach, right on the sand. It's just started to get warm enough to do that.

Riley nods. "Yeah, I'm up for that."

When I get upstairs, Dave's in the lobby. He gives my brush cut a fluff, and I grab his wrist and turn his arm back, play fighting. We giggle, then freeze when Riley comes up the stairs and says, "See ya this weekend, Bart."

Dave and I stand there until he leaves and the doors fall shut behind him.

"Everything cool?" Dave asks.

"Yeah. Well, yes and no."

He raises an eyebrow. "Rosa Waves trouble? It looks like you were handling it in there."

"Yeah, nothing like that. I just don't want you to think ... that I wasn't into it. Last night."

"Yeah, you were pretty clearly into it." Dave half smiles.

"I'm glad it happened, but—"

"But there's Erika. I know. You said so last night." Dave looks at me for a long moment. "Come on, Bart. Don't look so burdened. Don't worry—I don't feel like you used me."

"You sure?"

"Who's to say I didn't use you?" Dave grins as he backs away toward the doors to the parking lot.

● ● ●

Saturday is gorgeous. Riley and I start at China Beach and hike the Juan de Fuca trail all the way to Sombrio Beach, spotting eagles and sea otters. Riley stops every now and then to take a photo. An eagle right over our heads. Extreme close-up macro shot of these tiny flowers that will produce berries this summer, coming out on the vines.

At Bear Beach, we scrabble along, hopping from stone to stone.

"Hey, wait up."

I turn back and Riley's got his lens out again. I figure he's going to take a picture of the stones the size of bread loaves all over the beach, worn smooth by the surf. But he focuses the lens on me. I stick my tongue out.

"You jerk. You wrecked it."

"You're not sending any pictures of me to the yearbook, are you?"

"No. I don't take pictures for the stupid yearbook."

"You used to."

Riley shrugs. Casey was on yearbook. I guess he dropped it after they split.

"Okay, fine. I'll give you a picture." I drop my pack and shake out my legs. Then I run ahead and launch myself from a big rock into a grand jeté. I hear Riley's lens snap a bunch of times in rapid succession.

"That's cool," he says, reviewing the pics on the display. "But, dude, if you break an ankle on this beach, I am *not* carrying you out."

"Fine. Leave me to die alone." I put my pack on and give him a shove. He shoves me back.

We talk all the way to Loss Creek, an hour from our campsite. Then we're mostly quiet until we get to Sombrio. We pitch our tent and start a fire, eat chorizo and ramen, and toast marshmallows while we watch the sun set.

We've talked about everything except what I feel like I have to tell Riley. We poke at the fire, and Riley yawns.

"Time to hit the sack?"

He nods. So we turn in, and I stare at the ceiling of the tent, at the pattern of tree bits that have fallen on the fly.

"So, do you still think synchro's gay?" I ask.

"Well, sure. You're doing it, right?"

"Eff you."

"I'm just giving you a hard time. No. I don't think it's gay. It's pretty cool."

"Will you come to the watershow? The club puts something on at the end of the year. I just hope I can get Erika to swim with me."

"She's still not talking to you?"

"Oh, she'll talk. But she won't swim."

"Sorry."

"Yeah. I was such an asshole." I go up on one elbow and look at Riley. He's got his eyes closed, so it's easier. "You know, I've figured some stuff out. I really, really love Erika."

"Good for you," Riley mumbles.

"You know when we decided we'd ask the girls to go to the barbecue with us?"

"Yeah." Riley yawns.

"It wasn't because I wanted to cover up for anything. I wasn't just trying to be straight. I really wanted to be with a girl."

"Mmm-hmm? Your point?"

I sigh. "I just didn't want ... Okay, you asked me that day if there was anything going on with me, like—" I sigh again. Why is it so freaking hard for me to put this into words? "Okay, you know when you said synchro's gay, and you told Geoff I was doing it to go after a girl?" Riley doesn't say anything, so I continue. "I really didn't want you to think that's why I was doing it."

Riley's still silent.

"Because it's really important to me. It's like—I tried synchro, and it was *exactly* what I should be doing."

Riley rolls over, his back to me. "Mmm-hmm," he mumbles into his pillow.

"So—okay, you still awake? I'm serious, dude. This is big news."

"Mmmph."

"You know Dave from the dive team?"

"Mmm." Riley rolls back.

"We hooked up. A little. And it ... didn't suck. But it made me realize how much I missed Erika. I guess it made me realize a lot of things."

Riley's silent, his eyes still shut.

"Like, I guess you weren't wrong when you thought I was bi."

He takes his arm out of the sleeping bag and flips me the bird.

"You're such an idiot, Bart. I knew all that a long time ago. Now will you let me get some goddamned sleep?" But he's smiling. And then I am. Because I guess, all along, he just wanted me to be honest with myself.

I just hope Erika feels the same way when I tell her.

THIRTY-SEVEN

Mom's got a day off, so she drops me at the pool for practice. "It's been nice to have you home more, Bart. It's been a good week."

"Thanks, Mom."

"You put a lot of years in at that pool, you know ... It's not a bad thing that you're scaling back on your training for a while. Maybe you can try a solo."

"Maybe."

"I know you miss your duet."

"Her. I miss her."

She takes a deep breath that turns into a sigh. She adjusts the rearview mirror. I can see it on her face—she's trying to figure out the right thing to say.

"If it gets too awkward with the girls, I want you to know you don't have to stick this out. You don't have to keep going to the synchro club. You know, Cragg told me he'd have you back on the Rosa Waves, if you wanted. He's seen you go all in with synchro. He knows you weren't just screwing around."

I laugh. "I'm not going back to the lane pool, Mom."

"Okay." She laughs. "I didn't think so. I just want you to know I'll support you, whatever you decide."

I feel my throat catch, and tears start. Exhausted, I guess.

"Oh, Bart. I know that *synchro* is what's in your heart."

"*She's* in my heart."

Mom smiles at me. "Okay, then. Don't stop trying."

• • •

Our club's team routine didn't quite make it past the qualifier, but Erika and Chelsea's solo routines made it to nationals. So the rest of us are going to end practice early and watch the live stream on Sunny's laptop.

All I have to train for now is the club's end-of-year watershow. I have an idea—something that will kick off the performance with a big visual impact. But will I even swim in it? With Chelsea staying out east to work with coaches there, my only option is to swim the free duet with Erika.

I tell Julia about my watershow kickoff plan.

"I like it."

"Jules, can you help me convince Erika?"

She hangs on the wall, doing these little jump twists on the ledge. "I can't convince that girl to do anything. Least of all make up with a boy who broke her heart."

"She doesn't have to make up with me. She just has to swim with me."

Julia stops her jumping and looks right at me. "Aw. Look at your face."

"What?"

"Bart, you're like a lost little puppy dog."

"Well. My heart's broken too."

"God, I can't stand this."

Sunny claps her hands and tells us to stop lounging, get swimming. "You've got half an hour before I start streaming the event. Make the most of it!"

Julia takes off for her laps, but I stay at the side.

"Bart? Are you all right?" Sunny asks.

I shrug. Since coming back from the qualifier a month ago, I've been training. Lots of figures, lots of land training. Strength, flexibility. Laps of sculling. But no routines. Everyone else has routines to work on right up 'til the end of the season, and even if they're not at the national championships like Erika and Chelsea, they'll still get to swim for the small audience at the club's watershow.

"Why don't you swim in Chelsea's spot in the team routine?"

"Yeah?"

"Yeah. She won't be back for it, and the girls would love to keep the choreography together. You've been watching them practise all year, you should be able to pick it up."

I smile. "Thanks, Sunny."

"Okay, now go! Do your laps. We'll practise team after we watch the solos."

When it's time, we all get out and dry off, and sit huddled around Sunny's laptop. Chelsea's called first, and when we see her, we shout and clap and cheer like we're there.

But when Erika swims, I'm quiet.

Erika's footwork at the start of her solo is like she's skating figure eights. Her grace and expression have us still. But it's so different from when I started watching the girls in the dive tank back when I was a racer. Now, I see *myself* in her movements. I know them, and I feel like I belong inside them. I watch her, and I can feel my own muscles twitching as I visualize going through the figures.

Then the combination of the music and her artistry ... I can't help it, but my eyes start to water. Then I catch the girls watching me. They've been watching me watching Erika, seeing me so caught up. Now I'm embarrassed.

I wipe the tears away from my eyes. On the screen, Erika spins, emerges, a hand outstretched like she's beckoning me into the pool with her.

Julia and Kyoka put their arms around me. Jules leans over and whispers in my ear, "You should have been there too, Bart." She squeezes my shoulder hard, and that little pinch of pain is the only thing that stops more tears from coming.

I text Erika as soon as the event is done.

> Told ya you'd kill it. Nicely done.

My phone buzzes.

> I haven't told Sunny yet. But this is a picture of a retired synchro swimmer. What a mess, eh?

I wait for the photo to pop up on my screen. Then I smile to see Erika, red goggle grooves around bloodshot eyes. An inch of black hair standing up on her head. One leg lifted high in a standing split, toes pointed.

> U can't retire. What about next year?

Nothing.

> I have an idea for the watershow. please please please swim duet with me?

> Don't tell me what I can't do. We're back day after tomorrow. Meet me at the pool before practice?

> :(

> I'll be there

I look around and think about what everyone here at the pool would say if they saw her solo. Or if they could just see us perform again. They would wonder how she could even think about quitting something she was so good at.

The team gets back in the pool. I throw myself into the routine, blocking out any thought but keeping the right distance from the swimmers surrounding me. The music. The count. How high I can launch Kyoka out of the water on our lifts.

• • •

On the way out of the pool the night before the girls get back, Dave sees me walking through the parking lot.

"Whoa. Why the long face?"

"I think Erika's quitting synchro."

"Aw." Dave throws an arm over my shoulders. "We could do something to take your mind off that."

I groan. "Please don't tempt me."

Dave puts his lips to my ear, and whispers. I let him pull me off course, pull me to wherever he's going, thinking about how I would love to feel the way I felt the other night. But the force of how much I want to be with Erika stops me.

I take Dave's hand, and unwrap it from my shoulders. "Dave, I can't. You know I can't."

He sighs. "Okay. I know you're not in *love* with me. *Lust* maybe." He gives a sad smile. "Well, my loss, her gain—if she ever figures it out."

On the way home, I check to see if Bill May's written me back, like I've done every day. There's nothing. Maybe I stepped over a line. After all, he doesn't really *know* me. I'm just another guy swimming synchro, in a different country, even. Why would I write him all that stuff? I just needed somebody who knows to say, "It's okay. Keep at it. Everything will work out for the best." Who better than the greatest male synchro swimmer in the world?

When I get home, I call for Mom as soon as I open the front door, but I don't hear anything.

"Mom?" I call again at the bottom of the stairs, but there's no answer. So I dump my wet towels in the washing machine and go up to my room. I put on some music with a slow, moody electric guitar and let my head empty, let my thoughts fall completely into my body. I drop into a front split and stay there, stretching out. Then I grab some books. I lift my front foot onto a couple books and check my back foot position. Then I come out of the split, set up the books for the back foot, and get back into position. Full oversplits. I don't care if it hurts.

I just sink in, just breathe. And when I look up, there's my perfect posture in the mirror—there's my extension, my grace. I lift my slender arms. Then my face cracks into an ugly grimace, and the tears come.

THIRTY-EIGHT

Erika's waiting for me in the lobby of the aquatic centre in street clothes, carrying nothing but a purse.

I let myself get a little happy that she finally wants to talk—at least until I see the look on her face.

"You look furious."

"I'm just hungry."

"Come on, let's go to the caf."

We start walking toward the little café that serves healthy fare—chickpea soups and sandwiches with alfalfa sprouts on multigrain rolls. We take our trays of food out to the patio, but all the tables are taken. Everyone's desperate for sun on one of the first warm days, and for the smell of fresh, non-chlorinated air. So Erika sits on the ground, leaning her back against the building. I drop down beside her.

I take a few bites of my sandwich, then ask her.

"Erika, do you wish I never came to the club?"

"How can you even ask me that?"

"Well, why are you quitting?"

Erika puts her sandwich down. "Retiring, Bart."

"Why are you retiring? To get away from me? Because I'll go find somewhere else to swim if that's it. I'll go up island or something."

She shakes her head. "No, you don't have to go to freaking Nanaimo. I'm not leaving because of you. You know, I've just swum enough meets and got as good as I'm going to get. So there's no reason for me to go to another national meet."

"Now that your solo made it to nationals?"

She nods. "That was my last goal ..."

"Except for the mixed duet."

"Yeah."

We keep eating until Erika breaks the silence.

"You know, you're the reason I decided not to retire at the *start* of this year."

"You weren't even going to swim this season?"

"Not after last year. Amanda put so much pressure on Chels and me. I didn't swim in the watershow. We came back from trials, and I just stopped. Julia begged me to come back with her in the fall, and Mom really wanted me to go to trials again, so I did. But I just wasn't into it those first couple of weeks, before you came. I was totally going to stop. And when you came to the Try It ... Well, Jules and I'd watched the mixed duets at worlds when it was on in the summer, and I started thinking if I could just do something different, if I could do *that,* I'd still love synchro. Then it looked like it was going to happen, with you ... so I stayed. I decided I could keep up all the sacrifice, and swim with the team, do another solo ... I'd just do it all because we were going to ..." Her voice cuts out, and she shakes her head.

"What sacrifice?"

"Oh, you know. You know we give up everything when we do a sport like this. Just think of the friendships that never were because you could never have anyone over, because you always had to be at the pool. Or all the other things we miss out on."

"Like?"

"I don't know ... music lessons. I never had time to learn an instrument. Playing baseball. Going to beach parties. Family dinners. Just ..." She sighs. "Meeting someone, even. Just *life,* Bart."

"Synchro kept you from all that?"

"Yes!" She sighs again, runs her hands through the inch or two of black hair that's long enough to lie flat now, and drops her hands to her sides. "Didn't racing do that to you?"

There's not much I can think of missing back then. I had Riley. I had Mom. And ... meeting someone?

"I didn't even *kiss* anyone until I joined synchro."

"You didn't?"

"But it wasn't because I was training all the time. I guess nobody considered me dating material before. And ... baseball just bores me." I laugh a little.

"So I was your first kiss?" she asks quietly.

I nod.

"You never told me that."

"You never told me I'm the reason you swam this year."

"So I was your first. That makes Chelsea your second."

I close my eyes. "Yes. And ... Dave was my third." I open my eyes, and Erika's looking at me now—she's not shocked or upset.

"Yeah?"

"Yeah. But me and Dave was just a one-time thing."

"Oh?"

"I dreamt about you the night after Dave and I got together. He's not the one I'm in love with."

Erika frowns, and goes back to her sandwich. We eat, not talking, until she breaks the silence again.

"You know, you never told me why you stopped dancing."

I swallow. I look out at the sky and the generous blue of the day.

"The same reason guys didn't show up to the qualifier."

Erika looks at me like she's trying to figure that out—then her look transforms into something else, more like sympathy.

"Don't quit, Erika. Don't let what happened keep you from doing what you want next year. I don't want you to swim with anyone else, but ... if you want to find another partner, just do it. You should keep going."

She shakes her head.

"Yes, come on. You still have this goal left. Why would you quit?"

"Like I told you. There's other stuff out there I want to do. I mean, why am I doing this? What's the point of me holding my breath for three minutes, or spending so much time with my feet sticking out of the water? 'Cause it's so ridiculous, when you think of it like that, right? I'm so over it.

I *was* over it. Until you joined." Erika's eyes go red.

I take her hand. Even with everything that's come between Erika and me, there's still a spark of energy that connects us physically. It's not extinguished. I still feel it.

Her phone buzzes in her pocket, but she ignores it. "When you joined ... that's when I fell back in love."

"With synchro?"

She gives me a sad smile. Her phone buzzes again.

"Hey. Hey." I wipe a tear from her cheek with my thumb. "Erika ..."

"Don't say it unless you mean it, Lively."

"Okay. Hey, look at me." I keep my hand on her face, connected again. "I love you." And for the first time since I messed this all up, I feel our energy fields stitch back up together. It feels amazing, and I want it to go on forever. But another insistent buzz from her pocket breaks the spell.

"Jesus, *what?*" she says, pulling her phone out, and I drop my hand.

"What is it?"

"It's Sunny. Something about a letter from FINA. She's begging me to show up to practice."

I look at her with the best puppy-dog eyes I can pull off.

She pushes me so I fall over a little. "Oh, good grief. Okay."

• • •

When Erika and I walk onto the deck, the girls are seated in a circle around Sunny. She waves us over. Erika takes off her shoes and holds them in her hand, and it makes me inexplicably happy to see her naked toes again.

"Girls ... and Bart. I've got a message from FINA." She shakes out a letter.

Erika and Julia exchange a look.

"'Dear Bart Lively and the members of the Rosa Pacific Synchro Club.'

"'First of all, thank you for sending the video of your mixed pair performance at your provincial competition, and to Erika Tanaka, Chelsea Gates, and Bart Lively for supporting this new event that has been inspiring so many in our sport. We enjoyed watching your routines immensely.'

"'Bart, we want you to know that your submission in support of mixed duet routines at the Olympics is not the only one of its kind. We have had similar communications from clubs in other provinces, and this demonstrates an exciting new interest in mixed events.'"

Sunny folds up the letter. "You sent them videos?" she asks.

"I thought they should see what the rules are keeping out of competition at a high level."

"Well, they wrote back. And within the year too." Sunny raises her eyebrows. "You should consider yourself lucky."

"Sure," I say, "but their letter didn't say anything. It just says blah blah, lots of people think mixed duets are cool. That's it."

Sunny stuffs the letter back in the envelope. "Change happens a little bit at a time." She looks right at Erika, then at me. "Bart, I know you were disappointed with what happened at the end of this competition season. But every season's different. You never know what the next year will bring. You should be so proud of all your progress. Don't you think so, girls?"

Then she pulls the letter out of the envelope again. "Oh, what else did I see here? Something about ... Oh, yeah, 'We would encourage your club to submit a mixed pair routine to the Western Summer Open, where a representative from FINA will address the synchronized swimming community.'"

I look at Erika, and the girls look at me, and they look at Erika, wide eyed. Kyoka lets out a little squeal.

"Um, excuse me?" I raise my hand. "Did they just set aside a spot for me to swim a duet in California? A mixed duet, from *our club*?"

"It looks that way, yes." Sunny says. "Except—Chelsea's in Montreal now. And she's not coming back for the games, so your pair's out ..." She looks at Erika. "I don't know what you'll do."

"Well, does it have to be competed at nationals? Is there a minimum score?"

Sunny looks at the letter again. "Yes, requirements ... They want all participants to have a minimum figure score in a sanctioned meet."

"What score?"

Sunny smiles at me.

"What score!" I walk around behind her, and reach out and snap the letter out of her hands as she laughs at me.

"Oh my ... Erika, we've got it. We've got it!" I look over at her. Erika stands there in her jeans and sweater, getting flushed in the pool's humid air. Her arms are crossed over her chest. But she's got this little reluctant grin that I can see she's trying to squelch.

The girls look at her, and look at me. Then Sunny tells them to get lost and go warm up. Before she goes, Jules reaches her arm out to Erika—and pulls her into a hug. She whispers something I can't hear into her ear, then leaves Erika fidgeting with the tassel on her purse, staring into the water of the dive tank.

I walk up to her and plead with my eyes.

"You want to do this, right?" I stop and look into her brown eyes, holding me steady, calming my excitement. "The Western Open! Come on. California! We've got to show them 'Breathing Underwater.'" I reach for her hand. "Will you swim with me, Erika? Will you swim our duet?"

She looks at me with that reluctant smile for a moment, and then lets out a groan and goes over to Sunny. "Can I borrow some gear?"

THIRTY-NINE

I shut off my alarm at 4 a.m., get on my bike, and head to the pool. Ever since I watched Erika's solo, her choreography's whispered in my ear, saying, *You really want to try me out.* And as we all know now, I'm a bit sensitive to seduction. So I crank my phone loud enough to hear "River" when my head's out of the water. My version is a different cover with acoustic guitar. The singer's voice is raucous, then soothing, laden with emotion the whole way through. It's effing perfect for this morning.

The opening notes of the guitar build, grow louder. I let the water blur my vision, and pike into the first figure. The bottom of the pool is a sunken dance floor, and I'm floating above it—drawing perfect circles, trailing my hand on the water's surface.

Like every morning, I think about Erika. Maybe there's no coming back from what I did to mess up what we started, but I wish so hard that I could rewind to the last morning we spent up on the dive tower. There's still so much I don't know about her—and I miss our movements mirroring each other. I miss being that close.

I surface from a vertical spin and see motion on the deck. I blink hard, and see her before I submerge again. I could be hallucinating, since I think about her every morning.

I keep going. The song carries all my grief and regret, and every time I surface, I see her. I blink hard to get the water out of my eyes, but she's still there—Erika, black hair, exquisite frame draped in grey sweats. She stops and watches me swim the whole thing.

The final notes of the guitar ring through the pool.

"Again," she says.

I tread water, looking into her eyes, waiting for the song to start over. The first notes begin, and I go over into heron. And this time, every surfacing brings my eyes to hers, to my judge.

"Again."

I'm panting, and I've only put in about ten seconds between the song repeating—but I go again. The sweeping, gentle, circular motions wind down, and the guitar plays out its last notes. When I surface this time, Erika picks up the phone and stops the music.

"You're swimming my solo," she says.

"Nowhere near as well as you." I breathe hard, catching my breath from all the vertical work.

"Can I show you something?"

Erika pulls off her sweats and slips into the pool. "On the vertical to the boost? Tuck in your lower spine and then snap out with your arms here."

I try the move again, and Erika says, "Better. But let me show you. Start the music?"

I get out and start my playlist. *River, fifteen times.* Erika starts swimming, and her movements are the same—sharp, yet soft. The same movements that made my jaw drop when I used to watch her from the other pool. Every motion with a clean ending.

She pops up halfway through the song. "You see?"

"Uh, yeah."

"Were you paying attention?"

"Yes, totally."

"It's the transition into the boost. Here. Just watch." Erika egg beaters in place, waiting for the right spot in the music. Her hands drill out the movements she'd be swimming if she weren't just waiting for the right moment.

The song reaches the chorus again, and the singer faces up to how she's selfish and sad—and Erika goes into heron. She spins, and pikes, ready for the boost—and I see it. She split sculls, and it keeps her body aligned. And her movement has a clear, clean end.

I swim out, and Erika paddles away a little, giving me space I don't want.

"Now let's go. From the count."

We paddle side by side, hand drilling until the song comes around again and we go over together, in sync. Erika's solo becomes a duet, our bodies mirroring each other. And the singer's wistful longing that she didn't screw it all up becomes my own.

We corkscrew down through our final spin, feet flying, then surface.

"What do you think?"

I sit up on the edge of the pool. "You're coaching me. I think that means you want us to keep going."

Erika lifts herself up to sit beside me, our legs in the water. The effect of her body next to mine has not changed. I am still hypersensitive, every pore in my skin screaming, *She's sitting next to you!* The pinkish light of dawn comes through the glass roof, lightening up the pool. I take her hand.

"Erika. I'm sorry."

She nods. "I know."

We stay together, just swishing our feet in the water.

"You know, I was so done at the end of last season. If we do this, it's going to be so hard. It means way more years, and it's already so hard." Erika's eyes fill with tears again. "I'm not like Chelsea. I'm not made of steel like she is."

"Hey." I put my arm around her shoulders and pull her into a hug.

"And I don't know if I'm who you should swim with. You changed when you started swimming with Chelsea. You started improving so fast with her." Erika's voice catches. "I don't know if I can do that for you." It's a few seconds before she can speak again. "You know you could go to junior worlds with her next year if you wanted."

"Well ... I don't want to. I want to go with you."

Whatever I just said, it cracks Erika—and she starts to cry.

"Bart, I don't know if I can do it."

"*I* know you can. I know *we* can."

"And I'm still mad at you for kissing her." Erika pushes me away with a manic laugh-cry. "God, Chelsea Gates. How am I even supposed to swim with you?"

I take her wrists and pull myself back toward her. "You're going to have to. At the Western Open, anyway."

"Right."

"Swim with me."

"I already told you I would. I'll do it."

"No. Not just the Open. I mean *swim with me,* Erika. All the way to worlds. All the way to the Olympics. You and me."

She lets out a deep sigh.

"Please?"

"I just want us to go back to the way it was at the beginning."

"Before we got together?"

Erika reaches up and brushes a tear off my cheek. "I don't know. Am I even your type?"

"Ha! Am I *your* type?"

Erika shakes her head. "Stop."

"Tell me. If you had a type, what would it be?"

Erika takes a deep breath. "Feminine boys with slender arms and big, wide grins."

She watches my lips when she says that. She puts her hand on my forearm, slides it up and measures the width of my elbow between her fingers, then slides them higher. She leans her head in like she's going to kiss my neck, then just bites the air next to my skin. A shiver runs through my whole body, and I watch her slip into the water with a kind of awe. How did she just flick the switch on inside of me? Now all I want is more of her.

I slip into the water, and stand on the ledge. "Come here." I pull her back toward me and put my lips to hers. It's a tentative, closed-lip kiss to start, then we relax into it, and we're kissing deeply, and her hands close around the back of my neck. I don't want to stop. When we come up for air, Erika says, "We should practise. We haven't swum 'Breathing Underwater' in ..."

"Weeks. I know. But first, this." I lean in to kiss her again. It's been so long since we've kissed. I need to fit in weeks of not kissing.

"You start that, and we won't get to practise."

"It's already started." We kiss again, and Erika lets her hand brush from my neck down my back, and I think I will die.

She pulls away. "Wait." She hoists herself on deck. "Come on, Bart. I'm going to start our music."

I groan.

"Come *on*."

She crouches down and hauls on my arm, so I get out, and I'm just laughing, because I don't even know how I could try to hide my erection.

"Oh, geez."

"Um ... seriously, can we do, like, just *one* run-through? And then I want to go up to the dive tower."

"What's with you and divers?" she teases.

"Hey. No fair." I draw her into a kiss.

"It's okay. Can't blame you, really. They are total eye candy."

We stand at the edge of the pool together, waiting for the rise of synth, the beat, and the count that we dive on. Soon it will be Sunday morning, and the tank will be full of swimmers. The littles—the ten and unders—they'll be in this corner. Our national team will be there, in the centre. But for now, we still have all this water to ourselves.

We run through, remembering the routine, remembering each other, all the distances and transitions. And when we're done, I take her by the hand and walk up the steps. We stop when we get to the landing where we spent those mornings. Erika goes to sit down, but I tug on her hand and keep going. Up the last flight. Up to the top platform, to the gate.

"What are you even doing?" She laughs.

I'm kind of making it up as I go along. I need to do something—something that will show her how much I mean this. I need to do something to show Erika that I'm going to take all the risk to be her partner, and go for this.

My legs are jelly. Every cell in my body wants to return to safety, curling up in the last landing before the top. But I force my hand to open the gate and force my feet to step onto the rubber carpet. I force myself to walk to the end.

I turn around and open my arms to her.

"You don't have to do this," Erika says, walking out to me.

"I'll be all right. Come on."

Erika walks out to meet me, and I wrap her in a hug, cuddle up close, and shut my eyes.

"Bart, you're shaking!"

"I know."

She grips me harder.

"I know it's a risk, Erika. We could both rank, but there might not be a competition for me. Or you could go to trials next year and not make it."

"Or we could make it all the way to nationals, but what if they don't include our event at junior worlds? And seriously, if I swim another year? I'm going to risk my sanity. And ... getting decent grades. And any chance of ever playing an instrument."

"Oh, come on, you can take up the fucking trumpet when you're older."

She laughs, and I open my eyes to watch her dimples appear.

"And what if we make it to worlds," I start, "but they don't let guys swim at the Olympics? You could go that far, Erika, and have to leave me behind."

"That would be the hardest thing."

I turn my head slowly and look down at the water below. My breath comes quicker. "For both of us." I look back into her eyes. "But I've got you if you've got me."

"I'm not letting go."

"I'm just going to take a step."

I step closer to the edge, tugging her with me. "I have to close my eyes again. Just for a bit."

"Then close them. I've got you."

I feel her embrace me tight, then let go a little at a time, until I'm standing on my own.

"You totally don't have to do this."

She says that, but she doesn't know what I'll do for her now. That I'd climb up a *hundred*-metre platform to show her.

But can I jump off a ten-metre one?

I have to. Because if I climb down the stairs now, who's to say that I won't back down when we're training hard before nationals? Or when I get booed from the stands, or told for the hundredth time I'm in the wrong place? Or if we get as far as we know we can, and they tell Erika she can go on—but I can't?

I have to jump for her. I have to for *me*.

I open my eyes. We are right at the edge. Erika stands three feet away, arms straight, knees bent just a little, ready to jump too. I swallow hard.

I say, "*Go.*"

FORTY

On the morning of the Western Summer Open, I start with silver eye-shadow, sweeping it up from my lash line all the way to my brows. Next, the liquid eyeliner. I've been practising to get that steady, straight line. While I do my makeup, I think about a conversation I had with Julia at the last GSA meeting before school ended—if you're a guy and you want to do a sport that's a massive athletic challenge but also a beautiful, graceful performance art, you have to pay this big penalty for letting your masculinity slip. You take flak. You don't get to go to the Olympics.

I say, screw it. It's time the pool and the wider world admitted that there are many ways to be a boy. I brush on my accent shadow, then use my lash curler. Then waterproof mascara—three coats.

●●●

Our sport is 98 percent female. Actually, at home in Canada it's more like 99.8 percent. But today, here at this beautiful open-air pool, I'm not the only guy.

Erika's eyes pop when I come out of the change room gelled, painted, and glittered.

"What, too much?"

"Never."

The FINA address is planned for just before the mixed duet event, so we have to wait on deck after warm-up.

"Thank God it's July in California," she says. "At least I won't freeze during the speech."

The FINA rep takes the microphone and begins. It is a brilliantly sunny, hot day. We're squinting in the sun's intense rays, and our skin's covered in zinc and diaper rash cream so we don't get burned.

"As you know, last year we featured the mixed duet at international competition for the first time."

Erika takes a sip from her water bottle, and just about spits it out. "Look who it *is!*"

"What? Who?"

"The guy in the warm-ups, to the left of the empty chair."

"Oh my God, it's Bill May!"

"Holy crap, this is a bigger deal than I thought!"

I laugh. "Oh, yeah. And look who's sitting with him." It's Christina Jones ... they're the pair that took gold for the technical mixed duet at the world championships last year.

"It's really them!"

The speaker talks about a couple of clubs from western North America that are working to open up the sport for guys. It's not just Bill fighting for it now. Here, and around the world, there is pressure for inclusion in the Olympics.

"It's a tipping point," the rep says. "And we are happy to announce that at the recent FINA Congress, the synchronized swimming technical committee confirmed that we will be submitting a proposal to the International Olympic Committee to include the mixed duet event at the next Summer Olympic Games ..." Her words are overtaken by applause from the audience.

Erika squeezes my hand hard. "Did you hear that, Bart? Did you hear that?"

"Yeah!" I can't wipe the grin off my face. "It's so much closer! Just one more step."

"Yeah, but do you hear everyone *clapping* for it?"

She holds my gaze for a moment, then I lean over and give her a kiss.

The speaker introduces Bill and Christina, who tell a little of their story about coming back from retirement after their hopes of swimming a mixed duet at the Olympics were long gone.

And something gets me about Bill. He could have been so choked about getting as far as he did and not making it to the Olympics. He could have been so mad or hopeless. But instead, he just talks about how much he loves synchro, how grateful he is that he got to come out of retirement and compete.

"And now we would like to begin our next event, the junior mixed duet."

We're the first pair. Erika puts her lips to mine briefly, and I can feel the nerves behind her kiss. So I take her hand, squeeze it hard, and don't let go. We walk up to the bulkhead holding hands, wearing our glittery blue-and-silver suits. Assuming our position at the start of the bulkhead, we bow our heads as if in prayer. The whistle goes. Our heads snap up, and a huge cheer rises up from the stands.

We march in sync to the centre and take our pose. We crouch over, waiting for our music. When we hear the first beat, we unfurl our bodies from fetal position to standing and tumble out, somersaulting into the water.

When we listened to the song over and over in the last weeks of practice, we realized that our big highlight didn't fit the lyrics. *I'm the weight, you're the kite*. But Erika and I both know that she's my weight.

Now when we go under, nobody except the two of us knows that she's going to be *my* boost.

Breathless, I get my feet on her shoulders and engage my core, waiting for the lift. She rocket thrusts me all the way out of the water, so that I'm ever so briefly standing tall on its surface, arms outstretched.

I'm there for a split second, but it feels like forever. I face a set of stands more full than even the ones at the qualifier. I'm alone out of the water, with all eyes on my body, hanging out there with enough time to wait for judgment. For someone to hurl abuse from the stands.

Down we go again. The underwater world saves me. It surrounds me with its comfort, just the rush of bubbles and the music coming clearly through. But then we come up, and the stands are shouting and clapping.

They loved our lift—they just *loved* it.

I see Sunny next to Bill and Christina, nodding to the music, enjoying the routine she's helped create over the past year. They all cheer us on.

And we hit every beat. We're crisp and fast and kick-ass.

At the last note, everyone in the stands claps, and Bill and Christina shout, "Bravo!" Sunny comes over and gives us high-fives.

I'm so excited, I don't even hear our score.

Erika and I dry off quickly, pull team jackets over our still-damp bodies, and find a place in the bleachers to watch the other duets. We shout and clap and cheer along with everyone else, and when they're done, I take Erika's hand and run down to the deck.

"Where are we *going?*"

"You want to meet them, don't you?"

"I—I don't know what to say."

"That doesn't matter!"

We grab Julia on the way, and Kyoka. The four of us head over to Bill and Christina, and they're already swarmed with other swimmers.

Bill looks over the crowd of heads and sees me. "Hey," he says.

"Hey," I say back. It feels ... weird to talk to him in person. To see him this close up.

"Thanks for your letter to FINA," Bill says. "The last time I contacted them, they told me about you and the other mixed duets coming today, and we knew we had to come see your event."

"This is ... so great," I start to gush. "I just wish we got to see you swim today."

"Aw, today's your day. So I hear you're a natural."

"Oh, I've got a long way to go."

"Sure, but you're here."

"Yeah, I'm here." I mirror Bill's grin.

We let the other pairs get a word in with them, and then Erika goes to find her parents. I look for Mom in the stands, but I don't see her.

"Bart?"

I turn around. "Mom! There you are."

"That was so great. You two always work so hard. And Bart?" Mom puts a hand on my arm. "You look really happy."

"I am." I give her a hug and see Dad standing behind her. I freeze. But then he opens his arms like he wants a hug too.

"You came all this way?"

"I said I'd come see you swim."

I hug Dad. He doesn't let go. "You were great, Bart. I don't know how you even do half of that stuff."

"Well, come to the pool with me sometime and I'll show you."

He lets me go. "Yeah, right. I think your old man would drown if he tried that."

There's a little smudge of my makeup on his cheek. I rub it off, and he laughs.

"So you know I'm going to keep doing synchro next year, right? I'm not headed back to racing."

"Yeah, well, after that performance, I should hope not."

Mom looks at him, her eyes wide.

"Yeah," he says. "It would be a waste."

I hug him again.

Some of the other synchro parents come down on deck to meet Bill, and talk to Sunny, and congratulate us. They talk about the announcement, and Sunny asks, half joking, if anyone has any brothers they could bring to the club next year.

As we're breaking up and making plans for rides to dinner, Bill nods me over to have a word. "Hey, Bart. I'm sorry I didn't write back—I was travelling and couldn't pick up my messages. I'm glad it worked out with you and your partner."

"Me too."

"I'm sorry about your nationals."

"I just wanted to keep going, you know?"

Bill nods. "You will."

"It'll get easier, right?"

Bill shakes his head. "No, you just get stronger. Just keep thinking about the boys who are ten and want to be in this sport. Think of how differently it'll go for them if they see a guy like you or me when they're that age."

"I will."

Bill holds his hand out. "Until I see you again."

When I meet up with the girls later at the restaurant, all of us in matching jackets with pink lettering, I'm still thinking of what Bill said. I wonder if I'd seen an older guy in my dance studio, if I would have toughed it out. If I would have stayed. I don't know—maybe I would have, if I loved it as much as I love synchro now.

FORTY-ONE

Chelsea is back home for Christmas break, so she and her mom have come to watch our club's watershow.

"Hi, Chelsea. How's your season so far?"

"It's been good. Really hard. But good." It's so weird for all of us to be suited up and made up—and for Chelsea to be here on deck in street clothes. "Hey, Bart, I don't know if Sunny told you ..." She looks guilty.

"Chels, is this is about your new mixed duet partner?"

"Yeah. He's just moved from New Brunswick."

"Ask him where he was in March, dammit. Stood me up."

"Well, now you and Erika have a little competition for this season." She leans in and whispers, "Just the way you like it, right?"

I push her away, laughing. "I'm happy for you. Tell André I wish him the best, and we'll see him at the qualifier."

Amanda Gates removes her shoes at the door to the deck so she can walk out and give Sunny a hug. Kyoka's mom sees her and comes over for the hug party. Then they pass right by me, headed for the stands. They don't say anything to me or look my way. I guess some things don't change.

Chelsea rolls her eyes.

"Bart, you coming out with us all after?"

"Yeah, the brunch?"

"I'll give you all the dirt on the national gig."

"I'd like that. Thanks. Hey, Chels?"

"Yeah?"

"Thanks for coming."

This watershow is mostly for fun. We're only three months into practising our routines for this year, so some are just partials anyway, but it gives us an audience.

I step out of the change room wearing my new duet suit—a black, bejewelled Speedo. And I pass Coach Cragg.

"Nice suit."

"Thanks."

"Hey, when's your event?"

"Our duet? About halfway through."

"Around ten? Riley and I'll come watch. Break a leg."

Cragg goes back to the guys in the lanes, and Riley waves. I wave back. I look up into the stands filling up with our friends and family, and spot Dave and his new boyfriend, and give them a wave. They whistle back, and Dave shouts, "You look hot!" The grandparents in the row ahead of them turn around and stare. I laugh.

The synchro school's coach is AWOL, and about twenty kids under ten are wandering around not knowing where they should go.

"Bart, can you help?" Sunny asks, as she speed-walks down the deck carrying an armful of streamers.

"Yeah, of course."

I hold out my arm between two little guys getting into a wrestling match. "Hey, Mitchy, Ian, you guys gotta line up at the bulkhead for the start of the show! You're going to kill it, right?"

Mitchell and Ian, seven and eight, hold their hands up so I can give them each a high-five. They grin ear to ear.

On her way back, Sunny stops and says, "They're here because you are, you know."

I blow her a kiss and get the other littles lined up for the procession around the dive tank that the club does at the beginning of every watershow.

But first, Erika, Julia, and I climb the stairs of the dive tower. Today, we're kicking off the show with the "Bart entrance," as the girls called it after I debuted it at the end of last season. We tape down one end of a streamer to a dive platform or board and hold the other end—so when we jump in, we trail a streamer of colour through the air. And today? All of us are taking a big dive, two at a time. When we're done, we'll have decorated the tower with a hanging curtain of colour.

"Hey, did you hear Chelsea's got a mixed duet partner out east?" I ask.

"No way!" Jules says. "Well, she gets to eat her cake too now. Doesn't she?"

I laugh. "True."

The other girls from the team take their positions on the lower boards. Sunny runs up the stairs, taping down the start of a streamer roll onto each swimmer's platform. Erika and I have the top. I've got the red streamer. Erika has the yellow. Jules has purple, just below us.

"Are you ready, Erika?"

"Yeah. I'm ready."

When Sunny starts the music, there's no curtain to rise, no spotlights to light. Instead, we pick up our streamers and leap, sending ribbons of colour through the air that follow us into the pool.

ACKNOWLEDGMENTS

I'd like to thank Brian Lam and Arsenal Pulp Press for taking a chance on Bart's story. I was waiting for the bus home from work on a cold January evening, and your offer didn't just make my day—it made my decade! Thank you also to Shirarose Wilensky, for your careful and thoughtful editing—and to Colin Thomas, whose insight and guidance were key to getting the story to this stage. Thank you to Oliver McPartlin for the design, and Cynara Geissler for marketing and promoting *Synchro Boy*.

I want to acknowledge the Victoria synchro club for providing inspiration, and Stefanie Dickson and Brenda Scott, for your coaching. Thank you to Katherine O'Connor and Kristen Chen for putting up with me continually screwing up the counts. Thank you to all the Victoria Synchro and University of Victoria synchro girls whose swims have had me in awe throughout the years. Without the years of watching you from the stands, and my year under the water, this book wouldn't exist. With all that noted, all details of the Rosa Pacific Synchro Club's year of competition are imagined, and any mistakes are my own.

I also want to acknowledge Bill May, Robert Prévost, Aleksandr Maltsev, Atsushi Abe, and all the other men of synchro, as well as their duet partners, for their inspiration—their passion and dedication to the sport were the seeds of Bart's story.

So many thanks to Leanne Baugh, Jill and Sophie Marshall, and Peter Carver for reading earlier drafts and giving me feedback—and special thanks to Jill for the racing swimming insights, and for all the walks around the lakes.

Thank you to Tim and Sandy Mitchell for all the times you've let me shut myself in a room for a weekend, for understanding that it was important, and for your emotional support. I love you! Radish! Happy New Year!

Thank you to my Open School BC friends, for being so flexible, and so supportive.

And a big thank you to Karen Rivers, for always answering my questions, and for pointing me to Colin. And huge thanks to Michael V. Smith and Melanie Little, for pointing me in the right direction to find the right home for *Synchro Boy*, and for always asking how the writing is going. Thank you to Glenda Lee Jury and Marthèse Cassar for getting it—and to everyone else who had faith in me, even when my own faith slipped.

Jennifer Callioux Photography

Shannon McFerran studied writing at the University of Victoria and earned an MFA in creative writing from the University of British Columbia. She has published short stories in literary magazines and a YA anthology. *Synchro Boy* is her first novel. She lives in Victoria, BC.